THE REVOLUTION

WILL NOT BE RATED G

A Romance

THE REVOLUTION
WILL NOT BE RATED G

A Romance

Keya Chatterjee

GREEN WRITERS PRESS *Brattleboro, Vermont*

Printed in the United States

10 9 8 7 6 5 4 3 2 1

Green Writers Press is a Vermont-based publisher whose mission is to spread a message of hope and renewal through the words and images we publish. Throughout we will adhere to our commitment to preserving and protecting the natural resources of the earth. To that end, a percentage of our proceeds will be donated to environmental activist groups and social justice organizations. Green Writers Press gratefully acknowledges support from individual donors, friends, and readers to help support the environment and our publishing initiative.

Giving Voice to Writers & Artists Who Will Make the World a Better Place
Green Writers Press | Brattleboro, Vermont
www.greenwriterspress.com

ISBN: 979-8-9914134-3-5

Cover design by Allison Pineault
ALL IMAGES: ISTOCKPHOTO.COM

PRINTED AT KASE PRINTERS, ON FSC-CERTIFIED PAPER AND PRINTED WITH SOY-BASED INK, DEDICATED TO SOUND ENVIRONMENTAL PRACTICES AND MAKING ONGOING EFFORTS TO REDUCE OUR CARBON FOOTPRINT. WITH PAPER AS A CORE PART OF OUR BUSINESS, KASE IS COMMITTED TO IMPLEMENTING POLICIES THAT FACILITATE CONSERVATION AND SUSTAINABLE PRACTICES. KASE SOURCES PRINTING PAPERS FROM RESPONSIBLE MILLS AND DISTRIBUTORS THAT ARE CERTIFIED WITH AT LEAST ONE CERTIFICATION FROM AN INDEPENDENT THIRD PARTY VERIFICATION, SOURCED DIRECTLY FROM RESPONSIBLY MANAGED FORESTS. WE ALSO MAKE ONGOING EFFORTS TO REDUCE OUR CARBON FOOTPRINT, REUSE ENERGY AND RESOURCES, MINIMIZE WASTE DURING THE MANUFACTURING PROCESS, AND RECYCLE 100% OF SCRAPS, TRASH, CARTRIDGES, EQUIPMENT, AND SOLVENTS WHENEVER POSSIBLE. WE ARE A FAMILY-RUN BUSINESS, LOCATED IN HUDSON, NEW HAMPSHIRE.

CONTENTS

THE REVOLUTION

WILL NOT BE RATED G

A Romance

1.
"IT IS OUR DUTY TO FIGHT FOR OUR FREEDOM"

—Assata Shakur
(response)

Ten days before Eamon

Aria Petros walked into the party in a borrowed bronze gown and the highest heels she could operate. She approached the check-in table and picked up the card corresponding to the name she'd been given. She was prepared for a facial recognition scan, but security was light. She put her clutch through the scanner and entered the reception with only a quick nod to the staff and security, ignoring her natural instinct to thank each worker and strike up a recruitment conversation.

Aria was an organizer and trainer for Expectus, not a spy; but she was also a team player. She had gotten to where she was because she did what was needed when it was needed. Tonight, she was charged with scoping out this diplomatic reception, and she planned to play the part to perfection.

Aria memorized key features of the gilded ballroom. Her surroundings were a caricature of Upland life, complete with crystal chandeliers, high ceilings, and baroque-framed portraits of President Donner. The men were in a mix of tuxedos and dress uniforms. The women's attire was varied enough that Aria blended in easily to the mix of sparkly champagne-colored jumpsuits, beautiful golden gele headdresses, and silken hand-loomed saris. Aria looked around and saw banners welcoming guests to the "Earth and Mars Reception."

Every aspect of this "Earth and Mars Reception," from the decor to the dress code, was designed to reinforce the authority of the Donner Administration. The presence of military personnel was intended as a show of strength to inspire political loyalty and fear. In Aria, it inspired a contempt that was only matched by her contempt for their obsession with plundering Earth while colonizing Mars.

Expectus was one week away from landing what they hoped would be a decisive blow against the Donner Administration. Aria's scoping mission would lay the cornerstone for their week of actions, building to the crescendo coming in a matter of days.

Aria stopped to get out her mirror and freshen the deep red lipstick that Poppy told her complemented her caramel skin. She turned and angled her compact. "Smudged," she mumbled while powdering her upper lip and snapping photos of each entrance. Aria was thorough; now she needed to get to the roof. Once she could see the setup and get enough information about the security, the Expectus team could use that information to maximize disruption the next day. Presumably, Poppy had assigned Aria and Noona to do this job personally, rather than one of their thousands of trained action-scoping leads, because this mission was make or break for starting the week with a sense of momentum.

Aria now saw Noona coming towards her, dressed as a caterer. The buzz of the party would prevent them from being overheard by audio surveillance, but they would need to limit their conversation to avoid raising suspicion.

"Red or white?" Noona asked, and then whispered, "The stairs to the roof are just behind the trellis." Noona leaned her head slightly towards a partition behind a table that held an ice sculpture and a chocolate fountain. Aria smiled and silently thanked Noona.

Noona had been Aria's best friend since they started high school together. Aria had always been welcome in her large Korean family gatherings, and Noona was Aria's strongest tie to the past. They were two of only three people of color at Duke Ellington High, named after the Black jazz musician. By the class of 2030 graduation, Aria was the *only* Black girl, as the daughter of an Ethiopian mom and Indian dad. Other than their small friend group, all their fellow students with darker skin had dropped out of Ellington and switched to Lowland schools, for safety reasons.

Half the country is starving, and these jerks have an ice sculpture and a chocolate fountain. Aria raised her eyebrows with a barely perceptible eye roll. Noona would know what she was thinking. She grabbed a glass of white wine and began to move towards the chocolate fountain table. She stopped when she heard Noona behind her.

"Ma'am you dropped this," Noona said—her code phrase for something going wrong. Aria turned around.

"Oh, thank you!" she said, grabbing a napkin Noona was holding out, and giving Noona a questioning look.

"Don't freak out," Noona whispered quickly, "but Neil Rao is here. He's in the circle of people schmoozing behind you. You should leave, or at least try to get upstairs without him noticing."

"It's fine," Aria said under her breath. "I'll be fine." She put her hand on the shoulder of Noona's black polyester catering uniform for just a moment to steady herself. The scratch of warmth emanating from Noona calmed Aria.

Neil Rao was the son of Secretary of State Simone Rao, one of the most dangerous people in the Donner Administration. A lot had happened in the twelve years since Aria had known Neil in high school. Aria's life had fallen apart at the same time that DC and most urban centers had formally split more firmly into Upland and Lowland. DC's split almost looked like a yin and yang symbol, with Lowland filling the southern part of DC and wrapping around to the Northeast parts of DC, with enclaves in the woods of the Northwest and all the way over to Adams Morgan where Lowland had held ground. The name was a misnomer, since parts were quite high elevation, but none of Lowland was as fancy as Upland, which included the federal district, Georgetown, Dupont Circle, Chevy Chase, and all along Connecticut Ave. Neil had been having fun as an Uplander with access to power, wealth and unlimited food, while Aria had spent twelve years crisscrossing the country by land and giving trainings to places that had been cut off by the Upland governments. She had helped activists in hundreds of places across the continent deal with food shortages and violence from the state. In fact, Aria was on a training trip when she was called back by Poppy for this week.

For the most part, in UplandUS, the darker your skin, the more likely you'd get thrown out. This party was safe for Aria and Noona since it was so international. It was safe for Neil because he was their token dark-skinned Uplander. Aria was disappointed in Neil for playing the part of "the dusky stud who thrived under fascism" for them. He had been smart in high school. He had to know the Donner Administration was pillaging Mother Earth, stealing food, and hoarding luxuries for themselves.

While greed and racism dominated the Donners' domestic politics, Aria had to admit the BRUINS attending this party were a rainbow coalition of sorts, with luminous skin and extravagant clothes from each of the BRUINS nations of Brazil, Russia, UplandUS, India, Nigeria, and South Africa in the mix. It was no wonder they needed Neil and his mother in the Donner Administration. Without them, they would not have a single person of color to talk with their only trading partners.

Was Neil actually in the administration, helping them? Her curiosity got the better of her and she scanned the room. She realized her mistake as soon as her gaze landed on Neil. He turned and looked right at her. She froze. Aria crunched her eyes closed and took a deep breath, wanting to believe, like an infant, that if she couldn't see the room, no one in the room could see her. She needed to calm down before she started drawing attention to herself. She needed a way out. She searched her mind for an empowering thought pattern. *I am the resistance. I am strong. My community respects me and will protect me. I am a confident, queer Black woman. I am not to be trifled with.* None of her reassuring thoughts seemed right for a mantra because she didn't believe them herself. Aria was about to be caught and ruin everything.

Stop it. I'll be fine, she thought to herself, landing on a mantra. *I'm fine. I'm fine.*

A blond woman looking like a BP logo in her green sequin dress approached Neil and said something before proceeding to hang on his every word. She was giggling and trying to move his hand to her dress, showing him how the shade of green changed depending on the direction of the sequin. Aria imagined that incessant flirting had been the norm for Neil ever since he was dubbed the "most eligible bachelor in Upland." Aria had followed Neil in the State Media enough to know that he had stopped touring with bands and was now modeling luxury watches.

A decade earlier, two years after they had parted ways, Aria had been in Lowland Cleveland giving an organizer training and saw that Neil was playing there that night.

"You won't believe this," she'd told the trainees. "Neil Rao has the gall to come to Lowland Cleveland to play in a show."

Aria's announcement had sparked outrage from the Expectus trainees, and they hatched a plan to sit in the audience and unfurl a banner against the Donner Administration. Aria was proud of them for using the lessons from her training where she had shared how the Danish population had socially ostracized Nazis. She'd helped the activists paint their banner and talked them through safety protocols while it dried, but then she made her excuses and left Cleveland as fast as she could.

She'd been evading Neil for more than a decade.

Despite her reassurances to herself, Aria was not, in fact, fine. Neil, on the other hand, was *fine.* He looked even better in person than he did on the airbrushed magazine covers and billboards. Aria tore her eyes away but not before she took in the filled-out version of the boy she'd loved as a child. He was still beautiful with his long, black lashes; but he'd also grown handsome. He had a perfectly trimmed short black beard that accentuated his jawline. As he spoke, she noticed his smile was polite but hadn't spread to his eyes. He had a drink in his left hand, and no ring on his finger. Aria was frozen in place staring at Neil's hands and Neil's face. She remembered the last time they saw each other. It was right before the last time she saw her parents. Before they were murdered. Aria needed to get out of there. The smart thing to do would be to leave calmly without drawing attention to herself; but then she wouldn't complete the mission. That was unacceptable. The very thought of it made her heart pound so loudly she could hear it in addition to feeling it rattling in her rib cage. Her breathing was uneven. She remembered the stage fright she had as a kid, and knew she was in danger of passing out. *I do not have time for a panic attack. I'm fine.*

Aria took a long, steady breath. *I'm fine.* Neil didn't seem to recognize her, so she turned slightly away and continued towards the roof. She needed to finish this mission as fast as she could in her ridiculous heels.

"The lemonade is the perfect mix of sweet and tangy," Noona said. Their code phrase shook Aria from her internal spiraling. Really, Nightshade? Memory erasure sure, but what about the risk? Noona wouldn't have considered such a drastic step had she not believed that Neil had identified one of them.

But Aria was wearing a long, loose wavy wig that Poppy had lent her. She had lost weight from malnutrition. She had makeup on, which she never did when she wasn't undercover. Noona was surely being overly cautious. *It was still possible Neil wouldn't recognize her*. The thought passed Aria's mind, just as she sensed someone behind her and heard the voice of an old friend.

"Long time no see, Aria."

2.

"IT IS OUR DUTY TO FIGHT FOR OUR FREEDOM"

—Assata Shakur
(call from the past)

April 19, 2030

Long before Neil Rao and Aria Petros found themselves at the same diplomatic reception, they were classmates at Duke Ellington School of the Arts. Like any good school of the arts, theirs was full of drama.

Aria was first cello in the orchestra. She loved to improvise, compose, and perform solo. She'd taken dozens of master classes from Yo-Yo Ma, on the piece he was most famous for, "Bach's Suite No. 1." She could play the piece in her sleep. She was so good that she had taken the risk to stay at Ellington even when everyone else in her community pulled out of Upland schools after the series of police and military raids that had taken out so many students and teachers. She and her best friend, Noona, were the only kids left who commuted from what they'd started to call "Lowland," across town, across a checkpoint, and downhill from Union Station.

Neil was the only other student of color in their class, but he was the son of the Governor of Upland DC, Simone Rao, who President Donner had named to that position after he had attempted to take over DC and was only able to take a few neighborhoods. Neil was a talented violinist, a class clown, and the Homecoming King. He always had an armed guard with him at school, and he was always giving that armed guard the slip to go hang out with another girl. Neil, Aria, and Noona had been friends since freshman year, but at some point, Neil had started to realize that walking Aria to the checkpoint after orchestra rehearsal was the best part of his day. It was two hours when he should have been practicing, but he wouldn't give up that time with Aria for anything. He wanted to escalate with Aria, but he wasn't sure how to.

One day, Neil found Aria in a practice room playing with her eyes closed, and realized it was his golden opportunity. She was repeating a short passage over and over. She was so focused she didn't even hear Neil walk in, until he started humming along with her, "Duh-duh-duh-duh-do-do-do do." Neil had perfect pitch, which was perfectly annoying to Aria. He loved annoying her, and didn't care that it made him a stereotypical lovesick teenage boy.

"I have to go meet my mom for some dumb thing, but I can still walk with you to the checkpoint if we leave now."

"The bell doesn't ring for fifteen minutes. They won't let us out."

Neil scoffed. "You're not usually such a rule follower, Aria."

"Let me play through start to finish once."

"Okay, then we go out the back door?"

"Sure."

Aria played the piece from beginning to end with her eyes closed. When she opened them, Neil sat on the floor in front of her. She'd really nailed it. It was so beautiful, Neil had actual tears in his eyes.

"How was my intonation?"

"Can I kiss you?"

"Was it that good?"

"It was."

"You'll be my first kiss, so make it good." Aria smiled, which Neil took as an invitation along with her words. Neil smiled back, stood up, leaned over her cello, brought his face right up to hers, and gently brushed her lips with his. He wanted so badly to feel her body pressing against his, but he didn't want to touch a twenty-thousand-dollar borrowed instrument without permission.

"This isn't fair. I need to kiss you again when you aren't holding your cello as a line of defense."

"Oh, should we set a date for that?"

"Let's do it at our senior prom. Will you go to prom with me, Aria Petros?" Neil asked.

3.
"IT IS OUR DUTY TO WIN"

—Assata Shakur
(response)

Ten days before Eamon

Aria had many attributes that made her an asset to Expectus, but the highest among them was her iron will. Aria had no formal rank. She never wanted that, despite all her parents had done to launch the movement. Aria was not a strategist. She had avoided high-profile actions for years because of Poppy's concerns for her safety. She mostly ran a bookstore that was a cover for the movement and led trainings.

Poppy, nevertheless, trusted her with high-risk, ad-hoc assignments. Aria wanted Poppy to need her in more intimate ways, but that wasn't their dynamic. Aria was in Poppy's inner circle, though, and she delivered when Poppy needed her most. Unlike other activists, Aria feared neither death nor imprisonment. Death would make her a martyr, and the cause was worth it. Imprisonment would land her with friends and give her a chance to deliver important messages. Aria had no family left that they could torture. If all went well, they would be abolishing prisons soon anyway.

If it didn't go well, being in prison would be the least of her problems.

Even with Neil Rao following behind her at the "Earth and Mars Reception," Aria was not worried for herself. She was worried for her friends. Failing to get the information back that night would mean that the action the next day would have a higher arrest count, and therefore not be the show of strength they needed to start the week off. The conditions were finally ripe for strikes and boycotts to take off in a serious way in nearly every Lowland region across the continent. Getting herself arrested would devastate Poppy just when Poppy had a million plates spinning in preparation for the revolution's crescendo. As a Black trans woman, it was too dangerous for Poppy to enter Upland. The Donner Administration had criminalized existence for trans and gay people. Poppy couldn't pass as cisgender, and besides, the current Expectus strategy was to make sure that no one in the Donner Administration knew what Poppy looked like after her surgeries, since Poppy had been their prime target for years. For many reasons, Aria and Noona had to be Poppy's eyes and ears in Upland tonight.

As Aria walked through the crowd, listening to snippets of conversation, she became more certain Neil would not want to make a scene at this huge diplomatic event. But there was no way to be sure of who he had become in the intervening years. Aria continued taking steps towards the entrance she had come through, hoping Neil would give up. She clarified her feelings: she wasn't afraid of the police state, she was, however, afraid of resurfacing trauma. Her logical brain reminded her that trauma didn't kill her the first time, and it wouldn't kill her now.

Neil put a hand on her shoulder from behind. She

couldn't keep walking away now. His touch pulled a part of Aria back in time twelve years. She turned slowly to find Neil shifting the two stemmed drinks he held so that he had one in each hand.

"Hi," she said, surprised at how calm she sounded. "It's been a long time. Neil, right?" Aria put out her hand to shake his, then remembered the drinks he was holding.

"Yes, love, my name is still Neil. How are you, Aria?" Neil was smirking.

"Aria?" she said, a last-ditch effort to convince him he'd mistaken her for someone else.

Neil grinned. "I couldn't place you at first. I mean, I could, but I wasn't totally sure it was you until I saw Noona, and then I was totally sure. Anyway, you don't even look like a … Susan," Neil said, tilting his head to read her name plate, "Anderson?" Neil laughed. Aria was trying to decide how much trouble she was in, while Neil began appraising her. His appraisal ended with a hunger in his eyes.

"Do you want to go to the roof and have a lemonade, Susan? It's been forever and I don't want you to lose your nerve and disappear before we can talk. Come on, please?" He sounded earnest.

"I already have my wine, but I'd love to see the roof."

"They've fixed all the lighting in this neighborhood in response to all the environmental activism, so there's an amazing view of some stars up there."

Eco-fascists do love their greenwashing. "I'd love to see the stars, but are we allowed? I see a lot of security." Aria had a particular disdain for eco-fascists justifying things like militarized borders and curfews in the name of climate action. The idea that Neil thought a fascist government forcing people off the streets at sundown was something to celebrate was another strike against him, but going to the roof was what she needed to do. Aria's intuition told her she was on the verge of getting the information she came to this party to get. Sure, it was possible Neil could isolate her on the roof and have her arrested, but the risk was much higher that he would report the run-in and have her picked up off the street later. The administration couldn't afford a scene at this event.

"Of course we're allowed," Neil said. "There are just two guards and I know them both well."

Neil seemed to trust her an inordinate amount for someone he hadn't seen in over a decade. He was nervously rambling and telling her everything she needed to know. Maybe this wasn't the disaster she feared.

"Tonight they'll tear down the party and put in the conference seating, and the larger wave of security will come in at dawn to be ready for mid-morning meetings," Neil said, as he led her behind the trellis to the stairs. "We can probably sneak anywhere we want tonight."

Aria walked up the stairs with Neil, with no more than a nod from him to the guards needed to get them through. At the top of three flights, they exited to a night of thick air. She looked around. This place was going to be a simple site to access for an action. There was a pedestrian bridge fewer than three feet away from the rooftop bar. They'd be able to prevent the meeting most likely and if they couldn't manage shutting it down, they could certainly disrupt any ability for the meeting attendees to hear each other with some megaphones, chants, and songs from that bridge.

"It's a nice terrace," Neil noted, looking at where Aria's gaze was going. "The stars are even nicer though," Neil said, looking up. Aria followed his gaze and saw that Neil was right. When they were kids, the daytime sky was sometimes blue and the nighttime sky had stars. In the past few years, the particulate matter from the fires in the West and South had blocked the stars altogether. Some of them were visible again tonight with the reduced light pollution. Ironic that these Uplanders were burning the planet with their oil, gas, and coal, while worried about making these gaseous balls in the sky more visible. Neil's complicity made him less attractive.

"It's beautiful."

"If I remember right, it's even nicer away from the terrace and bar lights." Neil gulped his drink down and placed his glass on a high-top table next to him. He walked across the roof and nimbly lifted his body up to a small platform that was a few feet higher and led to the part of the roof that held equipment. "I'm gonna check it out," Neil said, as he disappeared behind a stack of condenser units on the roof. They were for heat pumps, and were probably as old as Aria and Neil. They needed to be replaced. The heat pumps were not the only sign that this building had been electrified and weatherized during the brief window of time when climate change policy reflected a concern for people's wellbeing. Aria would have to let the action leads know not to do too much damage to the building itself. If they won the struggle and took over Upland, this building would be an asset.

Aria set her things down on the same high-top table where Neil had set his drinks. She took the free moment to retrieve from her clutch the phone-shaped microdrop that Gears had given her. She could contact Gears, Noona, and Poppy with it via text and photo. The device looked like a phone, but Gears said it worked more like a walkie-talkie for encrypted texts. Aria pulled it out and shot Gears a message with all she had learned and photos of the roof so they could plan the final action details before their spokesperson council later that night. She looked up and saw Neil returning just as she had finished sending her encrypted message, and returned the phone to her clutch. A sense of calm came over her as she realized that whatever else happened, her friends had all they needed to disrupt the meeting the next day.

"Nice antique you got there," Neil said, pointing at where her microdrop was.

"Nice watch you've got there," she said, pointing at Neil's Paxa watch. The luxury watch could feed all of Lowland DC for a year.

"Touché." Neil motioned Aria over with his arms, which she declined with a smiling shake of her head, realizing that few women would turn Neil down. His wide shoulders filled out his designer tuxedo perfectly and his eyes were filled with mischief.

"No way I'm climbing up to that part of the roof in these heels."

"Oh right. Well, take them off and I'll lift you up. The view's worth it." He jumped down from his perch, ran over to her, and grabbed her hand, sending a pulse of energy up her arm. His hand was familiar in a way Aria didn't expect. It was a firm hold, no sweat on his palms. Her smaller hand fit perfectly in his. It brought back the memory of how they held hands while Neil walked her home from school at the beginning of their senior year. Neil led her over to the platform. If she had been taller, she could have lifted herself up like she was getting out of a swimming pool, but the leverage she needed was just out of reach. Neil put his hands around Aria's rib cage, sending a tingling sensation up and down her sides. Her mind flashed to the tight hug Neil had given her after she'd told him that her parents had been arrested all those years ago. Her body remembered Neil; she couldn't deny that. Neil lifted her up just high enough so that she could lift herself the rest of the way. On the higher platform, Aria looked at the skyline. Her eyes glanced over the spot where the original water wall was built on 17th St NW to protect the White House. The buildings were much taller than they were back when that wall was built. Nonetheless, from the vantage point of the roof, she could also see the wall around Capitol Hill and Union Station, and just barely see a glimpse of Lowland on the other side of Union Station, where she lived. It was her home, and it was a place where the Donner Administration purposefully directed flood water to protect themselves.

Aria scanned the horizon and turned back towards Neil. She looked at Neil more closely than she had before, as he continued to look up at the stars. The new maturity in his chiseled jawline came with a few faint wrinkles around his eyes. Aria drank it in, then looked up at the sky as they stood there in comfortable silence. The moon was brighter than the stars and looked like an eyelid winking at her from across the sky. It seemed like a sign. Aria decided to speak.

"You're wondering why I'm here."

"No. I'm glad we're ready to have a real conversation, though. I've been worried about you since that night. You disappeared into thin air. I went to the vigil for your parents, you know. I was obsessed with finding you for the first few years. I can't believe that you found me after I finally stopped my search. I'm honored that you snuck into a party just to see me after all these years. Downstairs, I panicked that you'd chickened out. You were just standing there all gorgeous and confident, and then suddenly you were walking away from me, and pretending to be someone else. I've never turned in any girl who's snuck into a party to see me. And you're the first one I actually want to see, so I'm definitely not going to endanger whatever is happening here." Neil wore a seductive grin. He looked Aria up and down in a way that made her aware of both how revealing her dress was and that her pulse had gone up.

"So, what do you think?"

"What do I think about what?"

"About us."

"There is no 'us.'"

Neil grinned. "There could be. I like seeing you again. You're still easy on the eyes." The Nightshade didn't seem to have kicked in yet. If it had, it would have been satisfying to take Neil down a notch and clarify that her presence at the party had nothing whatsoever to do with him. He had a lot of nerve hitting on her. It was suspicious. She was keeping her mouth shut for now, as she was trained to do, and Neil was filling the space.

"I looked for you in every philharmonic concert program. I hired string quartets for events hoping you'd show up with your cello. I contacted Juilliard. I did everything short of asking my mom to check the surveillance logs to find out what happened to you after that night. How are you? Are you okay? Are you still playing?"

When Aria didn't respond, Neil kept talking. "I wonder if someone snuck alcohol in this lemonade, or maybe I shouldn't have had that Johnnie Walker that jerk handed me downstairs. I don't know what's going on. I'm getting old. Maybe my body doesn't process alcohol the way it used to. I need to sit down. Sit with me?" Neil lowered himself on the ledge and leaned back. Aria joined him, realizing that Noona must have given him a pretty strong dose of Nightshade if he was wobbly just a few minutes after he had deftly hopped up on the ledge and helped her up. *How was she going to get him downstairs and out of here?* She should be forming an exit strategy now that she had communicated the information they needed for the morning.

"Maybe we should head back down, Neil?"

"Can't. I need to sit and sober up for a bit. Stay with me." Aria imagined leaving him drunk on the roof, and the possibility that he would chase her down the stairs and through the party being far too loud. She settled back on her elbows next to Neil, eliciting another seductive grin. *Sigh.* It couldn't hurt to stay for a bit and cavort with the enemy, especially since he wasn't going to remember. There was so much Aria found she wanted to say to Neil, but she still wasn't sure who he had become or if the Nightshade had kicked in.

"What about you? Still playing your violin?"

"YUP!" he said. "Oh, that was too loud. Yup," he whispered. "I played the fiddle in a bluegrass band and bass guitar in a rock band too."

"Interesting. Why didn't you play in an orchestra and use your mom's connections to get a placement in an Upland town that's intact? Or just take a job with your mom?"

Neil's words weren't slurring yet, but his response sounded like a drunk's ramblings. It was Aria's first time seeing Nightshade at work, but so far, his behaviors matched what she'd been told to expect. "As it happens, I did end up taking a boring, stupid, morally corrupt job with my mom after failing as a musician and realizing I can't model forever, BUT, it's temporary. I'm not a bad person, Aria. I live in the part of Georgetown that's still there up the hill. I still go out on my kayak when the water is clean enough. Remember how you always screamed when you got in a kayak like you were afraid of falling in? Remember we used to get around the checkpoint on that thing. God, you were adorable. I mean, you are adorable. Can I kiss you?" Aria shook her head "no," thinking that she needed to tell Noona to go a lot lighter on the drugs next time she spiked a drink.

"We were never really together, Neil. Or did you forget ditching me and going to prom with Sadie? And, no, I don't think it would be a good idea to kiss. You're drunk."

"I'm not drunk, Aria, I'm just intoxicated by you," he said, intently.

"No one is that corny sober," Aria replied.

Neil started rambling again. His words were running together now. "I'may be m'first time drunk in years," Neil held up two fingers, and continued, "but i's also m'first Ari-time inna gajillion years." Neil held up ten fingers, and his torso wobbled a bit when it lost the stability of a hand on the concrete below him. He looked like he was regrouping to talk again, this time more slowly. "Anyway, I wanted to kiss you when I saw you at the party and I hadn't had even a sip to drink then. So why can't we kiss?" Neil gasped with sudden realization. "Are you married? Who gave you that ring?"

Aria felt confident at this point that Neil wasn't going to remember this in the morning. "I'll tell you some things if you want."

"I want. Yes, I want."

Aria leaned in and whispered in his ear, "Okay but I have to clip this on your shirt first." Aria reached in her bag and got a lead clip designed to cut the sound from the recording devices that were woven into every white button-down shirt. She leaned over him and clipped it between his fourth and fifth buttons where the microphone would be muffled. She took a tiny magnet and stuck it to Neil's watch. She had already said too much with the recording devices running. Luckily the recordings were only kept for 24 hours, and they had a person on the inside to delete the audio sooner if needed. Tonight's audio from this party was getting replaced with recorded party sounds every thirty minutes or so. Gears also had programmed the Upland algorithms to never flag the presence of Expectus' inner circle. As a blond-haired femme of European-descent, Gears had somehow flirted their way into hacking every bit of the surveillance state. Nonetheless, Aria took the precautions she was trained to take.

As Aria put the clip and magnet in place, Neil stared down her dress, practically drooling, admiring the view of her breasts. Aria's nipples tightened in response. He wasn't physically touching her, but the way he was looking at her made Aria feel like he wanted to devour her. A memory flashed of Neil's head under her dress. Aria leaned back, scooched slightly away, and took a deep breath.

They weren't being monitored now thanks to the lead clip and magnet. Neil wouldn't remember anything about the night, thanks to the Nightshade.

"Do you want to come home with me, Aria?"

Aria laughed. Neil could barely sit up, although he seemed to have sobered up enough to speak clearly again. He might pass out at any moment, if she understood Nightshade correctly. He definitely was in no condition to be propositioning her.

"That's not where this is going, Neil. We are completely incompatible. Just look at your watch. Here's the key difference between us: you care about commodities. I care about communities."

Neil was not picking up the rejection that Aria was putting down. "I'd be happy to use some of my com-mo-dit-ies to be in com-mun-ity with you, Aria." Aria rolled her eyes. Neil slowly took off his bow tie, staring at her, not losing eye contact for a moment, and then leaned back and lay staring at the sky, sighing.

Aria laughed and wondered if she would regret being so careless just to get something off her chest. *I am a close confidant of the most wanted leader of the Expectus movement and I'm sitting with the son of the current Secretary of State, who would like nothing more than to have Poppy killed.*

But Aria needed to know if Neil knew what happened with her parents. She was never going to have a drugged Neil and no listening devices again. She had imagined this conversation a million times. *Carpe diem.*

"Neil, I need to be serious for a minute. Given how you were raised, you may not care, but I think it's my fault my parents were killed. My theory is that when you invited me to prom, your mother had me, and them, investigated, and that's how they were caught and killed. Do you know anything about their case? Why were they arrested and killed so quickly?" A look of confusion surfaced through the drugged fog Neil was in. He sat up with some effort.

"What? What are you talking about?"

Neil was staring at Aria, shaking his head, and visibly trying to focus through the fog of alcohol and Nightshade. Aria had wanted to get the theory out without breaking down in tears, but the tears were already filling her eyes as she talked about her parents. She took another deep breath and looked at Neil, matching the intensity of his focus on her, and told him the story of her last visit with her parents.

"I never found out how they were caught. The thing is, I'm

sure it was your mom who had them investigated because she didn't want me to go on a date with you. That's how they were caught. Your mom researched me because you had asked me, a Black girl, to prom and it led her right to my parents. It's my fault they're dead. I was a terrible daughter," Aria finished. She had never even told Poppy that theory. Confessing her guilt had taken the breath out of her. The weight of her loss felt like a vice squeezing her body.

"I'm so sorry. I don't know if that's what happened. I asked my mom if she could help them that night, but she outright refused to lift a finger." Neil spoke slowly, clearly struggling to sound sober. "It's my fault too. I should have known better. I thought your parents ran a restaurant. I didn't know we were putting them at risk by being together. You didn't know they were at risk. It is not your fault. All I know is that my mom said she'd hurt you if I went to prom with you, so I broke off our date just to be safe. The truth is that she's done that kind of thing since then, but I'm learning how to maneuver around her. What happened to your parents is my fault, a little. It's my mom's fault a lot, but it's NOT your fault." Neil slid towards Aria and pulled her closer to him in an embrace. Aria let herself put her head on his shoulder. They sat there like that for a while, forcing Aria to reflect on the irony of letting the enemy comfort her. Neil was more than the enemy though. The comfort of his arms was a throwback to better times. "Thank you for telling me. I'm so sorry." Neil was staring down at Aria intently, but in a way that seemed to go in and out of focus.

"If only I could go back in time and unkiss you, unaccept your invitation to prom, and uninvite your mother's attention on our family," Aria said. But Aria did nothing to unravel herself from Neil. She leaned closer, putting more weight from her head onto his shoulder and then chest, allowing Neil to bundle her into his arms against his torso with her breath on his neck.

Aria was lying in Neil's arms in this way, with tears welling in her eyes when they heard the scraping of the heavy door to the roof opening. Aria jumped up and dragged Neil into a shadow, and then turned back to get her shoes, which she'd left on the lower part of the roof, but Neil grabbed her arm before she could get back down. Then they both heard his mother's strident voice and two sets of footsteps.

"Well, if he didn't come up here, I don't know where he is. He promised me that he would work the Exxon lackeys to convince them to not make a scene this week, and, typically, he got drunk and wandered off with some woman instead. What are we going to do with him?"

Neil widened his eyes and put his fingers to his lips motioning for Aria to be quiet, as though that was necessary at this moment. They were pressed together in a corner with the woman who had her parents killed in eyesight. She was not about to make a sound.

4.
"IT IS OUR DUTY TO WIN"

—Assata Shakur
(call)

Spring of 2030

Aria was going to Juilliard in the fall. The senior showcase was her swan song. Her high school years were politically tumultuous, but she had locked in and focused on her goals. The Sibelius piece showed off her strengths. Her opening cello solo was intense. Romantic. Ominous. Foreboding. She knew from the face of their conductor, Doc Malone, that she'd nailed it. Aria was proud of the instruction Doc had given the orchestra at their last rehearsal. "Follow Aria's lead. Match her tone. I know we haven't had snow here in years, but use your imaginations. Picture Sibelius composing this in the dead of winter in Finland and capture the intensity of the loneliness and longing." It was bold of Doc to hold up Aria as an example to the whole orchestra. The administration had told teachers to be harsh on Lowland kids to try to get them to drop out; and Upland kids often complained to their parents if that wasn't happening.

Aria rose to the challenge that the praise presented for her, nailing her opening solo. She was so focused that night on getting everything right that she hadn't had a chance to find her parents in the crowd before the lights had gone down. They were always there at the end, with their flowers and their unconditional love. Like a baby that had never been dropped, Aria was free to hurl her center of gravity beyond the arms that held her. That confidence gave Aria the space she needed to pour herself into her music and not only get into Juilliard, but be offered a starting spot as first cello in their orchestra.

Aria was physically and emotionally in motion when the orchestra arrived at the part of the piece that was a call-and-response between Aria on cello and Neil on violin. Aria chaffed in annoyance at her friend, thinking about all the drama Neil had caused by unseating Ella Webster as concertmaster.

Aria poured her annoyance into their musical banter. Her eyebrows furrowed with focus. Her head and body jerked with the emotion of the piece, even as her arms and legs steadied the instrument that lay between her legs. Her fingers flew up and down the neck with the light force that the music demanded.

As the whole orchestra took over from Aria and Neil's musical banter, Aria told herself the drama with Neil and Ella was typical high school drama that would end as soon as Aria started at Juilliard. Then the flute solo ended, bringing Aria's attention back to the piece. Aria's second solo was coming up. Although she had every moment of the piece memorized, she counted the remaining rests to increase her confidence. At the end of her solo, she got the tight smile and nod she knew well from Doc Malone. This time Doc had tears in her eyes. It was a difficult piece for a high school orchestra, even at an arts school, and they'd nailed it.

As the applause rang out, Aria searched the edges of the darkness for her parents. They usually sat on the left in the middle, giving them the best view around the conductor of the first cello seat. Aria collected her music, searching row by row. There were guards in every row, presumably related to Neil, but no sign of her parents. She took her solo bow on Doc's cue and listened for the embarrassing whistle that always came from her dad when Aria was called out for attention. No whistle. Aria filed off stage after the full orchestra took a bow and looked back one more time. Maybe the pass she'd given them for parents to attend the concert hadn't gotten them through the checkpoint?

Aria's best friend Noona was in the audience with her family. Her younger brother played the trumpet, but Noona would have come just to see Aria too. Noona made a panicked gesture and mouthed that she was coming on stage. She pushed past her applauding family, running down the aisle and up the steps of the stage, into the wings where the curtains could hide their conversation from view, if not from the audio surveillance on their phones.

"Look," Noona handed Aria her phone and pointed at the news bubble that had popped up on the screen. Aria clicked through to the article.

> Traitors Arrested. Police apprehended Elizabeth and Suresh Petros earlier today for leading a conspiracy to overthrow the Upland Government. The two had established an elaborate front as restaurant operators in Lowland DC, where they had been holding illegal meetings and operating the Lowland government food apparatus, all

> while making plans to assassinate President Donner and steal from Upland. "Public safety has been restored with this arrest," stated Upland DC Governor, Simone Rao.

Aria stopped reading. Her mind flooded with questions. When did this happen? Where were her parents? Would she ever see them again? She'd never asked her parents outright what their roles were, but she'd always known that they were active in Lowland politics. They seemed to know everyone, and everyone knew them. They were never shy about their political views around liberation and had raised Aria to be vocal herself. Aria knew with absolute certainty that her parents had no plans to harm anyone, much less kill President Donner, as much as they loathed the man. They were devoted to nonviolent activism for strategic reasons. It would be absurd if it wasn't so terrifying. For the first time in her life, Aria wished she had a sibling or someone else in her family to call. She was an only child of only children, and all her extended family was in India or Ethiopia. She needed help here and now. She hesitated for a second, but then let her mind go to Neil. He could be a smug asshole, but he had connections. *His mother is quoted in this piece.* Aria took Noona's phone and waved her to join in pursuit of Neil, ignoring Ella, who was motioning her over from across the green room.

"Have you seen this?" Aria thrust the phone at Neil.

"Congratulations to you too. I made you sound pretty good, eh?"

"Shut up and read it, Neil," Aria demanded, giving him a second to get the gist. "Those are my parents. They didn't show up tonight." Aria suddenly teared up at the thought that they weren't there with flowers to greet her. She felt shame at her flash of selfishness. "I need to find them."

Neil looked up from reading the article, returned the phone to Noona, and embraced Aria, letting her body melt into his. "My God. What can I do?"

Noona answered immediately. "Do you know anyone who can take Aria to them? What about your guard?"

Neil's mother was Upland DC Governor, and she was the one who still allowed Lowland kids to attend Ellington, presumably, and had even managed to keep the name Ellington. Neil always had one or more guards with him at school. He may have mistreated Aria by breaking off their prom date, but they had been friends for four years. He was her first love and he had claimed that she was his first love, too, even though he'd had plenty of girlfriends before Aria. Surely, he would help her.

"Please, Neil. I'm begging you."

Neil motioned over his guard, the one who was the most ever-present, who Aria always thought of as the strong, swarthy one. His slicked-back black wavy hair and strong set jaw produced a no-nonsense vibration that parted the sea of chatting orchestra kids without him having to say a word. Kids and teachers were patting Aria on the back and congratulating her, but backed off silently with nods of appreciation as the guard approached. Aria handed Noona her beloved cello in a daze and asked her to take it and also to tell Ella what was happening. Aria, Neil, and his guard stood in a bubble of urgency that muffled the buzz around them.

"What's up, kiddo?"

"It's sensitive," Neil said. The guard nodded and took a rolled-up lead bag off of his utility belt, where he placed his watch and Neil's as well as both of their phones. "It's about the girl," Neil added, indicating Aria's phone, which the guard took and secured.

"You're the Petros kid."

Aria nodded.

"I'm sorry. There's nothing I can do."

"Do you know where they are?" Neil asked.

"Yes, but you don't want to get mixed up in this, and they won't be held there for long."

Neil intervened. "She wants to see them, and we're going to make that happen. If you don't help her, I'll figure out how to do it myself."

Aria was relieved that Neil was going to help. She looked at the guard, dubious about how helpful a white Donner Administration employee was really going to be. "If you aren't going to help, give us our phones back. We'll look up where every prison is and go to them all."

The guard looked at Neil and Aria with a mix of exasperation and sympathy. "Let me confirm where they are. I'll try to get you in for a few minutes, but it won't be believable if Neil is there. It'll just be you and me sneaking in."

"You can trust Anthony," Neil assured Aria. He held her hand and squeezed it.

Breaking into the detention facility to see her parents involved being blindfolded and manhandled—albeit gently—by the guard. He'd told her that it was going to be hard on her to be snuck in, but Aria was determined. When her blindfold came off, Aria blinked. As her eyes adjusted, she made out a fluorescently lit room full of desks and security guards, most of them holding the arm of a detainee. Aria was the only prisoner who could see how many others were there; everyone else had both their faces covered and their ankles and wrists bound. None of them were her parents. Aria looked down to see she was wearing an oversized T-shirt, likely of the guard's, over the black formal dress she'd worn for her solo. Neil's guard was taking her in under the pretense of her being a prisoner. Either that or she really was an idiot, and he was arresting her. Suddenly she realized that she only knew this guy's first name, Anthony. She had put her life in Anthony's hands based on Neil's trust, and she hoped he was right to trust him.

"Got a Lowland kid for breaking curfew," the guard barked as he pushed her through another door and into a hallway. He then spoke softly. "You have five minutes." Anthony scanned his pupil on the eye sensor, opening a door that held Beth and Shuri, Aria's Ema and Baba.

When the door opened, cockroaches scattered across the floor to the edge of the cell. Aria almost didn't recognize her own parents huddled together. The metallic smell of blood pierced through the smell of ammonia in the dark, cramped room. The walls were scratched with names and tick marks tracking days. Her parents were wearing regular clothes they wore to work at their restaurant, but their bodies and their clothes were as battered as the room they were locked in. They looked confused and so unlike their normal calm and competent selves. Aria fell into their arms and sobbed at the sight of their bruises and dried blood. "You shouldn't be here," her father said in his practical Indian dad way, as her mother rubbed her back. "It's not safe."

"I needed to see you. A guard snuck me in and will sneak me out soon."

"Then let's use the time wisely and hope you get out of here after that. All we can do is hope she gets out. Take this."

Aria's mother took off her ring and put it on Aria's finger. "Listen to me, sweetheart. I'm so sorry that we are abandoning you this way. Take the ring and remember you are loved. There is so much we did not have a chance to tell you and to teach you."

"What do you mean abandoning me? I'm not leaving you in here."

"Drop this Aria, please. You'll only make yourself a target. You are a Black woman moving in a world where that alone makes you a target. I know you, and I beg you, do not do anything rash. Play the long game. I'm sorry we didn't prepare you better, but I beg you, do not act alone, ever. Remember Anka, the server at our restaurant? She was arrested and executed with no trial six months ago for organizing against Donner. We've been trying to make her story public through our community, but few people even remember what *Habeas corpus* is supposed to mean in Upland. There's no due process, just swift punishment for what they see as treason. I can't imagine it will be different for us, especially with Simone Rao involved. I don't want you caught up in this. It's going to be hard but you need to continue your plans for now. Go to Juilliard. Live your life."

Why were they giving up? They were all she had. Aria felt a flash of how alone she would be without them and spoke through her tears. "No, Ema. They can't kill anyone unless they're trying to cross an international border. I know Neil Rao, remember? I'll find out where his mother is right now and demand you be released. It's my duty as your daughter. It's the dharma Baba is always talking about. I'll fight for your freedom."

Aria's father responded. "It is not your duty to fight for us, beta. That would be folly. It is your duty to fight for *your* freedom and *your* generation's freedom. Those duties are as ancient as the Gita and as recent as Assata Shakur. I know you are thinking of what we taught you about her, but this is a different time. We can't escape like Assata did. We won't be able to get out of here, of this. Stay away from Simone Rao. We saw her there, watching from her armored vehicle when they broke down the door of the restaurant, set it afire, and arrested us. She is a self-loathing murderer and I want you nowhere near her crosshairs. She is now claiming that every checkpoint to a Lowland community is an international border. They've been saying they would do it for a while, but now they have done it. The sham judge told us."

"I don't care what the judge said. This is illegal and I'll stop it."

Aria's mother whispered in her ear. "I believe you, sweetie, but not by yourself and not in time to save us. Please don't talk about this anymore here, and please don't worry about us." She looked at Aria's father before continuing. "We did our best to bend the arc of history towards justice. We've laid the groundwork that we could. We took care of you the best we could. I'm sorry we couldn't do more. It's up to you and the others now. Grieve for us. Say our names, but not for too long. You have a life to live."

Aria's father broke in. "I don't see why she should grieve. Remember what Lord Krishna says about death. 'Every human is destined to die. Do not grieve the unavoidable. The spirit is not destroyed when the body is destroyed.'" His voice cracked as he continued. "I am so, so proud of the woman you have become, my dear. It is your turn to live a full and beautiful life. You have so many people out there who love you. Sophie has some things you'll need for Juilliard. Do not take this whole burden on your shoulders.

Just do what you can. And, as always, listen to Ema's advice over mine where we disagree. My better half is smarter and more beautiful." Aria had heard her dad say that line about her mom to hundreds if not thousands of patrons at their restaurant over the years. She could not accept that this would be the last time she would hear it.

Why were her parents giving her contradictory advice on grieving, as though they were already dead? Why didn't they believe she could fix this? Didn't they know how much she loved them? Aria was crying too hard to speak and poured the ferocity of her love and appreciation through her hug. She hoped it came through. She spoke through tears when she could. "I'm so sorry I gave you such a hard time. I'm lucky to have you as parents. Thank you for everything. I beg you, please, please fight this. I'll fight for you on the outside."

"Shhh. My heart, enough of that talk. Find happiness and take care of yourself. Find your family."

Aria was sobbing again when the door opened. They were her only family she cared about or even knew. "Wait. We need just a few more minutes," her mom said, just before a bag slipped over Aria's head, abruptly ending her last sight of her parents. She felt her hands squeezed by her parents. The thud of the metal door closing was the last sound she heard before she lost consciousness.

Aria woke up before dawn in her family home. Anthony had warned her that he was going to inject her with something in order to get her out. She'd lost consciousness as he'd planned and presumably gotten her out of the detention center in an ambulance, as he had planned. Aria was not sure why he'd gone through so much trouble to help her, but she was grateful. She needed to make a plan to save her parents.

Aria knew instinctively that she should get out of the house before the sun rose. She found money, and a stash of documents in their "go bag" behind the shelf where her toy giraffe, Sophie, still sat after all these years. They didn't know anyone named Sophie, so this is what her dad was directing her to do, surely. Aria took the bag, remembering her parents' instructions on how to leave the house in an emergency. She climbed through the roof hatch and crawled across to the neighbor's roof. There were a few reporters on their street already and the sun wasn't even fully up. She climbed down to the balcony of the end unit, jumped down to the alley, and walked towards the nearest safe house she knew about. Although she had enough money in the go bag, she would never go on to attend Juilliard.

5.
"WE MUST LOVE EACH OTHER AND SUPPORT EACH OTHER"

—Assata Shakur
(response)

Ten days before Eamon

Neil had consumed enough alcohol in his life to know that the one drink he had had at the reception plus a couple lemonades should not have made him feel this disoriented. His head was heavy. He could only open one eye at a time, and every quick movement made the roof spin.

Neil had a lot of experience acting sober in front of his mother, and a propensity for acting on instinct. He was lucid enough to know Aria was scared and hurt, that he had Aria in his arms, and that his mother was nearby. Then he heard her voice again.

"Where does the tracker say he is? Did you get the audio back? I need to throw his shirts out and get a new set of mics, clearly. Remind me to fire the person who takes care of his wardrobe."

"Ma'am, the guards downstairs said he came up here, and

the tracker shows he is here. The tracker is in his shoes, so it's possible that he changed up here and left his clothes here, which would explain why they lost the audio feed on him."

If the roof would stop spinning for a second, Neil felt he could come up with a plan. The sound of footsteps approaching even closer let Neil know he had no time for planning. If Aria believed his mother had her parents killed, Neil believed her. Aria was frozen with fear. Neil knew his mother to be ruthless in the face of fear. He had to get her out of there, and there was no way out but through. Even wasted, he knew they couldn't make a run for it and hope to make it past his mother and the armed guard with his hand already on his weapon.

Neil made up his mind, loopy as it was. He looked at Aria, raising his eyebrows and tipping his head, silently asking for consent to act. He saw her nod "yes." Technically he saw two of her nod "yes," but he could only feel one of her, so he moved forward with the plan. He took off his cummerbund and started unbuttoning his shirt, handing the clip back to Aria. He unbuttoned his pants and realized he had a hard-on. He was pitiful. *How is that even possible with this much alcohol in my system?* All the better to make his mother back away, he supposed.

Aria touched Neil's side, reminding Neil of both their predicament, and why his dick was hard. He pulled Aria closer and caressed her cheek with his hand. He leaned over and pressed his lips to her neck, more sloppily than he meant to, and whispered in her ear louder than he meant to.

"Trust me." Aria looked annoyed but nodded again. Neil looked her in the eye as he shoved his pants to the ground. His vague plan was to shock his mother. Aria's eyes lowered to the erection visible through his boxers and then jerked back up to looking into Neil's eyes with a steadiness that eluded Neil. Neil pulled Aria into his half naked body, realizing she would feel his cock pressing against the crotch of her dress. Aria played along and scratched her nails down Neil's naked back. Even drunk and drugged, especially drunk and drugged, Neil could push his mother's buttons. Simone Rao hated sex, hated drugs, and hated her son as far as Neil could tell. Neil could not think clearly, but disappointing his mother was instinct.

Neil began the show at that point and groaned loudly, "You are so fucking hot!" He moaned loudly for show, trying to drown out the click-clack of his mother's heels coming quickly across the roof.

"NEIL. What are you doing? You are supposed to be downstairs working. I cannot allow you to blow a deal worth trillions of dollars. Are you drunk? Put your clothes on and step away from that whore!"

Aria tensed every muscle in her body against Neil. She was frozen again. Neil held her close, protecting Aria from having to turn her head, feeling her stiffness in their embrace. He turned so that Aria was protected from view and by the shadow of the equipment on the roof. He stepped towards his mother.

"Muhther," Neil said loudly, stepping out of the shadow. He was half naked in front of his mom. Right. No way out, but through. Neil willed his tongue to sound sober. Arrogance usually worked on his mom. Neil attempted a haughty tone, but his words came out stilted and he gave up halfway through. "We were not expecting an interruption, and this is most embarrassing. If you give us a moment we will get dressed and I'll introduce you to my fiancée, but you're gonna have to please apologize for calling her a whore." Neil's mother had taken off her shawl and was busy trying to shield her view of her son.

"What will people think? Your fiancée? What are you talking about, Neil? Put your clothes on now. Have you no shame? You are standing in your underwear on the roof of a public building in the middle of a critically important diplomatic event, and YOU want ME to apologize?"

Neil stepped towards his mother and to the side, forcing his mother to move her shawl to continue blocking her view. "Mother, I'm also standing in my underwear on billboards all over Upland. Give us five minutes to get dressed and we'll meet you downstairs." Maybe now she'd finally fire him.

"No. I'm not leaving until you tell me why you are referring to this Black whore as your fiancée." She was fixated on Aria in a way that made Neil growl. She'd never met Aria, but she might know what Aria looked like. She needed to leave.

"STOP calling her a whore," Neil belted out, all his muscles tensing. He walked towards his mother again, causing the guard to step forward. "If you must know, she is pregnant with your grandchild, so we got engaged last week. I gave her your mother's ring already and was going to tell you after your big meeting." Neil was saying whatever words would most piss off his mom. It was kind of fun, and it seemed to work. He needed to bring this to a close. "Mother, I've given you enough leeway. Give us a minute to gather ourselves or I will not talk to you about this at all and I will go straight to the media. In fact, I've got Becca at State News on speed dial. Shall I start a video call now?"

"Get dressed. Meet me in the conference room in five minutes. Bring the girl." With that, she spun around to the roof door, her guard following closely behind her.

Thank God. She was gone. He had done it. Neil felt a thick breeze and was reminded that he had no pants on. Walking unsteadily over to the pile of tuxedo, he was not sure he could face the challenge of pulling up his pants and pulling his shirt on. Aria motioned for him and handed him the lead clamp to put on the shirt in the pile. Neil could not manage that level of dexterity, so Aria came over and placed the clip on his shirt. Neil's moments of lucidity had taken all his energy. His head felt heavy. He needed help holding it up. He needed to call Anthony, his best friend and security detail.

"I need to get out of here," Aria said from behind him.

"I know. That door." Neil pointed around the corner. He spoke into his watch. "Caw Anny." His watch didn't respond, and Neil realized he must not have spoken clearly enough. Damn tongue. He tried again. "Call. Anthony." It worked that time. Neil tried to focus whatever brain cells he had left on speaking clearly. "Emergency," he said. Neil turned to Aria hoping she could fill in the rest.

"Hey, kid. Don't worry. I'm already in the back stairwell coming in now." The door swung open, and Anthony's larger-than-life presence was on the scene. Anthony's deep voice sent a calming wave through Neil's body. Neil could finally lower his guard and give into his exhaustion.

"It's you," Aria said, giving Neil a quick pat on the shoulder before leaving. Neil stayed on the roof, dozing in and out of consciousness. He had a vague notion that he needed to get dressed and retrieve Aria's shoes.

Neil woke up tangled in the satin sheets on his California king bed. He had a splitting headache and a foggy memory of encountering the high school girlfriend he'd been obsessed with finding, the night before. She was the first thing on his mind when he cracked his eyes open. He recalled how pleased he was that she'd snuck into the party to see him last night. He remembered locking eyes with her when he'd finally gotten her to turn around. He remembered telling her about his pet project of reducing light pollution in an effort to impress her, but everything after that was a blank.

The torch he'd carried for Aria had not gone out, apparently. It had shrunk down to a pilot light without Aria's oxygen, but as soon as he laid eyes on her, it wooshed into a raging fire. Aria was clearly not the same girl he'd pined after and fallen in love with in high school. The new version was tantalizingly familiar but also had an edge that she'd likely sharpened dealing with the aftermath of her parents' deaths.

Why had she finally sought him out? And what happened last night? He must have had some encounter with her that led him to drink himself into oblivion. Neil had been with a lot of women. He'd never resisted the long-legged busty models who threw themselves at him, offering him blow jobs and easy fucks, but those women were just warm bodies to him, just as he was nothing but a warm body and story for them to tell their friends. Aria was the only girl he'd been with who had also been his friend, who saw who he was beyond his body, and who certainly wanted nothing to do with his political connections.

Neil had imagined finding Aria so many times, but somehow he could not pull many memories of the actual finding of her from his brain. The most anticipated encounter of his life was a blank. Neil had blacked out a few times before, but this felt much worse than those previous times. He had brain fog and his head throbbed. He needed coffee. He also needed a new brain and body that he hadn't poisoned with alcohol, ideally. By the time his eyes were able to focus on the numbers on his watch it was already after 10 am. He was so far gone that he hadn't remembered until that moment that he was supposed to be working at his mother's meeting and at the pre-meeting breakfast at 8 am, so he quickly sent his mother a voice memo from his watch letting her know he was not feeling great and asking if he could rest a while.

The responding video message came quickly, projecting up an image of his mother's petite intensity from his phone.

> *"I'm dealing with this mess for the rest of the day but do not for one second think you are off the hook. We are talking about this so-called engagement tonight. You are being irresponsible, and you are in no way ready to be a father. We need to take care of this. One mess at a time. I do hope you didn't get caught up in the riots this morning. Send me the recording from yesterday's meeting and we can go over both work and your personal entanglements tonight. Be home at 8 sharp for dinner and a talk."*

What the fuck was his mother on about now? An engagement? Becoming a father? A riot? At least it seemed like the meeting wasn't happening. Neil had been blackmailed by his mother into taking this job, after his mother had also blackmailed all his bandmates into replacing him and finding a new bass player. She'd given Neil the choice of either working for her or she'd deplete his bank accounts and stop paying his rent so that he'd need to live with her. She had the power to do it and he'd seen her do worse to people who crossed her. No way in hell he was going to ever live with his mother again, so he was trying to keep the job for now, until he had a better plan.

His mom had said he was supposed to deliver the recording from yesterday's meeting, which should be easy enough, in theory. Neil had left the video files locked in the office he was using yesterday just before the reception. He'd go back and get them. Maybe something in them or at the site of the party would help him figure out who drugged him and why. At least he was off the hook for the meeting today. Neil opened his underwear and socks drawer and cursed his previous self for not doing laundry. He was down to the dregs. At least he had perfectly tailored clean suits hanging in his closet. For the first time, he was grateful that his mother had always insisted on handling his formal wear.

After getting dressed, chugging a gallon of water, a few cups of coffee, and a few aspirin, Neil's headache had dulled, and he felt nearly human again. He was too old for this. He needed to figure out what was going on and fast. He massaged his forehead and pushed on his eyes to make sure the pills had worked. He seemed better, but he was moving too slowly. It was now nearly noon and he had to get his files still as well as piece together what happened last night. He needed to call Anthony and find out what he knew. First, he needed some context. He found his bag in the corner of his room, with his computer. He opened the bag, and his laptop was there along with a pair of high heels. *What the hell?* Neil opened his computer and put on video of the state-owned news channel's morning coverage. It was biased, but it was the only news that was allowed by his mother's administration. Rebecca Donner was anchoring the news, and her familiar voice filled the room. She'd interviewed Neil dozens of times. He was the dark-skinned mascot for the Donner Administration that his mother trotted out every time she wanted to claim they can't possibly be racist.

Neil's mind returned to his brief encounter with Aria as he listened. Was it brief? Was it possible Aria was part of Expectus and had drugged him to get information out of him? He had just assumed that Aria had finally sought him out. His big head had played right into her dainty hands. Was she going to blackmail him with compromising photos or something? Aria had always been a quick study with a disciplined mind. It was one of the many things Neil loved about her. It seemed so unlike her to use her smarts to harm people, but she could have changed. She would have changed after her parents' deaths.

Neil went over the items in his bag again and wondered how he had recovered it from the coat check. The shoes must be Aria's. Neil resisted the urge to smell them. *Don't be a creep.* Neil's brain was yielding little about the night before, but somehow delivered up a clear memory of kissing his way up Aria's skirt twelve years ago to find that Aria hadn't worn underwear to prom. His cock stiffened at the memory of the smell of Aria. After being with so many women, how was it that a memory of Aria from twelve years ago could make him hard in an instant? Neil re-committed to not being a creep and to be extra good. He even spared a second of sympathy for the twelve years of women whose only flaw had been that they were not Aria.

Most of Neil's memories of Aria were of her playing the cello with a passion that made everyone stop what they were doing and listen. He'd never met anyone who could improvise like Aria. There was never even a question that she'd get into Juilliard. She didn't just have technical talent and preparedness, she had a magical way of connecting through music to peoples' souls. She was incredible, and the times when they played together were the most zen moments of

Neil's life. He loved being in a band with his friends, but he'd never had that kind of electricity and connection with anyone else. They read each other's minds and fed off of each other. They made each other better.

But that hadn't exactly been the case the night before. Or had it? The bits Neil was learning about the night were bizarre. *Was Aria the fiancée his mother thought he had gotten pregnant?* Biology had never been Neil's best subject, but he was pretty sure that a woman he hadn't seen in twelve years and had never had actual sexual intercourse with outside of his dreams could not be pregnant with his child. He needed to find out what was going on, and the state media's coverage was the best he could do for information under the circumstances.

6.
"THE REVOLUTION WILL NOT BE TELEVISED"

—Gil Scott-Heron

Nine days before Eamon

The figures being projected into Neil's room were, in actuality, sitting across town behind a square desk, surrounded by hot lights that made the air conditioner in the building work twice as hard, spewing even more heat into the oven-like outside air. The co-anchors were not sitting in love seats, as they appeared to be in Neil's room, but rather in stiff chairs in what had years ago been the studios of Voice of America, and now were simply labeled "State Media."

Since the vast majority of the news was about extreme weather, meteorologist Joe Donner served as co-anchor. He was the grandson of President Donner, and also technically the Director of State Media. Not wanting to handle the non-weather news that would mostly be about his own family, Joe convinced his wife, Becca, to be his co-host. They were the last of the live anchors in the country, as their producer Laurie reminded them periodically. They would have been replaced by CGI anchors reading AI-drafted scripts, but President Donner liked showing off his grandson and his wholesome family.

That day, the news Becca had to read was of great interest to Upland and Lowland alike. They could see on the dashboard projected in the room that there were over 50 million viewers, which was almost equal to the population of Upland, though the much larger population of various Lowlands were likely tuning in as well. Rebecca read her AI-generated-script with far more talent than the CGI anchors ever could, and never betrayed her disdain for the AI's slant. No one in the public could guess that moments before she had looked over Joe's script, she had been sobbing. Becca was a consummate professional. Joe liked watching his wife work.

Rebecca Donner: A group of so-called "activists" from the radical terrorist group Expectus have yet again caused mayhem and damage to our national status and diplomatic activities. The dangerous riot and property destruction campaign began this morning before dawn with hundreds of radicals entering the meeting place where the oil and gas lease auctions were to take place with dignitaries from all the BRUINS nations present. The rioters chained some doors shut and used the brute-force of their bodies to blockade other doors. They damaged the building, attacked bystanders with paint, released stink bombs and dropped incendiary banners from the top of the building. Biological weapons were also detected, including a number of the infamous Lone Star Ticks that Expectus has released repeatedly, leaving most Uplanders with a severe allergic reaction to meat. Almost a dozen of the rioters were arrested and the police are still processing and charging rioters with treason as we speak. Other riots broke out all over Upland locations, at banking facilities, resulting in thousands of banking locations being closed for the day, just as the public is desperately trying to evacuate across Western Upland. The traitors from Expectus have shown utter disdain for the Donner Administration and for the security of Upland. As a reminder to our listeners, any act to subvert the government or sow discord is a punishable offense. The courts have made clear that due process can be waived for offenses related to treason to protect national security.

President Donner has deployed security forces to deal with these rebellions, and the White House issued a short statement: "This incident will not disrupt the normal functioning of Upland and all citizens will have access to necessary services. We urge all citizens to remain calm and vigilant. We must stand together against Expectus and their malicious intentions. Any information about the whereabouts of Expectus activists should be reported to authorities immediately. Rest assured that order will be restored. Let us stand united against this threat to our great nation."

Joe Donner: Thanks Becca for all that information and reassurance, and good morning listeners! I'm your meteorologist, Joe Donner, here with the latest updates. Skies are clear and the sun is shining brightly in some Upland locations. The heat index will reach over one-ten here in Upland DC, even with our overcast skies. If it were sunny conditions here, the temperatures would reach one-twenty! Thank goodness for these clouds that are a result of the prevailing winds carrying smoke from the West Coast to the East Coast.

Looking into the Atlantic now, as wind patterns change, Tropical Storm Eamon is on track to become Hurricane Eamon and pose a threat to the entire Eastern Seaboard in the next ten days according to our AI models. The landfall could be anywhere along the East Coast, but the majority of models show a direct hit to Annapolis, Maryland. State media was able to talk with the mayor.

After their producer, Laurie, played a virtual reality recording of the Mayor of Annapolis, Joe Donner finished reading the AI-bot-generated script, and got the all clear signal from Laurie. He also saw his wife smile and nod in response. "I gotta run to the bathroom, Dop, and then Laurie and I are grabbing lunch. You gonna join us?" Becca asked.

Becca had always called Joe "Doppler," or just "Dop," since he covered weather, and also, he suspected, because she hated the Donner family and all that it signified. The Donners were a family that most people in Upland would be thrilled to be married into. Not so for Becca, and if Joe was honest, he didn't really mind. It served his uptight family right to have a daughter-in-law who barely tolerated their presence.

"Go ahead without me." Joe didn't bother to look up from his papers. "I need to read over what nonsense the bots wrote for the segments on the perma-drought in the Middle East that we are supposedly also going to prevail over." Becca laughed, unclipped her microphone from her lapel, walked around the rectangular anchor desk and gave Joe a peck on the top of his head.

"Okay. Love you. See you at home. Let's remember to squeeze the kids extra tight tonight when they're back from school." Becca was visibly distressed again and teared up as she talked about hugging their kids. Joe wasn't sure how he could help. He silently chastised himself for being relieved that she was too distraught to be concerned with Joe's whereabouts. He reached up to give Becca a side hug and to rub her arm.

Becca and Joe had been together since college, where Becca studied film and Joe meteorology. They had two kids, a dog, two Paxa cars that were self-driving and electric, and had worked together at the state-owned station for over a decade, since the inception of the station, when all visual, audio, print, and online news stations were collapsed into one state channel that was sanctioned by President Donner. Joe hated that his grandfather had put him in charge. He hated managing people and having to make decisions. He hated getting angry calls from his grandfather and father when they didn't like the State Media coverage even though it was all generated by bots they had a hand in programming. Deep down, Joe knew it was nonsense that only white Christians should control the government or be in positions of power. His parents and his grandfather were on the wrong side of history, he suspected. Joe wanted nothing to do with any of that, and wished for a world where he could be with his lover, keep his family safe, do the weather reports, and not be in charge of State Media.

As Joe watched his wife walk out of the station, he reminded himself that his choices weren't all selfishness. It was too dangerous to uproot their family and move to Lowland, as Becca had wanted to do, rather than take their current State Media jobs. It wasn't just that they'd have to give up creature comforts and Joe would have to give up his lover; they'd also be risking their kids' lives. Becca had totally lost touch with her family out west when Paxa had geofenced and cut off cellular service to every Lowland across the country, but she seemed to be able to live with that for now. They didn't have much of a choice. Still, Joe felt a bit guilty for his role in isolating her. At least she had good friends like Laurie. Joe suspected Laurie was more than a good friend, and was happy for Becca.

Joe had pictured Becca's parents and sister when he had read the words on the newscast earlier. "*All of Washington, Idaho, and Oregon are already 48 hours into a 72-hour evacuation notice, with one full day left to evacuate, due to the expansion of the Mega-Fire.*" So many millions of lives were in danger. They needed more than one day to safely evacuate such a large area. Joe hoped Becca's family was safe. He liked her parents. His mother-in-law was smart, and funny, and she liked Joe. She could be dead now, for all they knew. He could only imagine that Becca was processing all of this with Laurie. He was glad they had each other. Joe needed a less verbal kind of outlet and he was itching for it at the moment. He sent a quick text message from his watch.

"Meet me in an hour," he said into his wrist. The response came quickly. "Affirmative" it said on his watch, to his relief. Joe had no other coping skills. He needed to get laid.

When Joe arrived at the hotel room at the Hinckley Hilton near their home in Kalorama, he immediately felt the stress of the day's news melt away. He lifted his thumb to the sensor on the hotel room door and entered. He was sure his family knew that he had rented this room. He had tried to imply a few times that he and Becca needed a private spot nearby but away from the kids and they hadn't pried beyond that. Joe's source of relief was already there; he could tell from the smell of cedar campfire cologne, and the light on in the bathroom. Joe slipped off his shoes, took off his clothes and stretched out on top of the covers to the bed with his hands behind his head and his feet lightly crossed, exactly as he knew his lover preferred.

No one in his family would ever accept that he was gay, so he hid it. Back when Joe's grandfather was Governor of Virginia, Joe had been playing hide-and-seek in the Governor's mansion, when he found his grandfather in bed with a man. Joe was too young to fully comprehend what he saw, but later, as a teenager, Joe remembered that day and tried to come out to his grandfather, suggesting that they might be the same. His grandfather had slapped him across the face, and said, "Kin or no kin, I will kill you if you say a word about this. You understand, boy?" Joe's ears still sometimes rang with those words. He had not raised his own sexuality or his grandfather's to anyone since then.

Given how closely everyone was watched these days, Joe's grandfather likely knew that Joe was not only gay, but had a long-time lover. His life was privileged enough that even if they knew, everyone turned a blind eye to his affair with a Secret Service agent who pleasured him exactly as he liked it.

That day was no exception. Joe felt satiated and ready to face his family's quiet grief about his in-laws likely being dead. It was yet another trauma he would never speak about with his own parents or grandparents.

Being submissive brought pleasure and made Joe forget about the world he was trapped in, a world where he was in charge of a station he didn't believe in, where his own family would not lift a finger to help his wife's family, and where his choices were to be closeted or to be caged.

Joe didn't believe he was in danger of imprisonment. What tortured him was the knowledge that he was putting people he cared about in danger. They were careful—careful to never use each other's real names, careful to never leave at the same time, careful to never greet each other from across the room on the rare occasions Joe attended official events with security. Joe couldn't stop, wouldn't stop, just because of the risk. He needed this. As he walked out of the hotel room, Joe tried not to imagine the person he loved walking into an office across town and being fired and arrested for sodomy, but he knew it could happen. It could be happening at that moment for all he knew. Joe steeled himself mentally. If push came to shove, Joe would do what he had to do to protect Anthony.

7.
"WE HAVE NOTHING TO LOSE BUT OUR CHAINS"

—Assata Shakur
(response)

Nine days before Eamon

How did I get here? Aria's right arm was attached to the inside of her lockbox by a metal chain bracelet with a carabiner at the end, which was hooked to a bar inside a heavy cylinder. She sat under a tree not far from where they had disrupted the meeting. Aria was normally meticulous about checking her equipment before an action, but her run-in with Secretary Rao the night before had shaken her focus.

The events of that morning were running in a loop in Aria's mind. It was solid action logic to prevent a meeting of dirty diplomats with stink bombs and paint made to look like oil. The advance team had entered through the roof door Aria left open the night before. They had chained the front and rear doors shut from the inside. She had to hand it to both the art and tactical teams. One of the photos from the inside action was definitely going to spread like fire—an entire wall of Donner portraits had been embellished with mustaches and horns that somehow matched the paint and style of the portraits. Security didn't even know Expectus was there until everyone on the inside had left the scene.

At that point, the blockades from the outside went into position and Aria joined the front team, locking herself to a window next to the main entrance. She wanted to make sure attendees and security were clear that they were not going to be able to enter. The security quickly shoved out people who were not chained. After one of the cops began throwing punches, the yellow team retreated back to Lowland, as planned. Aria had her phone out, visibly recording the police behavior, even though each lockbox was also fitted with a recording device. She'd hoped the visible recording would reduce violence. It did not. The cop that had been throwing punches had kicked the phone out of her hand, twisted her arm and spat in her face. She had been braced for a punch to her head when he suddenly retreated. It sounded to her like one of the Upland soldiers was screaming that they had seen a Lone Star Tick. The State Media psy-ops was so good that they actually were terrified of these tiny ticks and believed they constituted an emergency. Donner had made people afraid of all the wrong things. The claim of a tick sighting was enough to activate the protocol of clearing areas with biological weapons.

After that, the security, police, and military cleared out. They'd met their objective of preventing the meeting from taking place. They had footage of police violence towards nonviolent Expectus members to share through Lowland. The videos would increase ire at the Donnerites and get everyone in formation for the week ahead. They also had the highly amusing portraits mocking Donner that would drive President Donner mad and delight their base.

They'd done what they needed to do for the first action day. Aria wanted her team to get back to the meetup point and get re-deployed to any alternate meeting location the Donner Administration came up with. That was when Aria realized that her carabiner was stuck. She had grabbed a new kind of carabiner that morning that she had never used. When she'd tried it out, she could unscrew it with her thumb and pull it apart to release herself. Now she couldn't see the contraption inside the lockbox. She wasn't sure why it wasn't unscrewing and releasing, but it resisted all the centripetal force of her thumb. She was stuck to a window grate that the team had attached a lockbox to that morning. Her action buddy that morning was a relative novice, who was going by Branch. They had helped Aria unscrew the entire window grate and remove the lockbox. They carried the lockbox, with Aria's arm inside it, to a nearby Magnolia tree. There was no way Aria could sneak through the police perimeter back into Lowland with the lockbox attached to her arm. The chinks in the Upland armor were big, but not that big. Branch had wanted to stay with Aria, as was protocol.

"Sorry, Branch, we'll be in more danger here if there are two of us, and I'll be fine. I know this area like the back of my hand, and I've survived hotter days. The best way you can be an ally right now is to leave with the rest of the team while the biohazard perimeter and fog are still in place. I'll be fine until dark on my own, and then I'll sneak out. Go. Let the tactical team know where I am and that I'm fine." Branch didn't move, and was nodding to themselves seemingly in deep thought, so Aria added, "That's an order, not a request."

"Hmm. I was raised to protect any darker-skinned elder, but I'll cede to your preference this time, since you're the team lead," they'd said before leaving, clearly not understanding that Aria would have just had the rest of the team drag Branch off if they became difficult. It would have been torture to spend the day with the young activist calling her an elder and peppering her with questions. She wanted to be alone.

Now here she was with only $100 Upland Credits, a fake ID, and the small burner phone she'd retrieved fastened together in her tank top. She had a handful of peanuts in her back pocket she couldn't reach. It had gotten so hot that even if there hadn't been a biohazard perimeter, no one would be outside. Aria was hungry and thirsty, but she'd have to wait until it was dark enough that someone would be sent to get her, or until the police found her and arrested her.

What a mess. Aria thought of what Poppy would say. Poppy would remind her that surviving this situation was her specialty, or spe-see-ah-li-tee, as Poppy pronounced it with a fake British lilt. Aria was the disaster queen. She was calm in a crisis. Poppy would remind her of all that she had achieved during disasters. Like when she had gone to Los Angeles, days after the huge fire, when it became apparent the government was not going to help. Aria had coached their leadership to develop a recruitment plan for search and rescue. They'd figured out who to assign as team leaders, and strengthened their existing distributed structure. She trained teams in how to do a quick skills assessments to siphon volunteers off into food and water provision, shelter provision, healing provision, and peer therapy training. The LA cadre lead had given Aria a rustic "Triage Tiara" made of handwoven deer grass for her work. The nested set-up they piloted was replicated all over the West as unprecedented fires and heat waves broke out. Aria's work had saved thousands of lives. Aria not only knew what she needed to do to survive this, but she was the go-to source for how to survive heat, fires, and storms.

Aria assessed her wounds. She had some scratches and bruises. She was lucky that her wrist did not seem to be broken, or even sprained, from when the cop kicked the phone out of her hand. She was slowing her breath and focusing her mind by counting. She did a body scan, focusing her mind on her feet first. They were a little sore from wearing heels the night before. She moved to her calves and relaxed them, and did the same with her quadraceps and then tucked her tailbone. She unclenched her stomach and felt her lungs expand under her ribs. She rolled her shoulders back and then relaxed her biceps and triceps, and then forearms. Her wrist was not in as bad of shape as she'd feared, and she was able to relax the muscles in her hands before moving back up to do the same with her facial muscles and finally her scalp. Thoughts and emotions had begun to intrude when her body scan got to her wrist, so Aria began to picture each thought and its associated emotion floating away on a cloud. She pictured the guard who'd attacked her, and pinned his visage and her anger to an imaginary cloud and let it float away. Her thoughts were coming faster than she would have liked, but she kept her distance, observing them, pinning them to clouds, and allowing them to float off. She pictured Branch (mild annoyance), Poppy (embarrassment at her situation, but also pride in having left the roof door open), Noona (love), Secretary Rao (terror), Neil (suspicion and curiosity). Aria's mind wanted to linger on Neil to puzzle out her reaction, but she made that cloud float off, too, and moved to a gratitude meditation—lying under the tree, silently thanking the Magnolia for its shade, the Lone Star Ticks for terrifying Uplanders, her attacker for showing the world how violent Upland society was, Secretary Rao for her lax security, Neil for saving her from that roof, Branch for helping her get under the tree, Noona for being her best friend forever, and Poppy for taking care of her and guiding her.

Aria had been there for a few hours, running through her meditations. She had started thinking of the tree as "Maggie" as she thanked it. The heat had brought out the fragrance of Maggie's flowers. Aria thought of how trees have both male and female reproductive parts, and wondered which part smelled good. Noona would know. She was the one who'd told Aria about the tree sex parts to begin with, right when Aria had come out to her.

"Bi? Cool, so are most trees!" Noona had responded with enthusiasm, as they walked through the National Arboretum. She'd been a budding herbalist even then. Noona had gone on to explain that in most trees, the flowers had both male and female reproductive parts and were referred to as "bisexual."

"I'm a different kind of bisexual than the trees then," Aria told her. "I only have lady bits."

"Yes. Yes. Sorry to make it about the trees and not you. Let's talk about how this new bisexuality discovery feels. Have you kissed a girl, yet?"

"No. The only girl I know who's out is Ella, and I'm not sure I can just walk up to her and ask."

"I'm scared for you, Aria. It's one thing for lilly-white Ella to get in trouble for being gay every few weeks. It wouldn't even be great for me as an Asian girl, but, be honest with yourself; it would be another thing for you entirely as a Black girl."

"I can't just ignore it, though, Noona."

"And you're sure this isn't just a rebound thing from Neil breaking your heart?"

Aria had only confessed to Noona how heartbroken she was under the condition that Noona never bring it up and never say anything to Neil or anyone else. "Shh. Don't even say that. It's not about Neil! And you have to believe me. If my best friend doesn't believe me that I'm bi, no one will."

"Okay, okay. I believe you."

"You know that they have this mandatory re-education detention for everyone who comes out now? It's the gayest scene ever, I hear. You're going to have to sneak into one and see who's there!" Noona laughed, kicking off one of their long plotting sessions that ended with their decision that Aria needed to ask Ella to prom—both to see if she was bi, and to get her first rebound after Neil over with.

The rustling of two Cardinals chasing each other in the branches above brought Aria out of her memory. Aria hoped the birds would enjoy Maggie's seeds in a few months, but the seeds would only come if the heat let up and the seasons changed. They'd all have to survive Hurricane Eamon's wrath to get to fall. For now, the birds hadn't yet sensed the storm in the ten-day forecast, and were just using Maggie for shade, flying from limb to limb in search of a cool breeze. Aria watched as their motion shook free a pale pink petal that floated right onto her stomach. Aria picked it up with her free hand. The sweet smell was tempting, and Aria remembered Noona telling her that magnolia bark and flowers were good for headaches and stress relief.

"Thanks, Maggie," she whispered as she took a small bite of the petal. It was an unexpectedly refreshing treat, and

Aria decided to have a few more petals as they fell. Feeling calmer after her snack, Aria began jiggling the carabiner again to see if it would unstick. She stopped when she heard footsteps.

Aria held her breath to avoid making any noise. In an act of betrayal, her stomach growled more loudly than she thought possible. A laugh escaped her lips at the sound. Maggie's petals were lovely, but not exactly filling.

"Is someone under there?" Aria held her breath again. She glimpsed a flash of an expensive-looking bag set down and dress pants. At least it wasn't military or police. For some reason she was not shocked and almost expected it when the figure that ducked under Maggie's low limbs was Neil. She had conjured him. Or, more likely, he'd just heard her laugh. Or maybe he'd been looking for her at the site of the action? That would not be good. He was impeccably dressed, and obviously had not been kicked around or spat on that morning. Must be nice.

"You again."

"Are—" He started to talk just as she shushed him. She motioned with her one free hand that he needed to take off his shirt. The last thing she needed was her name and situation announced over the surveillance system. Neil looked confused, but grabbed his bag from outside the tree limb circumference and fully entered the shelter the low limbs created. He scrunched his nose, probably from the faint smell of urine that Aria had gotten used to over the past few hours. At least a few folks had taken advantage of Maggie's cover from view to piss on her. Aria wasn't clear on whether her growling stomach and involuntary laugh had led Neil to find her or if he'd been looking for a place to take a piss. At this point, it hardly mattered. He needed to not give her away.

Neil motioned at unbuttoning his shirt with a quizzical look on his face and Aria nodded and confirmed that was what she wanted him to do. He removed his shirt, revealing an undershirt that he had sweat through. Neil removed that as well, though that was unnecessary for avoiding surveillance. Aria reminded herself that she'd seen this before. Even if it was too dark to properly take in last night, Neil's bare chest had been on magazine covers and used to sell all manner of cologne and watches. Aria made eye contact, studiously averting her gaze from the rest of the asshole Adonis that she knew lay beneath his clothes. There was a time when Aria was closer to a young Neil than she even was to Noona. Noona and Aria's friend group has lots of people float in and out, but Neil lasted the longest. Although the threesome included the only three kids of color at the entire school, they were not misfits. On the contrary, they were loved by teachers and classmates alike, and they were devoted to each other. Their friend circle only crumbled when Neil dumped Aria.

The adult Neil started to strut and swing his shirt like he was doing a striptease while kneeling on a bunch of roots. Aria silently asked Maggie to trip him with her roots so she could get back to her mental reset and meditations and avoid crossing a line she didn't need to cross. *Been there. Done that.*

Aria had just asked a tree to trip Neil Rao, who was doing a striptease for her. Maybe she remembered wrong, and those magnolia petals were psychedelics? With the shirt microphone put away, Aria dug into her front pocket and found that she still had the tiny magnet from last night. She handed it to Neil and motioned for him to put it on his watch so they could talk without their conversation being broadcast.

"Neil, I'm grateful for your help last night, really I am, but you shouldn't be here. Humans are not meant for this kind of heat. Go home."

"I'm in the shade, so I guess we're good." Neil smiled. Aria tried another approach.

"Neil, I'm exhausted. Could you leave?"

"This rudeness is so unlike you." Neil said the words as though they were a challenge, as though he still knew her. But Aria was not one to give up.

"How's this, could you leave me in privacy, pretty please?" Neil sat down on his ass amongst the tree roots in response.

"You want privacy? I get it. But I also wanted to not be drugged last night, so I guess we're even. I'm not leaving. You owe me an explanation for why my mother thinks I'm engaged." Neil had her there.

"Okay, but for the record, you are the one who declared I was your barefoot and pregnant fiancée. No one made you say that."

Neil shook his head as though he was going to disagree with something Aria had said, but then changed course.

"Was the barefoot part related to why I stole your shoes?"

"What?"

"I have them right here," Neil said. He leaned back and unzipped the back compartment of his bag, pulling the pumps out.

"I forgot I left them on the roof. They would've slowed me down. Keep 'em. I prefer my combat boots." Aria clicked the heels of her combat boots together, wondering what Neil was doing walking around with her shoes. Did he think this was going to be a Cinderella story? They lived in a dystopia, not in a fairytale.

"How are *you* so clearheaded about what happened last night?" Neil asked.

"I didn't drink anything last night."

"Let me guess. You incapacitated me with drinks and drugs to get information for your Expectus buddies.... And now here you are, seemingly incapacitated." Neil pointed at Aria's right arm, which was still attached to the lockbox. He stared at the spot where her arm disappeared into the tube.

"Was that a threat?"

"It was an observation."

Aria was done playing games. They needed to get to the point of this conversation. "Look, if you are going to call your mommy or your Secret Service friends and tell them you found a Black traitor tied under a tree, just get it over with. I don't need any foreplay to your betrayal. I'm used to it."

"My betrayal? What the fuck is that supposed to mean, Aria? You poisoned me last night, for fuck's sake! And you now have your arm stuck in a tube outside a venue that is roped off because biological weapons were released!" Neil lifted his brows in disbelief. "I only got through because I've already been bitten and I have security clearance."

Aria laughed when Neil mentioned biological weapons. "Do you really think I carried a tick here with me this morning, Neil? I doubt whether the tick sighting was even real. Do you believe all the Donner Administration's bullshit?" Aria shook her head in disgust. "Honestly, if you aren't going to turn me in, would you please just leave me in peace under my tree?" It was past time for Neil to leave Aria to her communing with Maggie.

"You are the one who said no one should be out in this heat. And I'm still dehydrated from last night, thanks to you. Do you want me to die of heat exhaustion?" Aria laughed again.

"You really think your perfectly hydrated, well-nourished,

medically observed, Upland ass would die out there? Please. Your watch would call a drone for water before you even got thirsty."

Right on cue, probably in response to Aria's words, Neil's watch spoke. *"Communication signal lost. Bio signals indicate dehydration. Drink at least 3 fluid ounces of water immediately."* Aria rolled her eyes. Neil reached for the water bottle on the side of his bag. Aria could hear the ice cubes clinking together and she longed for a sip. Neil took a gulp, moaning with pleasure and savoring every drop as a show for Aria. She rolled her eyes again.

"You're not going to ask me for water?" Aria shook her head "no." She had done the math. She could survive until nighttime. But surviving meant that she needed to stay hidden. That watch needed to stop making unpredictable sounds.

"Leave. Or at least get rid of the watch. Now."

Neil took off his watch, handed the magnet back to Aria, opened his messenger bag, and placed the watch below a few layers. She shouldn't have given him the option to remove the watch and stay. Shirtless and watchless, Neil turned and looked Aria up and down.

"Aria, it seems to me that you are very willing to break the law, and you are very willing to risk death, but you are somehow equally unwilling to admit that you need anything from me." Neil crawled over to Aria with his water bottle in hand.

"I'm not afraid of you." As soon as she said it, Aria realized it evoked a common refrain of hers from high school when they'd relentlessly flirted. Memories Aria had neatly put away in a box, were now spilling out. She remembered saying it once in the cafeteria when Neil had been threatening to squeeze his water bottle all over her. "I'm not afraid of you." Before he'd had a chance to douse her, Aria had turned her body, grabbed his sweatshirt, and dumped a handful of ice from her drink down his shirt. Neil conceded and begged for a truce. This time, there was no way for Aria to gain the upper hand physically; but she could try to win this sparring match verbally.

"I know you're not afraid of me," Neil whispered in her ear. "But are you a little bit afraid that you want me?" Neil's breath in her ear sent a shiver down Aria's spine. She anticipated the feel of his beard on her neck and camouflaged her almost-moan with a deep breath.

She chose her words to distance herself from temptation. "You represent everything I hate: unearned luxury, elitism, materialism, disconnectedness."

Neil sat up. "That's not me, Aria. My mother is the one you should hate, not me."

"Who do you work for? How do you spend your time? You know what's happening to us in Lowland and you do nothing. Don't pretend you're any better than your mother." Aria had the advantage of remembering their conversation from the night before and knew that Neil worked for his mother.

Neil hung his head back and groaned in exasperation.

"I'm asking you to please leave now, and not say anything about me being here," Aria said. "That's all I need from you."

Neil put his head in his hands and then ran his palms down his face as he looked up at Aria.

"Can we start this conversation over?"

8.
"WE MUST LOVE EACH OTHER AND SUPPORT EACH OTHER"

—Assata Shakur
(call)

March 8, 2011

Before Secretary Simone Rao was the Governor of Upland DC, or the Secretary of State, she was just plain Mona, a working-class child of immigrants from New Jersey who lived with her husband, Paul, in a basement apartment in Edgewood DC. No one called her Mona anymore, though, and that basement was never where she planned to stay, of course.

Everything is going to change after today, she thought to herself as she lingered in their tiny plastic-box shower longer than Paul liked her to. She'd insisted on having actual sex that included intercourse without a condom that morning, rather than just the "getting each other off" Paul preferred. That counted as progress towards her plan to have one boy and one girl while she was still young.

On top of that, she was going to land a job today so they could pay for the rest of Paul's law degree from Howard. It wasn't Harvard, but it was the Black Harvard and it was a great jumping-off point for him to get a good clerkship, a job in the federal government and then jump over to the private sector to cash in on the experience in government. She just needed to get Paul on board with that plan.

Simone had splurged the day before to have her one pantsuit dry-cleaned and her hair blown out so she could slick it back in a tight bun. The lies on her cream-colored cardstock resume about her degree in Public Policy from Harvard were as shiny and new as her costume jewelry. Her makeup was perfect. She had to take a bus to a metro, and change lines to get to her interview, so she'd left plenty of time to make it to the Inheritance Institute.

"You look amazing, baby. They're going to snap you right up." Paul stood behind her the mirror in his sweatpants and snug T-shirt looking handsome even in his morning sloppiness. He reached around and embraced Simone from behind and she fixed where her necklace sat.

"You're going to wrinkle my pantsuit."

"It's seven in the morning. You have three hours until your interview, Simone. I could make you feel good again so you go in there with a big smile on your face and still leave plenty of time to iron that suit." Paul began to rub Simone's shoulders. She sank her head back onto his shoulder and looked up at him.

"No time. If we didn't live in the middle of nowhere, maybe, but we've done what we need to do for project pregnancy this morning already. We need to implement the next part of our plan first. Are you going to meet with your colleague to find out how he landed that clerkship with Justice Thomas?" Paul reached around, kissed her on the cheek, and looked at her in the mirror with a faraway stare.

"Let's not talk about that now when it's your big day, baby. Knock 'em dead."

Simone spent the bus ride to the metro ride drilling interview questions in her head and reading the *Wall Street Journal* hard copy she'd picked up at CVS so she'd know what her interviewers had just read. The position was as an executive assistant, but after being rejected from so many executive assistant positions, she realized that these were men who got off on having Ivy League kids doing their dry cleaning, so she made herself an Ivy Leage kid on paper. No one needed to know she went to NJ Technical Institute.

> *My biggest weakness is that I work too hard, and sometimes I'm like a dog with a bone when I'm trying to get a project done.*

> *In five years, I see myself being an indispendible asset to you, Mr. Donner, having anticipated and met your every need.*

She had a broken Blackberry she'd found in the street as a prop that she'd pretend to scroll through in the waiting room. *This was going to work.*

Once she was called into the interview room, it was clear that things were going well. Mr. Donner was lapping up her answers.

"You know we don't get too many people of color who embrace our conservative principles. What brought you to us?"

"To be honest, I voted for Obama the first time, but I'm liking Santorum now." Simone had read that Donner was a big Santorum donor. She didn't know anything about it other than that she wanted this job. "I've had enough of the Hopey Changey thing. I'm ready for a little changey to lower our tax rates, if you know what I mean." Edward Donner laughed. He was eating this up and she was going to have enough money for another pantsuit and real jewelry soon.

"I know exactly what you mean, young lady. I really appreciate you coming in. We'll check up on these references and I hope to be getting back to you with some news by the end of the week."

Simone left on cloud nine. Paul would be salty that she threw out that line on taxes, but what he didn't know wouldn't hurt him. She could see the future unfolding before her eyes. Paul would be a Black conservative judge or TV commentator. His career would be buoyed by the connections she'd have at the Inheritance Institute. She'd make enough money as an executive assistant that her kids might actually have an inheritance, unlike her. She promised her future kids that they would lack for nothing. She would fight every day to make sure they had their every need met.

9.
"WE HAVE NOTHING TO LOSE BUT OUR CHAINS"

—Assata Shakur
(refrain)

Nine days before Eamon

Neil's father had abandoned him as a baby, and his mother was unsavory, at best. He craved connection. He lived his life trying to get everyone else to love him, and mostly he'd succeeded. Women, especially white women, who found him "exotic," threw themselves at Neil. The female attention had gotten out of hand since his body had been plastered on billboards all over Upland for the past few years of his modeling career. Some Upland women took one look at Neil with his shirt off and his watch on and opened their wallets to buy their husbands Paxa watches; other women opened their legs in reaction. Neil didn't mind the physical connection, but he longed for an emotional connection. He used to have that with the woman in front of him, a woman who had always been authentic, and powerful, and real.

Neil knew he enjoyed unearned privileges; the watch was a symbol of that. The Donner Administration didn't have the support of a lot of people in Upland anymore after all the fires and storms, much less any people in Lowland. They could only stay in power so long that way, and Donner knew it. They needed a few people of color on their team to try to mask that they had created a white-Christian-ethno-state at gunpoint. Neil's ridiculous photo shoots for the state media gave them some of the cover they needed. Neil understood it was wrong. He couldn't bear to look at those magazines, the ads, or even the unavoidable billboards. Every film shoot, every interview, made him feel dirty. He wished he could get rid of the emotional discomfort without giving up the physical comforts of his life. He hated himself for enjoying the security of his life. To be fair, he had tried to escape; he had just never succeeded in his efforts to get out from under it all. His media exposure had stained him as one of them.

Sitting under that tree, hearing how Aria saw him, Neil wanted escape. He wanted out. He wanted to wrest control of his fate away from his mother. And he was determined to make Aria his getaway car.

He needed a big show of allegiance to Expectus so he'd be let into Lowland, where he could start a new life. The logical thing would be to offer to spy on his mother; but he was loath to go back to her with his tail between his legs. If he had to go back, he wanted to go back with Aria there to throw his mother off-balance. He had to figure out how to get Aria to help him.

Neil absentmindedly rubbed his wrist where his watch had been. His contract required him to wear the watch at all times in public, which meant there was a significant tan line. The watch-shaped mark suddenly felt like a stain. His mother would scream at him for not staying out of the sun to avoid getting darker. At the same time, the tan line marked him as privileged for even having a Paxa watch. His wrist felt lighter with the watch off. Not so much literally lighter since the watch was made of titanium, but emotionally lighter, less shackled. Neil pictured his wrist floating up and recalled how he and Aria used to make their arms float in the music library. They went to a masterclass once where the instructor was trying to show them how the brain affects the body and made them all do the arm floating trick. He lined up the handful of students standing between the wall of the music library and a heavy bookcase, and instructed them to push their arms against the immovable object; then observed them each as they walked out of the narrow tunnel to discover their arms involuntarily floating up. Neil and Aria had gone back so many times to that small enclave to trick their arms into rising and to use it as a moment to reset their posture before big solos. He could almost hear Aria giggling every time she did it, the memory was so clear.

Aria was not giggling now, though. Neil looked her over. She was looking away and taking deep breaths, obviously trying to stay calm. She was lying on the ground in a tank top and jeans, and he could see a bulge next to her breast with what looked like a rubber banded stack of credits, ID, and maybe a phone. She was banged up. She was also hot. Her skin was flushed, and her clothes were hugging her curves. Her hair was different from the party; it was in a low ponytail and left natural, as it had always been in high school, flirting with defiance of the school administration's grooming policy that outlawed afros. She had a rebel inside her even then. Although they were older, so much about her was still familiar.

He'd saved her the night before, apparently. He'd had a massive crush on her when they were kids. They were friends even before Neil filled out with muscles. She'd liked him when he was a scrawny kid, so surely he could get her to like him now.

"I'm an ass. I'm sorry for drinking water without offering you any. Please take some." Aria looked at Neil suspiciously. "You're dehydrated, Aria. Please just take it." Aria reached out with her free left hand and took the water bottle and started sipping. Remembering Maslow's hierarchy of needs, Neil offered food next.

"Thank you. I have some peanuts in my back pocket that I stupidly put just out of reach, and I have been trying to get them for a while."

"We don't need your crushed ass-peanuts. I grabbed lunch from Paxera on the way here. I have it in my bag, hold on." Neil immediately regretted mentioning Paxera. It was the successor to Starbucks, after that corporation had folded rather than giving into demands to become a worker cooperative. He recalled that Aria had always called Starbucks, "Twenty bucks," making fun of how much they charged and how little they paid.

Luckily, Aria didn't mention it. She must have been hungry."That is some magic bottomless messenger bag you've got," Aria commented as Neil got out his lunch and fork. He speared the pasta with his fork, making sure to get a good bit of sauce and some mozzarella. He offered her the bite of pasta. Aria opened her mouth just enough, leaned forward, and closed her lips around his fork, savoring the morsel. "Mmm." Aria closed her eyes, put her head back, and groaned with pleasure. Neil's groins tightened in response.

"That's pesto. I haven't tasted olive oil or pine nuts for years. It's so good."

"Glad you find something I have on offer enjoyable," Neil said. Aria reached out with her free left hand for the fork. "You can't get much with one hand. I'll feed you. It's more efficient."

"Take some for yourself too," Aria said, with food still in her mouth.

"I plan to give you as much as you'll take first," Neil said, holding Aria's gaze.

Aria shrugged. "Suit yourself."

Neil fed Aria attentively, making sure not to make her wait for a single bite, and giving her water between bites. He used a clean handkerchief from his pants pocket to wipe her mouth periodically. He wanted to lick off the bits of pesto, but moved slowly, first wiping the small spill up with his finger and then sucking the saltiness off of his finger once he was sure Aria was watching. Now that she had food and water, she might be more open to helping him. *What was she thinking?*

"Penny for your thoughts."

"No thank you, Mr. Capitalist. I appreciate the food and everything but my thoughts are not for sale for any Upland Credits. Also, you do know that pennies don't exist anymore."

That did not work. "Okay. Do you want to hear my thoughts?"

"Not really."

Neil was amused. He appreciated Aria's prickliness, and that she was a survivor. "This whole situation is wild. You are literally chained to a tube under a tree, and you think you have the leverage here. The wild part is that you're right."

"Why? Why are you helping me?" Neil got the feeling Aria did not like feeling helpless.

"You have something I want." Neil wasn't getting anywhere being coy, so he tried being direct. "I want you to get me free from my mother."

"If you want to be free of your mother, just leave Upland and go to Lowland. You don't need me for that."

Neil laughed and wished he could be that naive. "I used to think it could be that easy. I even tried it. I booked my band at a Lowland venue and planned to escape my life after the show. Long story short, it didn't work."

"What do you mean it didn't work?"

"There was a big banner and chanting that was targeting me, and the tour ended early. To make matters worse, my band broke up, thanks to my mom personally threatening them all after it went down. She told me after that that if I ever went to Lowland again, she'd have every musician I ever worked with arrested."

"Still not trying to win any 'mother of the year' awards, I guess. Was that in Lowland Cleveland that happened by any chance?"

"It was. How did you guess that?"

Aria paused. "I was in Cleveland."

"You were in the audience?"

"No, I left before the action, but I set things in motion."

Neil was stunned. Every day he fought the feeling of being undeserving, of being unloved. He told himself that just because his father didn't love him and disappeared before he was born didn't mean he was unlovable. Knowing that someone he cared about so much, thought him so worthless, broke his heart a little. "Fuck. You. Do you hate me that much? Why would you do that to me? And it wasn't just me, my band members all became targets after that." Aria stared at him silently, which made Neil more exasperated. "First you drugged me last night and now you tell me that you kept me from escaping Upland. Why, Aria?"

Aria sighed. "Last night, I didn't trust you to keep your mouth shut about seeing us. We drugged you to keep us safe."

Neil glared at Aria, waiting for more.

"Back in Cleveland, I didn't think about how the protest would affect you. I saw an opportunity to hurt the Donner Administration and I took it."

Neil softened his gaze, still waiting. He still thought he was owed an apology, but this new Aria seemed like someone who would refuse to apologize.

"It wasn't meant to hurt you either time, but I can see that it did. I'm sorry."

Neil was not used to people apologizing to him. When he called his mom or her cronies out on their behavior, they doubled down, demanding their own apologies. Aria was either being open and honest, or she was doing a great job seeming like she was being open and honest. In any case, Neil's hackles were lowering. It still hurt, what she'd done, but at least she wasn't trying to pretend she hadn't done it. "I don't know how to react."

Aria spoke gently after a while. "Well, you can forgive me and accept the apology, or you can choose not to. You can also decide later if you need time to process. That's up to you."

"Do you want me to accept your apology?"

"Sure. That's why I made it, but also I don't control that. I did what I did. If I knew it would harm people as much as you say it did, maybe I wouldn't have done it. But I don't have a time machine, and it's done. All I can do is apologize and try to fix it. I am sorry."

Neil saw an opening to make his case. "I forgive you, but you didn't need to drug me to keep safe. If you work with me, if you talk to me, I can keep us safe. We can work together."

"And how exactly would you keep us safe?"

"I know how to use the media against my mother now. Trust me, they are shaking in their boots about the public turning against them—especially Donner, but as a by-product, my mother too. I've got tons of contacts in the state media. I know how to work that angle better than anyone."

Aria stared at Neil for a while, but didn't follow up on what he'd said about the state media coverage protecting them. She wriggled her arm around and was messing with the tube that held her right arm, moving it so her arm and the tube were in a new position. "I'm glad it's this hot, or other people might be out here despite the biohazard warning, but I'm getting heat grump. You still have that ice I heard clinking around?"

"Yup." Neil shook an ice cube from his bottle into his hand and slid it over Aria's jawline and behind her ear to her neck, watching the ice—and her resistance to him—melt away.

"Feel free to use more than one at a time." Neil ran another ice cube along the straps of her tank top across the tops of her breasts, letting the meltwater drip down her cleavage, watching Aria's nipples pebble against her tank top. Neil's hands itched to palm her breasts, but he kept his hand on the frozen cube. He looked at Aria's face as he continued moving the ice cubes back and forth across her chest and neck.

"I could do this all day," Neil said, deciding she was relaxed enough that she might be open to his elevator pitch.

"You're right, you know, that I've been complicit in what my mother is doing, but I've tried to get away, and I'm ready to try again. We could use the pregnant fiancée setup I apparently came up with last night. We could introduce you to the media as my fiancée to make sure they can't just disappear you without a public outcry from across Lowland. I'll make it clear that if they hurt you it will backfire on them. Even if they figure out you've dallied with Expectus, they won't be able to harm you without soiling my image, which at least my mother won't do. All she cares about is our image. You could spy on my mom all you want and she'd have to live with it. It's a win-win, Aria. I get to have you as a fiancée and take down my mom, and you get to have me as a fiancé and take down my mom."

Neil moved the tiny remaining bit of ice cube back up to Aria's throat and her head dropped back. A gasp of pleasure slipped from her lips when Neil got out a fresh ice cube for her throat.

Finally, she responded to his pitch. "Why would we do all that Neil? No offense, but I have no interest in being your fiancée or in spying on your mom." She said, more focused on the sensation of the ice, than on the conversation.

Neil was confused. "I think I've been making some assumptions. Why *were* you at the party last night? Aren't you here because you were part of the Expectus action this morning?"

Aria tensed her body. "I don't need to spy on your mother; she says every hateful thing she thinks right in the public."

"But, don't you want to know where the next meeting is?" Neil added gently, "You can trust me. This is the perfect setup for you to take her down, Aria." Neil repeated his ice dance on the left side of Aria's jawline and her body was slowly relaxing again.

"I don't even understand your plan, Neil. We pretend we're getting married just to find out where meetings are taking place? Why are you pushing this? If you want out, just leave."

Neil had no idea how to "just leave." He was tired of being alone in the world. He wanted to do this with Aria. His words were not working to make the case, but he could see that what he was doing with the ice and his hands was working, so he made the move to straddle Aria's legs, with his knees on either side of her, continuing to move the second ice cube around until it melted. The sensation of having Aria between his legs sent all the blood in Neil's body straight to his cock. He came up with an excuse to touch her.

"You know you shouldn't keep a phone there. You'll get breast cancer. I'll take it out for you." Aria smirked.

"This is your real plan, isn't it? To feed me opulent food, arouse me with ice cubes and then have your way with me while I'm at your mercy?"

"Is it working?" Neil gently reached into the side of Aria's tank top and extracted her phone and items, placing them carefully on the roots of the magnolia. Aria arched her back into his hand as he did it and he lowered his head and licked the trickle of ice water that was falling between Aria's breasts. She tasted of salt, and smelled faintly of honeysuckle. He laid his head on her chest, listening to her heart. "Did we kiss last night on the roof?"

"No."

"I don't remember."

"Any of it?"

"No. I thought maybe we kissed. It's making me think

back. The first time we kissed it was so chaste. The second time we kissed, you were a bit tipsy at prom. Last night you say we didn't kiss, but I can't remember at all, and you do remember."

"We just pretended we were making out for your mom. You kissed my neck."

"I don't remember at all." Neil lifted his head, looking at Aria. "Just to keep it, you know, fair, can I kiss your neck again?" Aria unexpectedly nodded "yes." *This whole plan was going to work.* Neil ran his thumb along Aria's bottom lip. He lowered his lips first to her jawline, then he nipped her earlobe, letting his beard scratch at her neck, watching closely as she subtly exposed her neck more to feel more of the sensation. He kissed her neck, as promised, but he couldn't stop there. Neil lifted his lips to hers. His tongue grazed the line between her lips, and they parted. Careful not to put his weight on her, Neil leaned forward onto his knees. He ran his hands from the sides of Aria's breasts down to her waist. Her curves nearly undid him. Neil increased the pressure of his lips and kissed Aria deeply. Aria stretched her torso up and kissed him right back.

Only when the motion of Aria's tongue in his mouth subsided and she sighed, did Neil remove his lips. He was trembling down to his toes with want. His body craved something quick and noisy, but even if he could seduce her, they needed to be quiet under the circumstances. Anyway, his mind wanted something more from Aria. Something slow and quiet, a test of endurance. But what about Aria's body? What about her brain? He stared into her eyes and kissed her temple. Her free hand reached over and rubbed his forearm, back and forth. The effect was the same as if she was rubbing his shaft. She subtly increased her tempo, and shifted under him until his hard-on was between her thighs. As they stared into each others' eyes, they pushed into each other. Once. And then again. And again. They were musicians after all, and they both knew how to set and follow a rhythm. They'd always played well together. Neil heard music in his head to go along with their rhythm, he lowered closer to Aria with each thrust and kissed her neck, tasting her salt again. Aria grabbed Neil's hand, interlocking their fingers, and pulled his hand up next to her other trapped arm. With her arms over her head, and their rhythm intact, she was gasping in syncopation. She felt so good under him, he could explode, and then, she sped up. Neil closed his eyes and felt her body tighten, ready for release.

"Yes. Yes. Yes," she said, between the beats.

Neil, like the teenager he was when they met, exploded in his pants as she climaxed under him. They were both out of breath and flushed from the heat. If they weren't so dehydrated, they'd be dripping with sweat.

"I'm so sorry. I normally have more stamina. Was that okay?"

Aria smiled. "Yes," she breathed out again. "That was nice."

Neil wanted to try to go again, but that seemed to be Aria's sign she was done. For now. Aria let go of the grip she had on Neil's hand. Neil lifted himself up, looking down at Aria's skewed tank top and exposed right breast. Her arm was still stuck so he sat up and straightened her tank top into position, ignoring his urge to strip her bare. He leaned down on her and kissed her again.

Aria spoke into his lips. "This is nice, but both my legs and my arms are falling asleep." Neil jumped up to remove his weight, hitting his head on a lower branch of the tree.

"Ow."

"Shh."

"I'm not being any louder than you were being a minute ago. Some things are involuntary."

"Oh that was voluntary on my part." Aria was shaking her legs, and turned over onto her stomach, trying to move her arm, and was suddenly able to remove her arm from the tube. "Thank God." She was unstuck. She had seemed to enjoy the restraint when they were going at it, though. Neil tucked that information away for later, he hoped.

"You free now?"

"I guess we fucked it loose?" Aria sat up, stretching her neck and arms.

"How?"

Aria shrugged. "I just unhooked the carabiner with my thumb. It finally unstuck." She was grinning, removing a chain from around her wrist that had been attaching the carabiner to her. She stuffed the carabiner and chain in her jeans pocket. Neil was sitting half naked on the ground, watching her every move. She had a bulge in the crotch of her jeans. He had felt it when he was on top of her, but couldn't figure it out until he saw her standing up.

"Are you wearing a diaper?"

"Shut up."

"Are you sick?"

"No! I didn't know how long I was going to be here, okay. It was a precaution."

Neil had his hand down his pants and was cleaning himself up with the same handkerchief he had used when he'd been feeding Aria.

"So, I guess you don't need me to help clean you up when you've got that diaper to soak up all of your hot sex juices, eh."

"Shut up," she said, but she was laughing.

"Okay, I'll never mention it again if you take my proposal seriously for one minute? It's a good idea I had last night; the whole fiancée thing."

"Neil, get dressed and let's get out of here. Thank you for shaking my stuck carabiner loose. We can talk someplace that doesn't have a lockbox attached to a huge window grate," Aria said as she picked up her stuff and straightened herself, stretching and shaking out her left arm.

"Am I allowed to wear my shirt? "

"No. Put on your undershirt and leave the shirt and watch in your bag." Neil wanted to wrap his arms around Aria and insist that they nap under the tree until it cooled down more. She was already packing up to move, though, so instead he offered Aria his hand and they walked around to the other side of the tree to an opening and stepped into the afternoon sun. The heat was less dangerous now as the sun went down, but it was still hot as Hades. They held hands as they walked around the corner to a park bench. There were police, Secret Service, military, and every other form of cop car on the streets around them; but it was too hot for any to exit their vehicles. A few people driving by stared at Neil, recognizing him from the media, no doubt, and Neil saw Aria realize they were attracting too much attention.

"Neil, I had a really good time with you. Thank you for fucking my chains free. I have to get out of here."

"Let me put my number in your phone."

"Do not ever touch my gadgets again," she whispered. "That was a mistake. How do I know you're not an infiltrator?"

"I promise you, I'm not an infiltrator. You'd know it in your gut if I was. You know you would," Neil whispered back. His lips tightened, as he contemplated his next line.

"The only thing I want to infiltrate is your heart." Aria rolled her eyes, right on cue, but she did smile, which made Neil feel great. He loved getting a reaction from her. "Besides," Neil continued walking alongside Aria to try to keep up with her sudden increase in speed, "aren't spies supposed to dress as activists and be even more radical than everyone else and seed conflict by making fun of activists for not being hardcore enough?"

"Yes, but the fact that you know that is just another thing that makes you suspicious."

"Give me a break, I just read about COINTELPRO. That doesn't make me an infiltrator. I'm sure you've read the same stuff in the zines that get passed out. How about this, I won't touch your phone? I'll write my number on a piece of paper, and you can call me tomorrow. We can have dinner. We can have a dangerous liaison." Neil grinned. "Or we could just be sex buddies?" Neil tried out what he thought was an irresistible grin. He paused in the shade beside a tree, reached into his messenger bag, and pulled out a small Moleskine notebook and a Sharpie. He was relieved that Aria paused when he did and stood next to him. He ripped out a page and wrote his note.

"May I?" he asked and reached up to her shoulder. She nodded and he tucked the paper into the rubber banded bundle that held her ID and cash.

"I'll take your number in case I need to get in touch with you to get information, but we are absolutely never ever going to be sex buddies, whatever that is, Neil. I really have to go."

"I'll walk you to the checkpoint, like old times."

"Fine. But put on your button-down shirt then and don't say anything to give us away once it's on."

Neil pulled his shirt out of his bag and pulled it on, buttoning it as he walked. Once he was done, he texted Anthony which checkpoint they were headed to, and walked Aria there. They walked and talked as they had as kids. Neil was holding Aria's hand and turned his whole body to face her as often as he could.

"I'm not going to offer you a penny this time, but are you thinking about how much you've missed me?" Neil asked.

Aria shook her head. "How are you this cocky?"

"I have a mom who hates me and a dad who abandoned me as a baby. Between confidence and crying about it, I choose to be confident. What about you? How are you so attracted to this cocky?" Neil shook his body at Aria.

Aria laughed despite herself. "Stop it."

"You love it. Hey, are you dating anyone else?"

Aria laughed again, but didn't answer. This was going well and Neil was almost sad to see that Anthony was a few steps ahead of them at the gate. Before Neil had a chance to come up with an excuse to get Aria to stay, Anthony overrode the robotic security, and let Aria through. It would have to wait for another day. Neil walked halfway through the checkpoint and gave Aria a chaste kiss on the cheek and a big hug.

"Don't be a stranger," he whispered in her ear. "Please," he added as she pulled free. Aria walked through the checkpoint and down the hill, turning just once to blow him a kiss. The kiss gave Neil hope. He couldn't help himself. He pretended to catch it and hold it to his heart and then eat it sloppily, eliciting another eye roll and smile combo. It felt good to pull another smile out of her and Neil wondered what she'd look like when she read his note, and if she'd read it at all.

As soon as the checkpoint was out of sight, Aria pulled out the note and unfolded it. “I’ll find you,” it read, just above his phone number. Aria smiled at the thought before she tucked the paper away again. Earlier that day she would have read that note as a threat, but now, after their chatting, she found it endearingly naive. Sweet or not, Aria and Neil could not be together. Neil couldn’t have known that only Uplanders had access to things like Moleskine notebooks and Sharpies. He lived in another world, and as much as part of her wanted him to find her, she couldn’t imagine what would come of it.

10.
"WE HAVE NOTHING TO LOSE BUT OUR CHAINS"

—Assata Shakur
(call)

June 20, 2031

A year after her parent's deaths, Aria had abandoned the cello altogether. It reminded her too much of the life that was cut short when her parents were murdered. Survival meant blocking out what came before. It had been over a year, and, at Poppy's insistence, Aria had gotten out of bed every morning after returning from organizing an extended funeral. Poppy had made Aria a beautiful cross stitch with Mariame Kaba's quote, '*Let this radicalize you rather than lead you to despair.*' Somewhere along the way Aria had stopped calling her Aunt Poppy and stopped thinking about her that way. Poppy pushed Aria to change focus and run trainings in nonviolent direct action, noncompliance, mutual aid, and strategic escalation. Poppy trained Aria herself and took care to have dinner with her every night. Not even her parents had done that.

The act of training people to be enthusiastic helped Aria become not only a part of the living, but also a person who lived for the cause. She finally understood when she stood at the front of the room and when people applauded at the end of a training, why her parents were willing to give their lives for Expectus, and how the vigils she had planned helped their murder backfire on President Donner. She had undermined their effort to dehumanize her parents and make people think of them only as traitors. She had also revealed a deep and painful injustice to all of Lowland, and everyone in Lowlands across the US had one of those. Everyone was suffering at Donner's hands in one way or another.

"They want us to feel fear, they want us to feel chaos, and they want us to feel unbalanced—and instead we are going to prioritize joy," Aria announced in her trainings. "We're going to take up space, because this is our home, and we're going to organize so we have enough people that they understand that they really, really should not be messing with us. Who's with me?"

Aria felt she was becoming more of an equal to Poppy every time she got the crowd roaring, and so she said "yes" to every assignment she was given. The high of moving people into action was just as good as the applause after a great concerto. She needed Poppy to see her that way. She was willing to take on trainings nobody else wanted to do—planting the seeds for military and police defections that would be critical for their end game. Poppy told her that many of their trainers believed so deeply in the abolition of police and military that they were not willing to do the work to get defections. That was enough to convince Aria to take it on. After becoming an expert in training defectors in the summer of 2031, Aria was ready to move on to the next thing that was hard to recruit for: disasters that were likely to either land her with her parents or make Poppy realize that with the specific nineteen years Aria had lived, she was a grown-ass adult who was a viable partner. She was going to travel across the country to apprentice with experienced leaders, shore up defector trainings and ultimately land in the fire zone in the west. Aria was excited to learn from the Western Lowlands model. She'd heard so much about how they were succeeding at taking care of each other before, during, and after, large fires with mutual aid and survival pods.

As Aria finished up her last top secret orientation to Expectus for young people attempting to go undercover in the military and police, she picked up the papers and pens from the room, and sat down to pray. She had not prayed once since her parents had been killed, but something about leaving behind this long-ago abandoned church on H Street NE moved her to sit for a minute. *Lord, let these young people I just convinced to become police defectors have the courage to stay the course. Give them the wisdom to know how to appear incompetent and not insubordinate when they are given orders to kill innocent people. Let Noona stay safe at school and be able to achieve her vision of ending hunger in Lowland. Let Poppy's faith in Rev Ezekial's plans for mass defections in the military be well-founded. Let this trip to the Western Lowlands be fruitful. Let my blanket of grief keep me feeling close to my parents. Let me never forget what they died for.*

"You ready to head out?" Poppy knocked on the door to the sanctuary, and Aria rose from her spot, hoping it wasn't conspicuous that she was praying. It didn't seem like something Poppy would find impressive as a coping strategy. Poppy kept insisting Aria go to peer counseling. Aria feared that if she did, she would just get attached to another person who she'd lose. "You missed the facilitation team debrief. You knocked it out of the ballpark again, baby. Your story of self had them all in tears. You'll always be needed here. You can always decide to stay with us here." Poppy waved around the musty abandoned church.

Aria walked to the door of the sanctuary to be closer to Poppy. She reached out to embrace Poppy, and Poppy enveloped her in the doorway with her warmth and smell of lavender. She would take any opportunity to be held in Poppy's arms. It was the only place she felt safe anymore. Aria caressed Poppy's back and stepped in snugly. "Do *you* want me to stay?" Aria murmured into Poppy's ear, through her braids. Poppy gave her a firm squeeze that said, *I am a parent figure, not a lover,* released her embrace, and pulled Aria by the hand out the door to walk back to headquarters. "Come on, baby girl, let's get you moved."

Aria flushed at the rejection, feeling firmer in her decision to leave and prove herself to be the competent partner for Poppy she knew she could be.

Aria's success came quickly, as she expected. After a few years of apprenticing, Aria was one of the few Expectus activists who knew what was going on in other Lowlands. She had contacts everywhere, even if the only way to reach them was by talking to people physically, going from place to place. She brought Poppy back information about the numbers of childcare workers pledged to strike in Lowland Chicago, and the number of farmers pledged to strike in the bread basket. She knew who could be trusted to carry information, and she connected leaders in different places by creating chains of communication where everyone knew the person next to and behind them, but not enough to reveal the network to Donner spies. Aria never wanted a public role, but she knew she was critical. Her duty to avenge her parents' murders drove her to take risks and responsibilities that others avoided.

When Poppy called Aria back to Lowland DC in the summer of 2042, and she saw Eamon was on the way and the fires were still burning out west, she understood what was happening. Conditions were ripe for the takedown of fascism. If Poppy was ever going to see Aria as a potential partner, it would be in these stressful conditions, where Aria shined. They were on the cusp of making their move and calling for a total shutdown of Lowland DC to push Donner and Rao into exile in Russia. Hundreds of other Lowlands were in formation to escalate at the same time, but it was the DC Lowland plan that was most critical for finally unseating Donner. Poppy needed Aria back home.

11.
"FORGET YOUR PERFECT OFFERING"

—Leonard Cohen

(Aria)

Six days before Eamon landfall

Aria cranked open the rolling shutters to reveal the large red Lowland Books decal on the windows of the bookstore that served as a front for Expectus operations. Poppy always poked fun at her for covering and uncovering the glass so far before a storm was coming in, but Aria wasn't taking any chances. In the early days of Lowland, windows were constantly broken in skirmishes with Upland police, and Aria got in the habit of being protective of the bookstore's large windows as soon as she was put in charge of the store. Besides that, the sound of the metal going up and down reminded Aria of her parents' restaurant. Every time she heard the shutters hit that middle D note on the way down, she remembered how impressed her parents were that she could identify a note in metal clanking after just one semester of music theory. "Our job is done! Our daughter is a musical prodigy and can find beauty in a rusty security gate," her father had proclaimed, as her mother gave her a squeeze that felt celebratory. They had started each day with the clinking up and ended each day with the sound of the metal coming down. So much about Aria's parents was a mystery that she reveled in the parts she could claim to know and she aimed to recreate them in her own life, including standing in front of the shop and greeting neighbors in the morning.

Outside the bookstore that morning, the artistry and ritual surrounding the start of hurricane preparedness were underway. Aria loved how murals that usually disappeared into the background became visible again to her during hurricane prep as they were moved around to cover the most vulnerable surfaces. The "Black Lives Matter" in bold black and white popped into the foreground, bringing with it the memory of Neil looking stunning in his tuxedo. The "Climate Justice Now" written in a circle around a muscled, Black feminine arm flexing and holding a bouquet of sunflowers and wind turbines suddenly reminding her of Neil's muscled forearms and biceps, instead of reminding her of Poppy, as it usually did. Noona constantly told her that her obsessive crush on Poppy was limerence born of trauma, not love. Maybe that's what this old and now new again thing was with Neil too.

Aria's mind was still on Neil inside the bookstore, as she inspected the glistening shelves, straightened piles of books, and noted to herself which books were newly banned in Upland, and should be labeled as such. It was the vast majority of the store at this point. Uplanders often came to Lowland to get copies. Aria's mind drifted from her tasks, when her eyes landed on the small "Uplander Reads" section, and the magazine 'Men's Rights' with Neil on the cover, posing with a dumbbell and a sexy grin. "Upland's Most Eligible Bachelor Shares His Workout Routine." Aria wanted to know more about Neil than the magazine or her encounter could tell her. Impulsively, she picked up her phone, opened her most secure Expectus app, and called the research department."Hey Pinky, it's Aria. Can you get me everything you have on Neil Rao for the past few years?"

"I have a lot on him from other requests. I can probably get it to you tomorrow. We're slammed today researching everything and everyone in Hurricane Eamon's path and the readiness of the hubs and unions for the general strike. I've got an AI report running on the trifecta of Upland storms, heavy rains in DC, and storm surge. I've also got a surveillance team on the dozen detainees who Upland is claiming are Expectus activists, and they are making progress on tracking who they are and their current whereabouts. Poppy is cleared for those details if you need them. How urgent is the Neil Rao thing?"

Pinky was busy. Aria had gotten too distracted thinking that Neil Rao could somehow be of use. Her life had a purpose. This moment was what she had been preparing people for over the last decade. She needed to focus on finishing what her parents had started. Everything they wanted, everything she wanted, was within reach and here she was taking precious resources to find out about Neil Rao.

"You know what, Pinky—you have a lot on your plate. Don't worry about the Neil thing."

"I-I can do both, Aria. I have a big team. I'll get b-back to you." With that, Pinky hung up on her, never being one for niceties. Pinky only stuttered when overwhelmed. She shouldn't have bothered Pinky.

As she hung up, Aria saw Noona approaching and felt warmth and relief fill her body at the sight of her best friend.

"How on Earth did you get away at lunch prep with Eamon coming?" Aria asked. Though Noona had been an art major at their arts high school, she was the head chef for all of DC Lowland and had coordinated all infiltration in the food service and catering industries for the past few years.

"I've got so many recruits after Hurricane Alberto. I've got two dozen people apprenticing under Laila on recovering food waste alone. People who've been food-deprived love to be first in line for all the calories we have, and we're rolling in peanut butter, sweet potato, and eggs right now from the farmers. I've also got heaps of purslane, dandelion greens, and lamb's quarters, thanks to the foragers."

"Anyone interesting lately?" It was rare for Noona to hook up with anyone, but when she did, it was usually one of the foragers bringing her something to cook with that turned her on.

"Nope. I'm keeping focused on the work ahead until Eamon's behind us at least. Besides, it seems like maybe for once I can live vicariously through *your* sex life, rather than you through mine." *Did Noona know about Neil*? "And speaking of our high school friends that refuse to disappear forever, I see Sadie over there flirting with the new guy. Did you tell her about running into Neil?"

"I think we're better off keeping your herbal foray under wraps, don't you?"

"Aria, I had to protect us. What if he remembered us the next day and told his mother? Besides, I think I've finally got the dosage perfect! Did he get euphoric before he fell asleep? Was he hallucinating at all? I want to hear everything." Aria had missed her friend over the past couple of days. She looked around the bookstore, reassuring herself it would be fine for her and Noona to sneak away.

Sadie was about to start her disability community storm prep meeting, and Cole was helping her. Their heads were together as they tweaked the agenda written up on a large white paper on an easel. Cole was at least five years younger than them. He said he'd come down from Canada to join the struggle about six months prior and had experience working in small businesses and managing barter credits. Aria had just had time to orient him before she'd left on her last training tour. He was competent enough to run the store in her absence. He didn't know about any of the false doors in the bookshelves, or that the entire used books section was a dead drop for their undercover agents.

In all honesty, Aria did not trust him. He was too dogged in his anti-Donner sentiment and made too many references to how arms and violence might need to be part of the solution. She didn't want to come off as ageist against a passionate youth recruit, but, just in case, she had flagged for Pinky that he might be an infiltrator. Even if he was an agent provocateur, there was really no harm he could do managing the bookstore. Aria called out to him.

"Noona and I will be upstairs prepping for our meeting tonight. Can you take care of the front desk and any barters and help Sadie with the meeting? If anyone is looking for me, just take a message. I'll be back in a few hours."

"Yes, comrade," Cole answered, using a new moniker. Aria had had to tell him three times that morning to not call her "leader."

With the bookstore taken care of, Aria dragged Noona up the eight flights of stairs to her small quarters, where she shut her door, hung a lead curtain, put their phones into a secure bag, played white noise, and, finally, offered her friend a foot rub. It was the least she could do for the woman who was feeding them all, and she knew Noona loved a good foot massage almost as much as she loved when people spilled tea, so to speak. Aria had both for her.

"Aggh. That feels so good that you're distracting me from your story. Pause the massage so we can focus for a minute," Noona said as Aria dug her knuckle into the pressure points in the arch of Noona's foot.

"Let me at least do your other foot first."

Aria rubbed Noona's other foot and she finished catching her up on all that had happened, telling her best friend every salacious detail of Neil disrobing, twice. There was nothing so satisfying as having a friend gasp at all the right moments of a wild story.

"I can't remember the last time you hooked up with a dude. It was definitely before Beauty. Actually, is Neil actually the only man you've ever hooked up with?"

"No. But it's true I've mostly appreciated Expectus Women."

"Well, we Expectus women are super hot." Noona flicked her straight black hair with her hand, making Aria smile.

"Truth. I remember the first time I heard Beauty killing it doing political education in a political education training in Lowland LA and I was so turned on," Aria sighed. "The problem with Beauty is the same problem I've had with all women I've hooked up with—They're all competent organizers and planners and they're always trying to lock it down with me, while I'm out there trying to finish up my training and get back to DC. I mean, we have a fascist government to take down. I do not have time to play house."

"And you don't think Neil wants to play house?"

"I don't know." Noona had her "get real" face on and Aria didn't like where the conversation was going.

"And are you done trying to play house with Poppy? Because don't even try to tell me that isn't what you've been angling for." Noona had been trying to convince Aria to get over Poppy and move on for *years*.

"If Poppy let me in, let me take care of her, that would probably be a bigger contribution to Expectus than any trainings I could do or any action I've nailed. I still think that, if that's what you're asking."

"Have you told Poppy about Neil?" Noona asked just as someone knocked loudly on the door, cutting off the inquisition.

"Aria and Noona, I know you are in there, open the door," boomed Poppy. Aria scrambled to get their phones out of the lead bag, stash the curtain, and open the door while Noona put on her socks and shoes.

"Hi, Poppy," Aria exhaled at Poppy, trying not to seem out of breath. "We were just debriefing the action, so had our security protocols in place."

Poppy stood in the doorway, nearly filling its frame with the height added by her hair wrapped up in a colorful *dhuku*. Aria took in the sight of her and felt a surge of admiration for Poppy as well as the shame of having done things she knew she shouldn't have done. Only Poppy could make her feel this way. Aria straightened her spine and lifted her chin, attempting an opposite action.

Poppy looked at the pair of best friends with a smile and, after a pause, asked Noona if they could have some time alone for their own debrief.

"Of course. I need to get back down to the kitchen anyway. I'll see you both tonight at the spokesperson dinner."

She hugged Aria tightly and nodded at Poppy on her way out the door.

"You know we didn't have the reclamation team remove every bit of lead from every corner of Lowland just so you could gossip with your best friend," Poppy scolded. "But since you've got it all out, go ahead and put it back in place. We need to talk."

Aria dreaded the disapproval that she knew was coming, but she nonetheless put the security back in place and told Poppy the story of the past few days. They lived in a surveilled world. Poppy likely already knew the broad strokes. Poppy folded her arms, pursed her lips and clenched her jaw as she listened. She was not enjoying this story as much as Noona had.

"Let me get this straight. You were caught by Secretary Rao during your scoping mission, and you still participated in a high-risk role in the action the next day, operating against all protocols. Then you messed around with a hill elite who is the child of the most dangerous person alive, and ON TOP OF THAT you did not immediately alert me to the situation? Have I got most of this straight, Aria?" Aria nodded sheepishly.

"But Poppy, you and Noona are both always saying I should explore my sexual interests more. Remember?" Aria pointed at a copy of *Pleasure Activism* on the shelf behind her.

Poppy put her two hands on the scarf on her head and looked up at the ceiling as though she was praying. "Good Lord," she said under her breath to the ceiling before looking at Aria again. "The sex is irrelevant. You put yourself in incredible danger without a safety net for no reason. You failed to follow your training or even basic protocols. Your father's last words were to warn you not to act alone. The last thing he said to me was to take care of you."

Aria pushed aside her shame and defended herself. "It wasn't my fault the carabiner failed. I took it to Gears and the repair team, and they said it was old and faulty and couldn't be repaired even to their satisfaction. They melted it down for recycling. The only real danger came from bad equipment." Aria made the claim without really believing it herself. She hated that Poppy saw her more as a child than as a potential partner, and she hated that she sounded like a child even to her own ears.

"No, Aria. You should have checked your equipment. You appear to be dangerously distracted by Neil Rao. You've been playing with fire." Poppy began pacing as she often did when giving orders. With her height, and the compactness of the room, she could only manage three steps in either direction. Aria backed up and sat on the mattress to make space.

"I'm just remembering how both fragile and fierce you were when you showed up after your parents were killed. You're going to need that in the coming days. I just found out about an opportunity." Poppy said, leaning back against the wall, so she was not looking down at Aria at such a steep angle.

"What do you need me to do?"

"Some sleeper agents at the BRUINS meeting got me a message at great danger to themselves. Their resurfacing at this moment is a huge opportunity for us. I have reason to believe they know where massive stores of resources are being held. This could save a lot of lives after the transition."

"What kind of resources?"

"Seeds. Minerals. Lord knows what else. I need you to

go forward with the plan Neil sparked by announcing your engagement to his mother. You can come out to the media as his fiancée, and announce that you will be traveling together from now on and that you'll be joining the BRUINS meeting. With Eamon coming in, you can be our eyes and ears on the ground with Rao. If Eamon is as bad as our meteorologists are telling us the models predict, this is it Aria. Eamon is plus-sized, and slow as molasses. He's going to cause a lot of damage, unless you can get the final pieces of information we are missing from the two double agents—how to lower the water walls, and how to find and open these strategic reserves."

Aria mimicked Poppy's body language from a moment ago and looked at the ceiling before protesting. "How do you even know about the pregnancy lie? You know what, don't answer that. How on Earth would I get that information? I told Neil that I don't see the point of spying on Simone Rao, and I don't. I'm terrible at being undercover. Look at what a mess I just made of things. Besides, won't Rao know who I am as soon as she gets a good look at me and kill me before I find these sleeper agents?"

"She will recognize you. That part is risky. But that will get her off-balance too. Part of the mission is to keep Rao distracted, and you will do that beautifully. As far as getting the information, we have reason to believe that there will be people at the meeting who have what we need. You'll be briefed, but I don't want you knowing any more than you have to, for your own safety. You need to make a decision before we talk more about this."

There wasn't much of a choice. She'd have to go undercover in Upland, which was not her skillset. She'd face the constant threat of arrest and assault. She'd have to be among the people who inflict pain at what might be the most pivotal moment of her life, instead of in her own community with her friends. But she would also play a significant role in taking down Rao and Donner. If no one else was lined up to find out how to lower the water walls and access the seed reserves, what choice did she really have? This was the opportunity she'd been waiting for.

She'd have to pretend to be engaged to Neil, and she'd have to be convincing. Noona needed seed reserves desperately for her work. It was getting hard to feed everyone with what they had. Eamon was about to make it worse. This was a huge and fortuitous opportunity at just the right time.

Aria was going to have to go, but she needed some affirmation that she was the best person to do this. "Isn't there anyone more experienced who can go in?"

Poppy moved over and sat on the mattress next to Aria and used her code name, which was reserved for times when they were in the middle of an action, near law enforcement or surveillance. "Fields, you're the best person for this job. You're the only one who can get close enough to the parties we need to infiltrate. If you can't do it, we'll send someone else, but their chance of success will be far lower. You need to decide now. If you're scared or uncomfortable, then you don't have to do it. I'll send someone else in to get the information on the water walls and the reserves and hope they can do it. We have no way to get the information we need from them without sending someone in. If being with Neil feels threatening, it doesn't have to be you."

Aria leaned into Poppy, who put her arm around Aria.

"I'm not scared of Neil," Aria said, looking at the ceiling again. "I am scared of Secretary Rao, though. I don't see why Simone won't just have me shot as soon as I arrive. How could being with Neil protect me from that?"

Poppy looked Aria up and down, rubbing her arm. "Simone won't openly go after her son's fiancée. Anyone else we send in will be in more danger than you." Poppy sounded just like Neil in her assessment of Simone Rao. Aria would have to get over her fear of Secretary Rao. This was for her parents. This was about this incredible new opportunity to secure food for people and protecting the community from floods. She'd be saving lives and making Noona and Poppy's lives easier. Aria allowed herself to be comforted by Poppy's warm presence, grabbing one of her hands. "Okay. I won't be sloppy this time. I'll do whatever you need me to do."

Poppy stroked Aria's hair, lifted her chin, and looked her in the eyes. "Your parents would be so proud of you. This is going to work out with you and Neil, don't worry. Have fun, just not at the expense of the mission." Poppy playfully winked at Aria. And at that moment it finally sank in for Aria that she and Poppy were never going to happen. Poppy would always see her as a child.

"We need to see through this general strike and prevent it from turning into a massacre of our people. If we get to the other side, I can explain more about all the things I can't tell you today. Let's stay focused now. We're going to create the world we've always dreamed of, where we all take care of each other and share resources. We'll build the world your parents imagined for you, the things you always draw on those visioning boards—vertical gardens on every building, clean air, clean water, parks, schools, high-speed rail for all those training trips you take, and all the food we need. I need your help to get us to that world. I need you to step into your power as a future ancestor and as a daughter."

Aria nodded, touched at how much Poppy remembered of her vision boards. Poppy was right. She would do this if it was what Poppy needed from her, and what her parents needed from her from beyond the grave.

"Good girl," Poppy said, patting Aria's hand, then getting up from her seat and leaning against the wall near the door. "Maybe I should have told you this earlier in the conversation, but it turns out Neil actually walked into the bookstore right after you ran up here with Noona. We intercepted him and put him in an Expectus Orientation and then a Hurricane Eamon Search and Rescue prep training on the first floor." Aria was stunned. Poppy looked oddly emotional about the situation, and even seemed to be blinking back tears. Aria was touched that Poppy was so worried about her.

"Please remember, Aria, he cannot know anything more about me and my role as an elder in the movement. Understand that he is using you to get out of the world he's trapped in. You can use him right back, but that doesn't mean he can be trusted with any information that is not public. This is not a time to let security culture drop. Your job is to distract his mother with your scandalous engagement and find out from these sleeper agents how to lower the water walls and access those reserves."

Aria nodded. She was ready to do this.

"And Rao won't kill me?"

"Rao wants you dead, I'm sure, but she loves her son too. She doesn't act like it, but, trust me, Simone Rao is trying to protect her son. It's his feelings for you, and his realization that he needs you to get out of Upland, that will protect you from her. She's actually quite insecure. She's terrified of the public turning on her; I can see it in her face. As much as you might want to, do not squash Neil's feelings or any hope he has for your relationship to be real."

Poppy glossed over the point that Neil was using her, but Aria latched onto it. It hadn't occurred to Aria until then that Neil could be using her as much as she was using him. It made the situation seem more even to think of it that way.

"If Neil's been through the trainings, he already knows our plan for strikes and boycotts in the wake of this storm. Is that safe for him to know so much?"

Poppy nodded, and reminded Aria that they were not trying to keep the plan secret because they wanted millions to participate. People needed to be prepared to stop caring for Upland children, stop picking up trash, and sabotage self-driving transportation. They could be public because Upland didn't believe they could succeed against their military might.

"You can share anything you know with Neil except my role. Don't tell him about me. Everything sensitive about our escalation plans that needs to be kept from him, I've carefully kept from you, too, so that you don't have to worry about accidentally sharing things. I'm counting on you to extract this information before Eamon arrives. This is a massive lucky break for us that she called this BRUINS meeting and it means we have the opportunity to avoid a whole lot of death and suffering if you succeed."

"I'll do my best." This was not how Aria had imagined spending the final week of escalation. She thought she'd be at Poppy's side in Lowland DC, in the thick of it, not banished to some evil meeting in the middle of nowhere where there'd likely be an attempt on her life.

With Poppy standing, she was looking up at her again. "Do you forgive me for getting myself stuck at the action site?"

"You know the saying, Aria. Fail fast and fail forward. Don't be lax for this next bit. Head to the equipment shop and have Gears give you your kit for this mission, and then go and tell Neil how this is going to go down. You focus on your part and we'll do the rest, okay? This is the most important role of your life. Follow protocols. *Do* the things that you train everyone else to do." Poppy held Aria's gaze as she spoke seriously, then after a pause, her tone shifted suddenly to pep-talk mode.

"You got this. I love you. I trust you."

"I got this. I love you, too, and I trust you that this is the right move," Aria echoed, standing to hug Poppy goodbye and giving her a kiss on the cheek before Poppy slipped out the door. She never stayed for long after giving marching orders.

As Aria rinsed off in the shower a few minutes later, she had a premonition that she would never see Poppy again and teared up. Squeezing the water from her hair, gently, she shook off the feeling. She focused on getting ready, oiled her hair, brushed her teeth, packed a small backpack, and prepared her room for Hurricane Eamon relocation tenants who would need the space. She'd have to straighten her hair or wear a wig before being seen in Upland, but she'd worry about that later. She headed to go see Gears for her equipment and instructions then to meet Neil, as Poppy had instructed. At the bottom of the dim stairwell that opened to the hallway of training rooms, Aria realized she was scowling and "fixed her face," as her mom would have instructed her to do. She rolled her neck, shook out her shoulders, and checked her outfit. She looked good. This might be her last mission, and she was going to rock it. Game face on, Aria went to find Neil.

12.
"FORGET YOUR PERFECT OFFERING"

—Leonard Cohen
(Neil)

Six days before Eamon

Neil stood in the abandoned training room waiting for Aria, who he'd been told was on her way. All the molecules in his body, including those between his legs, were skittering in anticipation of seeing her again. This was his third opportunity to make his case to her, and he needed to get it right this time.

Neil distracted himself by taking in the murals of natural landscapes, butterflies, and birds. There were scenes of drum circles, dancing, and children playing. The largest, though, was a Guernica-esque mural showing the scene of federal troops being pushed back by masses of Lowland people outnumbering them. There were no landmarks. It could have been of any one of the many cities where this history had played out.

The sound of children playing across the hallway created dissonance with the scene in front of Neil. He heard the same group affirmations that closed out the training he had just taken:

> *We are a force for liberation. We are capable of taking care of each other. We all have a role to play. Together, we have wisdom. We will live full and beautiful lives. We know what is at stake. Everyone will have their opportunity to join us. We expect to succeed. Expect us.*

They were children talking about words and concepts that were definitely illegal, like liberation. Were those children taught a traditional curriculum? Did they do algebra and study literature? Did they learn to play instruments? Or were they receiving the same training Neil had just gotten, but over years instead of hours? Neil hoped they weren't being brainwashed into introducing themselves with their pronouns and referring to the Indigenous land they were on, as he'd been instructed to do in the training. His eyes landed back on the guiding principles on the wall:

1- *We protect each other, humanity, all beings, and Mother Earth with our deeds and words;*
2- *We stand on the shoulders of our ancestors and we strive to be honorable ancestors;*
3- *The most vulnerable among us must thrive for our community to succeed. Black- Trans- Disabled- Indigenous- women are the most threatened right now; if we design our world to give them dignity and agency, we will give everyone dignity and agency.*

Protect all beings? Hadn't it been Expectus activists from Lowland who had released the Lone Star Tick and made the majority of Upland, including him, allergic to meat? Wasn't that a step too far? Neil knew that they claimed the move had saved society from even worse impacts of climate change caused by the meat industry, but he also knew that there were medically vulnerable people who needed meat and dairy and suffered when the allergy hit them and they had to essentially become vegan. And could it possibly be true that all the assassination attempts on Donner and even his mother were lies or inside jobs? Surely some of that violence came from Expectus, despite their steadfast commitment to reject violence and oppression. They had been radicalizing people for years and surely held some responsibility for assassination attempts? At the very least, shouldn't Expectus' mistakes be addressed in the intro training he'd just taken, and on the walls too?

They'd said in the training everyone was welcome to raise questions and try things out, but Neil was an obvious outsider in a room filled with self-identified working-class and oppressed people. Neil wasn't shy. He'd asked the question at the end of orientation that he thought everyone was thinking.

"Don't mean to be an asshole, but I'm an underwear model for the company you just told us was oppressing us and stealing from us. Am I supposed to believe I can just quit my job and be welcomed here?"

The trainer looked around the room and made eye contact with some of the crowd of nearly a hundred new Expectus members. "What do you all think? Neil Rao says he's ready to seize the opportunity to join us in Lowland and leave Paxa behind. Are you all ready to take him up on that offer?"

Heads nodded immediately, but the room was silent until a voice yelled out from the back. "We're all in this together, brother!" At that, the crowd murmured in assent, and the trainer looked back at Neil.

"Everyone will have the opportunity to join us, Neil. We're happy to have you. We need more defectors from your ranks. Let's give a hand to Neil for having the courage to defect, friends." The applause and the smiles looked genuine.

Neil could imagine growing up and raising a family in this world. Something he'd never do if he thought his mother would get her hands on his kids. He wanted to have a life that his mom would call emasculating and offensive. His mom's disapproval made him want this life more. His mother lived rent-free in his head, but he wanted to evict her.

The training had exposed the underground government of Lowland DC for Neil to see for the first time in all its complexity. He couldn't believe that anyone off the street was allowed to walk in and get an orientation, but that's what the woman told him when he came asking for Aria. There was a plan for everything in Lowland DC he'd learned during the Search and Rescue training that followed—food, water, labor, education, arts, flood & fire preparation and response, housing, clothes, restorative justice, and health. Lowland DC may not have had a lot of food, medicine, clothes, or material possessions, but they took care of most of their people and were organized with what they had, or so they claimed. They had physical trade routes with other Lowlands, which was mind-boggling.

Neil had not expected such a welcome, but he'd come anyway. He had to. Anthony had not only given Neil an address for Aria, he'd confessed to Neil that Aria's parents were killed because of his mother's involvement. That piece of information was what drove Neil to finally leave. His mother wasn't just a pain in his ass; she had blood on her hands.

Neil had always suspected that was the case, but he'd finally asked Anthony point-blank in his apartment the day before because he was ready to hear the truth about the only parent he had ever known. Anthony stared into Neil's eyes with his arms crossed and then looked down at his left hand, made a fist, and subtly knocked it twice in the crook of his elbow. Neil's eyes widened at the ASL signal for "yes" that he and Anthony had used since he was a kid. He stumbled back a step, stunned by both the response and the risk Anthony was taking by revealing the truth. Anthony then patted Neil's bicep and handed him the small paper with Aria's name and an address. He gave Neil a tight hug and whispered, "see you soon, kid" in his ear.

Neil wasn't sure he would see Anthony soon. He was sorry for that, but he was not going back. It was no longer an option to work for his mother and go on the dates she set up with Upland women who wanted to be married to anyone connected to the Donner Administration.

The woman he wanted was on her way. Neil recognized the cadence of her walk and felt her presence behind him. He spun around to watch Aria opening the door. She looked like she was just finishing a photo shoot. She pulled at one of her damp curls, as she approached wearing a tank top, jeans, and combat boots. She had a backpack slung over one shoulder. She looked happy, confident, and sexy as hell.

"You found me," he said, reaching out to hug her. His body sighed with relief when she stepped into his arms and molded her body against his. Neil rubbed her back gently as they hugged. This was home. It was a warm and sexy spot, and he loved it. Neil reluctantly stepped back before Aria felt him bulging against her. He wanted to pull Aria into his lap and run his fingers across her clavicle, and then palm her pert breasts like he had under the tree, but she looked ready to go. The thought of her leaving without him rankled him. He wanted her, and not just to get out from his mother's grasp.

"Impressive place you've got. I hope you aren't planning to go anywhere when I just got here." Neil pointed at her backpack.

"As it turns out, I am going somewhere, and it's with you to wherever you're going. I'm taking you up on your offer to be pretend-engaged so I can spy on your mom."

Neil studied Aria's big brown eyes, wondering why she was suddenly on board with his suggestion that she had mocked just days earlier. "What changed? What did my mother do this time?"

"I can fill you in on more later, but it's getting late and I need to know where we are going and why. What's the next step to becoming a spy in Upland?"

Neil had expected to have to convince Aria to go on a date. Now she was offering to go with him wherever he was heading. She wanted him to go back to the one place he'd just sworn off—his mother's side.

"Why don't I join you here instead? You'll need more hands with Eamon coming. Everyone in the training seemed ready to welcome me into the fold to help with all the work going on here. I think I'd be good at search and rescue."

Aria was shaking her head slowly. She was not happy. "I wrote the script for that training. I know about every team you just learned about. That's not what we're doing. You're not turning your back on me again." *Oops.* Neil mouthed the word silently, wishing he could rewind his words. "This is just like you, Neil. You offer to take me to prom, and I rearrange everything to make it happen. You just changed your mind and took Sadie to prom instead. And now a decade later, you offer me a fake engagement as an opportunity to work together. You *begged* me to join you. Now that I'm saying yes, you change your mind? Seriously? What happened? Did you see Sadie upstairs and get reminded of how easy it is to screw Aria over?" Aria spun around to leave.

Neil was stunned by so many things Aria had just said, he couldn't absorb it all. "Wait a second, Aria. I was just making a suggestion that would get us away from my mom."

"And you're doing that coincidentally right after I say I'm ready to follow you and go to your mom, which, again, was *your* idea that you're now backing out of."

Neil needed to get back to the closeness he felt when they were embracing a moment ago, back into Aria's arms. "I'm not going back on my word. I said we could spy on my mom together, and that's what we'll do if you want. Sit down and talk to me." To his great relief, Aria turned back around and loudly scraped a metal folding chair towards her and sat down, settling her backpack on the floor between her legs. It was a far cry from his lap, but it was an improvement over storming out of the room.

"Fine. I'll sit and talk, but I need to know if you're in or not. This isn't like a prom date you can just cancel. This is real life and there are real stakes for me. I owe it to my parents to get this right."

Her parents. Her dead parents. Who his mother had a

hand in killing. Neil considered telling her what he'd just found out about his mother, but didn't have the courage to bring up his terrible genes and risk the conversation spiraling out of hand. "I'm in. I'm not backing out on you. I'm right here and we'll go wherever you want. But you just dropped a lot on me and I want to understand what is going on before we go." Neil pulled up a folding chair to face Aria's and sat down, rubbing his beard. He was going to lighten the mood if it killed him."Can I ask a few questions to make sure I understand?" Aria nodded and Neil continued.

"Okay, is Sadie really upstairs, and if so, can we sneak out from this floor somehow without running into her?" Aria laughed. It was working. He was de-escalating and she was staying there with him.

"Yes, Sadie is upstairs in the bookstore running a meeting for the disability justice community about how to deal with this disaster. We're friends now. Well, sort of friends. She's doing good work and we respect each other. She's been through a lot. It's a long story, but she was kicked out of Upland after she was disabled in a Paxa-truck crash. She has post concussion syndrome. She also has a kid she loves more than anything and she's no threat to you or I. We can sneak out if you want, but I promise, it's not necessary." Neil remembered Sadie as a self-obsessed girlfriend who cared about nothing but status and clothes and now she organized people with disabilities. The most shallow person he knew was making a bigger positive difference in the world than he had with all his good intentions and privilege.

"We're going to have to come back to the whole Sadie story later." Neil took a deep breath and shook his head, trying to take it all in. "Next question. Why are we going to spy on my mother? I thought you said there were easier ways to get information?"

"We found out that the BRUINS meeting has a few people who have information we need that could save a lot of lives, so we need in. The best option we had was me joining you and going with the ridiculous story you made up about us being engaged and pregnant," she said holding up one hand, palm up like a scale, and then held up the other and said, "And if I don't take this on, a lot more people will die in the wake of Eamon." She moved her hands up and down like the scales of justice, pretending to weigh which option was better.

"So I just got here, got oriented, realized this is where I want to be, and I have to go back to the place I hate?"

"Give me a break, Neil. You are a well-known model, and Upland's most eligible bachelor and you have always had everything you ever wanted in life. Compared to what people in Lowland have been through, asking you to live in the lap of luxury for a few more days is a minor inconvenience. We'll be back in Lowland putting your new Search and Rescue skills to work before you know it."

This was it. This was the opening he needed to turn Aria towards him. Neil scooched his chair closer to Aria, held her hands, and looked into her eyes. "Okay. I need you to hear me on something if we're going to do this. I took my mother's side over yours once as a kid and it was a mistake. That will never happen again. I'm sorry I hurt you when I was trying to protect you. I don't regret trying to do that, especially because I just found out she had a part in killing your parents, but I do regret not telling you what was going on and about her threats. I can't believe what she did to your parents. I knew she was ruthless, but murder is beyond what I thought she was capable of."

Aria blinked back tears. "Did you just find out about her role in killing my parents?"

"I found out yesterday and I left immediately."

"But you're willing to go back?" Neil kept holding Aria's hands, relieved that she believed that he had been in the dark. He surprised himself in how willing he was to go back, and he nodded slowly. Aria looked at him with a softness that hadn't been there since they had reunited. "It'll take forever to walk back to your place. I'll fill you in as we walk."

Neil stood, nodded, and picked up Aria's backpack. He could do this for her. "Do you need fake paperwork to get through the checkpoint?" Neil guessed he would be seeing Anthony pretty soon after all since this would never work without his help. Aria shook her head "no" and pulled a badge from the side pocket of her backpack. It looked incredibly real and had her real name on it.

"Not Susan Anderson this time?"

"Fuck Susan Anderson. I get to be me." Aria kissed the badge and clipped it to her pants. Her confidence buoyed Neil. "Do I look like an Uplander?"

"Not at all. I'll get you some clothes."

Aria batted her eyelashes at him. "Oh, I thought you'd like me more without clothes?"

Neil laughed as his cock twitched at the image. He gave the ASL knock for "yes" and "please" that he'd gotten her using in high school. This was going to be fun. "Let's go get our spy on. We can talk code names while we walk to the checkpoint."

"Come with me and let's at least say 'hi' to Sadie on the

way out. And I'm sure Noona will want to apologize to you about the whole drugging you thing. We can get some books from the bookstore too."

Neil got up to go with Aria. This wasn't the quiet start to a life with Aria in Lowland he'd hoped for, but life with Aria could never be that boring. So many things could go wrong, but holding Aria's hand walking out of that room, somehow everything felt right.

13.
"JUST RING THE BELLS THAT STILL CAN RING"

—Leonard Cohen
(Laurie/Gears)

Five days from Eamon landfall

Laurie stood behind the studio bots with her hands held up, framing how she wanted each person to appear for viewers in Upland. She directed the bots with audio commands to soften the lighting and move each of the cameras to be at eye level with both Becca in the armchair, and Aria and Neil on the sofa. To viewers across Upland, their holograms would appear to be in the room with them, whereas, for viewers in Lowland, the 2-D video of the studio would be played on tiny phone screens for some, and for many, they would only get the audio on their shortwave radios. Under normal circumstances, no one in Lowland would bother to tune into the State Media propaganda, but with Hurricane Eamon on the way, Lowlanders would tune in to stay on top of what the Donner Administration was saying. Plus, an interview with Neil Rao was likely to have universal appeal, especially an interview introducing his new fiancée. Laurie couldn't quite believe that her friend Aria Petros was that fiancee, and neither could Aria, from the look on her face. To be fair, Aria had only had about ten minutes to adjust since Gears had walked up to her, introduced herself as Laurie, and explained she'd be producing the interview.

"Alright. The lighting looks good and the prompter is all loaded with the questions. Becca, are you ready?" Becca Donner gave a thumbs up. Aria looked shell-shocked. It was Laurie's job as a producer to coax her out of it.

"Neil and Aria, are you ready? This will be recorded. It's not live, so if at any point you want to stop and re-do a take, just say so. There is a test audience of around a hundred people listening so that we can collect audience questions." The unstated reality that everyone knew was that the room was bugged. The Donner Administration could always release what they wanted. Gears had access to pulling and deleting footage and audio for almost every location in Upland, but she did not have that kind of access to recordings in the building where she worked. If Aria and Neil accidentally revealed this to be a fake relationship, there wasn't much Gears would be able to do to salvage the mission.

"Got it," Neil said to the room. He'd been following Aria with his eyes since they'd arrived, and anticipating her every need—getting her a glass of water once and extracting her from a conversation with the interns who were glaring at her another time. He'd walked her over to the sofa and encouraged her to take a breath. Maybe Gears was drunk on her own new-ish love for Becca, but there was something in the creases around Neil's eyes when he smiled at Aria that told her that at least for Neil, this was real.

"Are you okay?" Neil had asked Aria quietly, but the mic picked it up clearly for Gears. Aria nodded. She leaned back on the loveseat and inched closer to Neil so their legs were touching and held his hand. Neil kissed her lightly on the cheek, tucking back a lock of her recently blown-out hair. Good, Aria was getting into her role. She could do this. Gears gave her a thumbs up. Aria returned a solemn nod.

"We got this," Neil whispered, as though the mic wouldn't pick it up. Gears smiled reassuringly and willed Aria's success. She blew a kiss.

"You guys make an adorable couple."

Anthony stood in the corner guarding the door, reminding Gears that Aria would not be safe until the news was public. Once they were officially a couple, the hope was that it would be harder for Simone Rao to have Aria killed. For her own safety, Aria needed to get this right. As Aria's friend, Gears needed to get this right. This was essentially Expectus' only public communication before Eamon, and it had to be believable if they wanted people to follow the plan when Eamon came and escalate when they were called upon. If anyone could make them look good, it was Becca.

It was so cute how excited Becca had been to do the interview that morning. They'd woken up in bed together since Joe was "on a trip," spending the night with Anthony.

"You're letting me ask questions that are not generated by a bot? And I don't even know how they are going to answer. People are going to love it. I bet a lot of people don't even remember that news can be unscripted." Becca pulled on her robe and walked over to the bathroom. "You are determined to make me not hate this job and I love you for it," Becca said before starting to brush her teeth and apply her first layer of makeup.

Becca looked as gorgeous as ever and she was going to nail this interview. Gears was confident in everyone involved, other than Neil, and he was up first.

Becca Donner: Neil, all of Upland knows you already, but can you introduce us to your girlfriend?

Neil Rao: Of course, this is Aria Gelana Petros, the love of my life. For those who have their VR on, this is redundant to say, but Aria is the most beautiful girl I have ever met, inside and out.

Becca Donner: Good looks and a good heart! Tell us, is that how you snagged Neil?

Neil Rao: Aria didn't snag me, I snagged her, just so we're clear.

Aria Petros: Well, we snagged each other.

Neil was doing fine. He began to describe how he and Aria had become reacquainted at a fundraiser for their high school, which was a lie, but overall, he was sticking as closely to the truth as possible.

Gears hadn't been sure if the Upland audience could enjoy the banter between an interracial couple, even if they'd already embraced Neil as their own, but the comments from their test audience were starting to roll in and they were doing pretty well, even before moving to the music, which Becca began to tee up. This was going to be a perfect break for the audience from the nonstop Eamon coverage Joe was in the next studio projecting out live.

Becca Donner: Speaking of music, are you two going to share a tune with us today?

Neil Rao: We are! It's our little way of announcing our plans this fall.

Aria and Neil stood up and walked over to the spot in the studio where their cello and violin sat. They hadn't had time to practice so they'd decided to go with a piece they could both play in their sleep that sent the "We're Getting Married!" message, *Pachelbel's Canon.*

As they sat down, Gears reminded herself how good they sounded when they tuned and rehearsed a few measures. The cello part was repetitive and easy; Neil took on the hard job of the melody. His sound was as gorgeous as his face, though, and it was adorable how he winked and nodded to Aria to mark the transitions. They looked like a natural couple from the outside.

They sounded good together too. It had been a long time since Gears had seen Aria look so happy. The song was so old and yet so familiar. A flash of Gears's deceased older sister's wedding ceremony popped into her head, and she wouldn't be the only one with memories climbing to the surface. By the end of the piece, everyone in the studio had tears in their eyes. Becca broke the silence with applause.

Becca Donner: It's been a long time since we've had live music in the studio. Thank you. Tell me, am I guessing right that there are wedding bells coming up? When is the big day?

Neil Rao: We can't reveal everything at once!

Aria Petros: We'll come back on the show to share when we get back from the field, we promise.

Gears lunged to the control panel and managed to beep over most of the phrase "when we get back from the field" for the test audience and then deleted it entirely from the video that would play to a larger audience and all other recordings she had access to. It would be okay. That's why they weren't live. "*From the field*" evoked a mission they were on and was too close to the truth. Besides that, "Fields" was Aria's code name. Luckily Becca and Neil didn't even seem to realize the gaffe and had kept going.

Becca Donner: Your families must be so excited! What was your mother's reaction to the news of your engagement, Neil?

Neil Rao: She was thrilled, and especially can't wait to be a grandmother. We don't want to rush that piece of course!

Becca Donner: We're getting in some listener comments, I'll read the first one from our producer: *'I'm going to dub you Niaria and I hope you DO rush to have babies, you two would make beautiful babies!'* And Gina from Upland Atlanta asks, *'Will you two perform at my wedding?* And the final listener comment is anonymous. *'I never thought an Upland/Lowland relationship could work! You are giving me hope!'*

Many of the comments Gears sorted through from the Upland test audience used the "N-word." There were a depressing number of hateful racist messages about Aria and Black women in general. Only one viewer picked up on who Aria's parents were and questioned whether Neil should be marrying the daughter of executed traitors, which was not ideal. Gears had been hoping that most people had forgotten about Aria's parents, even if it was big news a dozen years ago.

The vast majority of the comments showed a lot of love for Aria and Neil. Gears had not realized how well-known Aria had become through her years of training. There were a few notes from every single urban center in their test audience. Personal notes for Aria were the majority of the comments coming in, wishing her well. *"You go girl! I did not peg you for the marrying an Uplander type, but I love seeing you so happy!" "This is Jenny from Lowland Minnesota. You look amazing! Love the hair AND the stud on your arm. You've come a long way, Fields!"* Gears quickly deleted that one from the system, and deleted one other that referred to Aria as Fields before she even read it. This was not good. Even if it was only one person, Gears didn't like that anyone had realized who Aria's parents were. She liked even less that a few people had realized Aria was Fields.

There was nothing to be done about it, though. They couldn't give up this opportunity and abort the mission. Aria would just have to move forward quickly. At least Aria and Neil were wildly popular. Neil's popularity was not news, but it was still good that no one was turning on him.

Gears decided they had what they needed. She needed to get this on air. She gave the signal to Becca, who thanked Neil and Aria for being on the show. Gears queued up the music and photo montage of their first year together that she had made up to create a past for them. She'd created one of them posing on a hike at Sugarloaf Mountain, one of them side-hugging at a table, and another of them biking down a street with a sunset behind them. They looked authentic, if she did say so herself. She panned back to the couple after the photos, because the way Neil was looking at Aria was even more convincing than her photo montage. Gears called it a wrap after Neil's last line.

"Here's to many more years," Neil said as he kissed Aria on the lips gently.

Gears put the piece in the queue. There was no need to edit further. She checked the window out of paranoia, although she knew Anthony would have alerted her if the military or police were approaching. It was almost eerily quiet outside. They were getting away with it, it seemed. The piece would air as soon as Joe finished reading the evacuation orders.

14.
"JUST RING THE BELLS THAT STILL CAN RING"

—Leonard Cohen
(Aria)

Three days from Eamon landfall

Aria and Neil boarded the first train of the day to Harpers Ferry from Union Station. The air smelled of burnt rubber from far-away fires in the West. By the time the train pulled out of the tunnel, the sun was starting to burn off some of the smog, but visibility was still limited, so the train ambled slowly through Brookland's front yard gardens that Aria had visited with Noona so many times, and into Upland Maryland. Aria knew Expectus had once tried to establish a Lowland enclave in Frederick, but the local activists were overwhelmed by militia forces and had to retreat to Lowland DC ultimately. They were going straight into a region with few allies.

The train was full of families trying to make an early move out of Eamon's path. Aria and Neil didn't have to deal with the crowds. At the station, they'd been whisked onto a golf cart and taken to the first-class car, where they had a private room with two red and gold upholstered benches. The old Amtrak trains had been sold to Paxa Corporation long ago, which had invested little in that part of their company. The car they were in was luxurious on the surface, but Aria could tell it was just a dressed-up train car from the early 2030s. Since Neil was their primary watch model, he rode for free. Aria had heard stories of Lowlanders being denied boarding even if they had bought tickets, but maybe because of their presence, she hadn't noticed anyone being turned away that morning. Of course, she might not have seen it since their chauffeured entrance was from the front of the train and everyone else boarded from the rear cars—a supposed perk of accompanying Neil to his mother's diplomatic retreat. It was all a far cry from the high-speed rail that Expectus envisioned. It was hardly the most important thing to worry about, but if the next week went well, the trains would be free of surveillance and free of fare within the decade.

Aria did not discuss any of this with Neil, of course. The listening device on Neil's shirt was picking up every word they said in their cozy room. In day-to-day life, Aria didn't think anyone but a bot was listening. Lowlanders outnumbered Uplanders and overwhelmed the surveillance system, especially since water shortages had started to limit their use of AI. Aria was also quite good at confusing the listening bots with her strategic use of sign language and coded language. Being with Neil was different. Aria knew his mom likely always had a human listening in on Neil and certainly did now that he supposedly had a new pregnant fiancée. Despite, or maybe because their private roomette was being surveilled, Aria and Neil continued the dialogue they had been having on the way to the station.

As they were leaving the bookstore the night before, Noona handed them a selection of books including *50 Questions to Answer Before Getting Married*, with a smile. Both Aria and Neil were surprised by how fun it was to answer the questions. They'd been good at improv together in high school drama class, and the rules of improv came back to them quickly: say, "yes, and," and "there are no mistakes."

"Do you believe in God?" Neil read from the book.

"I don't think so, but I'm open to finding out I'm wrong when I'm dead. You?"

"Agnostic too. Let the mystery be!" Neil referenced an old pop song they'd orchestrated for composition class together. This was a safe and even fun conversation for Aria. "I can't believe we're having a baby. Here's another question in the book: What characteristics do you most want to instill in your children?" Aria was impressed by how in-character Neil could stay.

"Maybe resilience?" Aria thought of her parents' efforts to encourage her to keep trying when she failed, even if she just tripped while running. Her parents were the ones that made her think she could pick herself up from anything. Them and Poppy. Aria wasn't going to talk about any of them in a surveilled spot, though. She surprised herself that she found she wanted to share those stories with Neil. She'd do it later, in private. Part of the reason Aria preferred queer relationships was the strength of the emotional connections she could find. It was weird to feel the same kind of desire to share her feelings with Neil.

"Definitely resilience. And independence too." Neil said, breaking the silence and referring to the characteristics of their fictional child.

They talked about their fears about their (not real) child's life in the climate crisis—with fire and hurricanes everywhere, and either too much or too little water. They talked about how many children they wanted. Aria touched her stomach and experienced her first ever pang of a biological ache to have a child. She was getting inexplicably teary-eyed. Biology was a bitch. An image flashed in her mind of her jumping Neil right there in the roomette and impregnating herself with his seed. She blinked it away and snuggled closer in their seat as she answered him.

"I just want to be the best mom I can to this baby," Aria said, getting into her role more. "I want this baby to be loved and I want to love it. I want to raise them to be fierce and kind at the same time. I'm pretty sure I'm going to fuck up the kid no matter what I try. I mean, we're bringing our baby into a messed up world that doesn't deserve them. I've always felt like a mom, so this is a dream come true for me, in one way, but it's also my worst nightmare to mess this up."

"You are going to be such an amazing mom, Aria," Neil said. "A sexy mom too." He had a smile in his eyes, and he kissed Aria's temple before moving on to the next page of the book. Neil's hand rubbed up Aria's torso, skimming the side of her breast in a way that made Aria squeeze her thighs together in anticipation.

As the conversation continued, Aria got closer and closer to Neil and took every opportunity to touch him. She surprised herself with her comfort level around Neil. She held his hand when they talked about what it meant to be a feminist and what chores and roles they thought they could and should play in a marriage. Aria found herself falling into fantasy, despite this being a mission, not a date, and despite how it seemed like a vision of matrimony from another time, without their very real differences in the way. She rubbed her hand along his forearm as they talked about marriage and whether they believed it was still important.

"There's a great bell hooks quote about marriage in a patriarchal society and how hard it is to keep your values," Aria shared.

"bell hooks. Is she a poet?"

"My favorite."

"Let's read some of her stuff together later," Neil said. "And figure out how to be the exception."

"May I?" Aria asked, as she offered to sit behind Neil and rub his shoulders as they talked about how they each handled conflict. Aria liked to have time and space for meditation and then talk enough to get to the root cause of the issue. Neil liked to have some space and time to process, too, and preferred to save deep conversations for after a good workout, when he could think more clearly.

Massage over, they leaned on each other as they went through the next chapters of the book, and laughed about how typical their answers were and how they had thought themselves to be far more original thinkers than what they were finding.

"What happened to the young artists we used to be?" Aria asked.

"I know, right? Who even are we right now?"

To Aria's surprise, the train ride was fun. There were no cameras that Aria could see, just microphones, so they didn't need to embrace each other more and more as they went through the book, but it was happening naturally. Aria liked that Neil was handsy. His hand had made it down past her belly button to palm between her legs. Aria leaned her head back with a small moan and Neil kissed her neck and moved his hand to lightly massage her inner thigh. Aria's pulse quickened.

Neil's back was to the window, and Aria leaned harder against him, grabbing the book of questions from him, and holding it so they could both see it. As they rode along, Neil's hands kept meandering as they recalled what they still needed to discuss from the book.

"Next question. How would we each handle ebbs and flows in our sex lives?" Neil raised with a smirk on his face.

"Let's explore that one tonight," Aria responded, lifting her eyebrows, and turning to smile at Neil.

"Okay, next question. What do we love about each other?"

"This is going to sound like it's about me and not you, but I love that you take care of me and you come after me. Like on the roof of that party, you protected me from your mom's view. You made sure I was safe." The image she'd invoked of Neil's body and their encounter on the roof made Aria buck her hips up against Neil's hand.

Aria wanted to also share that when she was stuck locked down under that tree he had been so concerned for her and making sure she had food and water, but the invisible ears didn't need to know all that. Their roomette was both intimate and public at the same time. The people listening should be made to squirm though, especially if it was Neil's mom herself doing the listening.

"I love how you take care of me in bed too. I think this book has us both on track to get lucky tonight."

"Not until tonight, huh?" Neil's hand moved gently up her side and grazed the side of her breast again. Aria pouted her lips at the loss of touch between her legs, and Neil kissed her temple again.

"If I start telling you what I love about you, we won't be waiting until tonight." Neil was hard and ready and yet he didn't even push himself against Aria. He picked her up. "Turn around." Aria knelt on the train bench, facing Neil, and he held her hands, staring at her with his deep brown eyes. His pupils were so large his eyes were almost black. His shirt was wrinkled. Aria wanted to rip it off, get rid of all the microphones, and pull Neil into her. Neil held her hands instead. "I love that you tell me what you need and what you want. You are sexy, you are gorgeous, and you are the most talented musician I've ever heard. You are braver than I could ever be. You always have been."

"That's not true, Neil. I could NEVER take on your mom and you did it without hesitation."

"That's true. It's easy to be brave when it comes to protecting you. I have a question not in the book."

"Is it one of your 'would you rather' questions?" Neil had loved those as a teenager.

"Sort of. Let's say we're in *Casablanca*. Am I Humphrey Bogart or Victor Laszlo?" Aria took a deep breath and recalibrated her body and mind to the conversational shift, thinking about the question, remembering sitting in the dark together in the back of their film class.

"You mean Rick Blaine or Victor Laszlo."

"Who's Rick Blaine?"

"Maybe you should've paid more attention to the movie if you want to ask me about it!" Aria laughed and swatted Neil's thigh, trying to be playful, but the hard muscle she found under her hand just reminded her of Neil being hard everywhere. She refocused her mind again. "Rick Blaine is Humphrey Bogart's character in the movie that you made fun of for weeks as being archaic."

"I have no idea how you remember that name from twelve years ago, but sure Rick Blaine. And for the record, I paid a lot of attention, but it was mostly to you."

"While we were dishing about Mr. Fibano?" Aria smiled at the memory of her and Neil on the bench in the back of the class, fitting into each others' indentations like peas in a pod, whispering about the spice level of each of Mr. Fibano's mannerisms. She hadn't once tried to jump Neil in their film class, which is what she wanted to do now, right here on the train. She wanted to feel their bodies pumping and the train rocking them together.

But the announcement came on the loudspeaker that they were approaching Harpers Ferry, and Aria realized it wasn't meant to be. She pulled her mind out of her lust and considered the question that Neil had asked about Victor Laszlo and Rick Blaine as she picked up her bag and straightened her clothes, watching Neil stand and shift his pants so his hard-on was less obvious.

Aria was disappointed they hadn't had time for more after getting so worked up, but she was glad there hadn't been time to answer Neil's question. This wasn't 1940-something, it was 2040-something. Aria didn't have to choose. She could have her cake and eat it too.

15.
"THERE IS A CRACK IN EVERYTHING"

—Leonard Cohen

(Aria)

Before opening the train door, the train conductor's right hand quickly went up and his fingers folded down to make a right angle, half of the ASL sign for "expect," meaning that he was with Expectus. That was Aria's sign. This man would be her "getaway driver." She memorized the fatherly face and trusted he would risk everything to get her out of there as soon as they had gathered the intel Expectus needed. She smiled and posed every few steps and looked at Neil with an adoration that came naturally after their time on the train. She and Neil had agreed that going public fast would be the best protection from Simone Rao, so she was ready for the cameras and questions coming at them from every direction as they alighted.

"Unfortunately, we don't have time for questions now because we need to get to the meeting opening, but we will be having a proper press conference at the end of the meeting. I hope you'll join us there," Neil announced to the crowd.

Anthony immediately blocked the crowd with his huge presence. Neil placed his hand on Aria's lower back and led her towards a wooded path that was cordoned off from public access. Being treated like royalty by both the state media and the public clearly buoyed Neil's confidence, and Aria hoped some of that confidence and none of the royalty would rub off on her.

The plan was coming together. Neil, as her inside guy, had gotten them access. The conductor was her getaway driver. Now they just needed to nab the information they needed and get out of there. Being in Harpers Ferry reminded Aria it was not necessarily an asset to have both the risk tolerance and the conviction of John Brown. What was to stop her from going down the path to martyrdom on this mission? The train station they'd just left was a replica of the one John Brown's crew had come to for help when they tried to steal the weapons at the Armory to free enslaved Black people. It was on higher ground than the original, to try to avoid the ravages of climate change.

Aria stole one last look behind her before they entered the forest, and saw families with huge suitcases making their way up the hill, running from Hurricane Eamon's wrath. They were packed as though they were never going to be able to go back home. There was an exhaustion and desperation to the scene.

They are why I am risking walking into this trap, Aria thought as they stepped out of sight into the dappled light of the forest. *I will do everything I can to succeed for my community and for my parents.*

Alone in the woods, Neil stopped and removed the mic on his shirt. Aria gawked as he removed his shirt unnecessarily slowly, all the while with his gaze on Aria. Aria broke eye contact, letting her eyes wander to safer territory, his neck, his mouth, his scruffy jaw. She wondered if he would shave before the reception or wear his scruffy beard. Neil stepped towards Aria once he'd removed his shirt and safely covered the microphone. There were no cameras now, no reason to pretend they were in love. *What was Neil doing?* Aria had known Neil forever and also not at all in his Upland persona. But none of that mattered. This was a distraction. She needed his insider knowledge more than his body.

"We should go over the plan while we're free to talk." Neil stepped closer again and Aria tilted her head, ready for a kiss that didn't come. *Did he still want to fuck her? He seemed to on the train. He was ready under the Magnolia tree.* Neil's stare slowly moved to the ground under a tree, up to the canopy, and back to Aria's eyes. She wasn't misreading him. There was technically no reason for Aria to ignore her deep attraction for the sake of the mission. But there was no reason to give into it before they even had time to review her plan. Aria coughed. "The plan."

"Right, the plan. Tell me the plan." The spell was broken.

Aria picked up a stick so she had something solid in her hands other than Neil, and she took a step back, holding the stick in front of her to create some space. "The basic mission is simple—we find the moles among the BRUINS. Poppy believes that there are at least two moles here, that they know each other, and that they know both where the seed and mineral reserves are located. Poppy had been in touch with them, but about a decade ago, both digital and analog communications were compromised, so the only way for us to talk to them is to go to this BRUINS meeting and find them in person. We only know they are here now at all because they left a cryptic message at an old dead drop spot that this BRUINS meeting has allies. Poppy thinks the moles may also know how to lower the water walls that will otherwise cause flooding in the poorest communities, and also the location of some strategic reserves. Our job is to get any critical information we find back to Gears." Neil looked skeptical but nodded, and Aria continued. "It relies on more luck than I'd like, but it's what we've got. Let's hope the double agents want to find us as much as we want to find them."

Neil watched while Aria pushed leaves with her stick into four piles. "We'll look for the mole by splitting up. I'll take the Indian diplomats tonight." Aria pointed to one pile of leaves. "And the Nigerians tomorrow," she said, pointing to another pile of leaves. "You'll take the Russian diplomats tonight and the South African diplomats tomorrow." The second two piles of leaves represented the Russians and South Africans. "If we still haven't found anything, we'll try the Brazilians next, but they are the least likely to be the double agents since their turn to authoritarianism happened so much later and the movement there has wrenched back power so many times."

"That's too bad. The only decent people I know in that bunch are the Brazilians. I'm not sure the others are going to tell us anything."

"All you need to do is make conversation and bring up the reserves. If it's the mole, they'll find you later and figure out a secure way to share the information. We'll plan to leave via this path and by train either tonight or tomorrow night at midnight, assuming we've gotten what we need by then. We want to get out of here before Eamon bears down on us."

Neil's face was unreadable. "And my mother?"

"You'll have to keep her at bay for this to work. That's all you." Neil nodded and looked somber at that assignment.

"And where do we deliver this information once we have it?"

"Gears set me up with jewelry that will record and transmit. We don't need to physically deliver information, we just need to get ourselves out of here before your mother gets to us for our own safety and sanity. We get the goods and we get out."

Neil started singing the *Mission Impossible* theme music, another throwback to their time at Ellington where they had the assignment in composition class to write their own theme music for classic movies. "Doon, Doon Doon, Doon, Duh Duh, Doon Doon Doon Doon. Duh Duh. Duhduhduh." Aria dropped her stick, and started walking down the path. They had enough of a plan.

"Let's get going."

When they arrived at their room at the Hilltop Hotel, they entered at the rear and used the back staircase to avoid the media. Their bags magically appeared in their room. Tchaikovsky's fourth symphony was playing and the balcony doors were open, providing a majestic view of the mountains and their inverted reflection over the meeting point of the Potomac and Shenandoah Rivers. The water was gushing around boulders, heading down the Potomac to the ocean, which was closer than it had ever been to this point thanks to rising seas from climate change. In addition to the view, the room was about twenty times the size of Aria's room above the bookstore, with a lounge area, a kitchen, a bedroom, and a bathroom that, on its own, was at least twice the size of Aria's room.

She wouldn't bother searching these huge rooms for devices. It was unlikely she'd find them all. Neil busied himself unpacking his garment bag in the closet.

"Tchaikovsky's fourth, huh," Aria asked, making small

talk for the audience on the other side of all the listening devices.

"I wanted you to be comfortable. Let me show you the cello they brought for you too." Neil reached out for Aria's hand.

Aria had a shared cello at the bookstore that she checked out sometimes and played in her room, but it was nothing as nice as the beautiful instrument that was in front of her when she unlatched the case in their suite. By joining Neil, she had entered a parallel universe where everything was plentiful and easy. Aria wondered what it would be like to not know, or not care, that the ease of Uplanders was on the backs of so much human suffering outside of Upland.

She took a moment to adjust the height of the stool and screw in the pin of the cello. She tuned the instrument for a few moments. When she was satisfied, she played along with the symphony that was piping through the speaker system. It came flooding back to her. She didn't even need music, though she noted that there was a thick book of sheet music on the stand in front of her.

When the symphony ended, she started to play Bach's Suite No. 1 from memory. Neil was sitting on the floor next to her, transfixed. He reached out and started rubbing Aria's leg. She stopped playing and wondered if she should read into Neil getting physical when there were listening devices, but being restrained back in the woods. Was being watched his kink or something? Quite a kink to have in the midst of a surveillance state. Aria longed to stay in that room and suss out how noisy he liked to be while people were listening. The reception downstairs was to begin in an hour, though, and that was her priority. They didn't have much time to get geared up and join the party. It was time to find the agents who would leak them information.

16.
"THERE IS A CRACK IN EVERYTHING"

—Leonard Cohen

(Neil)

Walking downstairs into the reception with Aria on his arm, Neil did not notice the view of the rivers. He did not notice the arched doorways to the room, nor did he notice the long, carved banquet tables made of cherrywood, the candelabras, or even the familiar faces waving and nodding their greetings. All his attention was on Aria. Neil was wearing a tuxedo with a fuscia bow tie and cummerbund to match Aria's sari. He had been braced for Aria to mock the sari and tux combo when he took it out of the garment bag and explained that he had a fashion assistant who'd picked it out. But she'd just laughed and asked if he knew how to operate the gear he'd ordered and then poked fun at him for never having heard the term fuschia, even after dating Sadie, whose visual art expression was almost entirely in that shade. The conversation didn't linger on Sadie, thankfully. Neil couldn't have contained his annoyance if they went back to harping on their high school prom. They had moved past all that finally, it seemed.

Getting Aria into the sari had taken both of their full concentrations. Aria had shivered when Neil tucked the fabric into her skirt and then leaned forward and rested her head in his neck, rubbing his trimmed beard with her palm. Unless he was mistaken, he was affecting her as much as she was affecting him. Neil couldn't wait to unwrap the yards upon yards of fabric. First, they had work to do.

The first group to catch them in conversation was a couple of Russian brothers and their waif-like fashion-obsessed girlfriends, who Neil had unfortunately known since he was a teenager. They had still been spoiled and reckless children when Neil had gotten stuck showing them around in their twenties. He had just barely kept them out of trouble by sheer luck on a couple nights, but then stopped agreeing to show them around when they started a massive fist fight in a Georgetown nightclub that Anthony had to break apart. The whole incident was covered up somehow, and Neil refused to ever "show them the town" again after that. If it weren't for his commitment to getting Aria intel, he'd avoid these two like the plague.

"Neil Rao, in the flesh! I heard a rumor you made an appearance at the Gala but I didn't find you. How are you doing, man? It's been a long time since we were wingmen for each other. Looks like we've all ended up with sexy girls now." The two women who hung on Nikolai and Dmitri asked Aria who she was wearing and began talking about fashion while the men peppered Neil with questions about how his mother planned to run the auctions at the end of the meeting. Aria was charming. She gushed over their style with such delight, even Neil almost believed she cared about fashion.

"I'm going to powder my nose. I'll be back in a moment," Aria said, starting the part of the evening where they would be separated. Neil kissed her on the cheek as she left and accepted the drink being handed to him by the brother he thought was Dmitri, but could have been Nikolai. His brain had blocked out memories of the blowhards in front of him for self-preservation, no doubt.

"A toast to Secretary Rao! You have an incredible mother, Mr. Rao."

After making small talk about his mother's no-nonsense diplomatic style, Neil made his move when they asked where his mother was.

"You know my mother, she loves to make an entrance," Neil told them.

"What could be so pressing that she would miss her own reception?" the brother Neil thought was Nikolai asked, more serious than Neil remembered them being in their youth.

"Ah, that's a tidbit of information I'm not supposed to share," Neil teased.

"Now you piqued my curiosity."

"Well, you'll have to ask her yourself. She told me she was looking forward to talking with you. I may be misremembering, but I thought she mentioned something about the mineral reserves."

The brothers' eyes turned dark and both of their brows furrowed. They looked angry. Neil knew that look and he didn't like it at all. They stepped closer to Neil. One of them fisted his lapel.

"Is Donner hoarding metals again?"

Neil had an urge to punch the guy, but there were two of them, they were huge, and punching wasn't his skill-set. If he went that route, they'd attract security and his mom would find out he'd asked about the reserves. Neil could see one of the guards in his peripheral vision put his hand on his weapon. He needed to calm these guys down. "Hoarding? No, no one is hoarding. I think it was the name of that musical band she thought you'd like, you know them, The Metal Reserves. Remember, we went to see them on the waterfront once."

The men looked suspiciously at Neil, but the big one let go of his lapel. Neil mumbled something about how rock music should be apolitical and then quickly excused himself and hurried to find Aria on the other side of the ballroom. The guard had relaxed back into position.

Neil spotted Aria on the balcony overlooking the river, her head leaning in towards another woman in a bright sari who seemed to be enjoying Aria's company much more than the Russians had been enjoying his. He could see two or three stars in the sky. Neil pictured the endless sea of stars that existed behind the curtain of dust, pollution, and the storm clouds that would be arriving tomorrow. He felt a stab of jealousy in his chest as he watched Aria against the beautiful background and with her beautiful companion.

Aria's jet-black hair was cascading down in waves and she was leaning into the other woman with short silver hair. They looked conspiratorial. Neil watched from across the room as they laughed together. Both women were slender and tall. As he watched them, Neil saw that they shared mannerisms, and bumped shoulders frequently. Then he noticed that they were smoking. How did he not know that Aria smoked? Neil found the habit off-putting and thought there should have been a question about it in that book of couples questions. He knew so much about her from being close in high school, from fucking her chains free under that tree, and from the hour they had spent getting reacquainted on the train. But there was a lot about her that was still a mystery.

Neil was about to walk over to the balcony to somehow silently point out that Simone Rao thought she was pregnant so she probably shouldn't smoke, when an older man in uniform emerged from the crowd and blocked his way. It was Anthony. He handed Neil a glass of water.

"Don't. Trust me. Don't act desperate."

Neil smiled at his guard. They hadn't had a chance to talk at the TV studio when Anthony was guarding the door the whole time as though someone was about to bust through.

"I was just going to check in with her."

"Do you want me to write up the scuffle with those Russians?"

Neil sometimes thought of Anthony as his best friend, but with the years between them, he was more like a father figure. Neil wondered whether Anthony was hurt that he hadn't asked for advice about Aria.

"I'm good. Those guys are just hotheads."

"You certainly are doing a good job making a splash."

It was true, Neil had checked the news on his watch. The public was obsessed with Neil and Aria and the media was referring to the pair as "Nearia." Pictures of them walking into the reception tonight were everywhere, Neil knew how Uplanders thought. Loving Neil and Aria as a couple made Uplanders feel they could not possibly be racist. Neil was banking on that sentiment keeping them alive and safe for the next few days. That, and Anthony's protection were the only thing they had going for them in this viper's nest.

17.
"THAT'S HOW THE LIGHT"

—Leonard Cohen

Aria's sari-laden gait was not smooth, and she had to resist the temptation to hike up the fabric to circle the room. One benefit was that she attracted the other sari-laden women, and was able to strike up a conversation with a person who turned out to be Preeti Gupta, the Minister of Coal for India, who approached and complimented her sari.

"I hate to be too personal, dear, but your pallu needs to be pinned. I have a few extra pins on my blouse; would you like me to pin the fabric back for you on the balcony?"

Aria couldn't believe how easy this was. Preeti was surely the mole if she was inviting her for a discussion outside. "I'd be honored for the help, Minister Gupta."

"Please, call me Preeti. And I have many years of practice with saris. I have so many here with me on this trip, you'd be welcome to borrow one for tomorrow."

"That's a generous offer, thank you, but Neil went through the trouble of getting a wardrobe delivered for me, so I'm all set."

Minister Gupta's eyes widened at Aria's mention of a wardrobe from Neil. "Is it serious with you and Neil? You did look natural together on TV. You were projected right onto my sofa in my hotel room here and the whole time I wanted to hug you both."

Aria's steps created more distance from Minister Gupta at the mention of a hug. She did not want to encourage Gupta's praise, but it kept going.

"I admit I've watched more than once. They have been replaying the interview constantly. You were magnetic. You two have what it takes to be a power couple. Is that what you want?"

Aria felt intruded upon. She didn't want to talk about Neil or a TV interview with this woman, but she needed to know what she knew.

"Neil and I were high school sweethearts."

"Young love, of course. Was it like Romeo and Juliet with both sides disapproving then?"

Aria stepped outside to the balcony behind Minister Gupta. They could theoretically speak privately here, if Gupta could be trusted.

"It was just a typically brief high school romance. The adult version is much better. Are you married? Do you have any advice for me about the coming months?" Aria discretely deployed the ASL Expectus sign but transitioned to pretending to play with her hair when she got no reaction from the Minister, who seemed entirely distracted and almost teary eyed.

"I was in love once, but never married. I envy you being at the start of something new. Do you aspire to have a relationship like the one your parents modeled for you? Did they have a love marriage?"

Aria was unclear what Gupta knew about her parents so volunteered nothing about their death at the hands of the Donner Administration. "My parents had a love marriage."

"My parents as well, and that was a very different time, before love marriages were so common. Maybe that's why I never married. I couldn't imagine finding something like what they had."

This conversation was lovely, but they were outside. This woman could be telling Aria everything she needed if she was the mole. *She must just be the Minister of Coal.*

"How did you get into politics?"

"The challenge is that I stumbled into it and then my work became so important that I could not stand the guilt of leaving it."

"Your work to displace indigenous communities to extract and burn coal?"

Shit. Aria braced herself for having just escalated their conversation, but Minister Gupta did not defend her work and simply leaned forward, resting her forearms on the railing and looking below and around, discreetly.

"That's not my life's work."

Aria rested her forearms on the balcony, mimicking Gupta's body language. She wanted Gupta to say more.

"Tell me a little about your life's work."

Preeti Gupta spent the next nearly thirty minutes telling Aria her life story. She shared about her mother and her father and her three brothers, and where they lived, and what her childhood was like, funny stories about growing up in Delhi, and a sad story about the death of her brother. She was a good storyteller, but Aria just wanted to know if she was the mole. "It sounds like your youngest brother was a real character. I'm sorry you lost him when he was so young. I guess you never know how long you have with anyone."

"No, you never know how long you'll have with a person. Let me fix this pallu for you."

Minister Gupta reached for the side of her blouse and extracted a safety pin. She took the fabric from Aria's shoulder and carefully pleated it with the safety pin in her mouth, before pushing the pin through the layers of fabric and brushing her fingers on Aria's shoulder to lift the blouse and pin the pallu down.

"That's how you do it. You did a great job, but you need to attach the pallu to the blouse."

Both the conversation and the pinning of the pallu were oddly intimate. *If there had been a secret to be spilled it would have spilled by now.*

Aria glanced behind her and saw Neil talking to Anthony. He was the hottest guy in the room hands down in his perfectly tailored tuxedo. She doubted he had gotten anything from the Russians. Neil made eye contact with her and she brought her thumb together with the tips of her first two fingers, indicating "no" for "no luck here." Neil made a different gesture back, that they had also used in high school to mean "no." It was a loose fist knocking from side-to-side. He then turned his fist and raised his eyebrows making a motion that evoked his cock and nodded "yes." Aria laughed despite herself and found she wanted to go and laugh with Neil.

Just as Aria took a step towards leaving the balcony, Preeti leaned forward and whispered. "Do not gesture any indication of this to him, dear, but I am on your side. We can talk more tomorrow." Aria's hand fell to her side, and she stilled as Minister Gupta passed her and walked back into the party.

18.
"THE LIGHT GETS IN"

—Leonard Cohen

Neil had been undressing Aria with his eyes the last half of the night, once he was sure his angry Russians had left the premises and he could relax. His hands were itching in anticipation of finishing what they'd started on the train and he'd wanted to continue in the woods. He finally had Aria back in their room. She was standing in front of a full-length mirror carefully removing her earrings. Neil approached behind her. They looked good together in the reflection. His cummerbund and bow tie matched the intricate border of her sari.

"Let me help you with that." Neil carefully unhooked the S clasp on her necklace, making sure to let his fingers brush the sensitive parts of her neck. She made eye contact with his reflection and smiled conspiratorially as he placed the necklace next to the earrings on the armoire. Neil wanted to unwrap Aria and then bury himself inside her.

"I've been anticipating removing this sari since we draped it." Neil unfastened the safety pin from the fabric on her shoulder that he had watched the woman downstairs pin onto Aria, and placed it on the table with the jewelry. The fabric from her torso fell and she caught it.

Aria had told Neil earlier that she hadn't worn Indian clothing since her parents died. Told him that her mother had learned how to wear a sari around her father's family, but died before she could teach Aria.

"How did it feel wearing it?"

"It made me miss my baba. He was always my biggest champion, you know? He thought I was the prettiest, most talented, smartest girl in the world. It's so self-centered, but it's hard for me not to have my dad out there somewhere, being my biggest champion no matter what." Aria shared the stories that had popped into her mind to share with Gupta. She found she wanted to share them more with Neil.

"I remember him from high school." Neil was brought back to the night Aria came to him in a panic—the night his mother had her parents arrested. He hated that he was affiliated with that hurt. Aria's mind was in a different place, though, it seemed.

"I'm lucky to have had him. I- I'm sorry to go on like that when you didn't get to grow up with your dad." Aria looked at Neil with sympathy.

"Don't apologize. I like hearing about your dad." Neil hesitated before revealing the truth to the listening devices. It was nothing he hadn't discussed in the open with his mother before, and he wanted to keep the conversation going with Aria.

"My mother told me that my father left when I was a toddler and claimed that I wasn't even his son when he abandoned us. I never knew him, and he's never gotten in touch. And you know my mother has never supported my music or my choices. I did the best I could under her thumb, and most importantly, I'm lucky enough that I've made it to you. You are my family now, Aria." His lies for the surveillance system were more true than his truths could have been without them listening.

Neil had untucked and unwrapped all of the fabric while he was speaking, and now held it behind Aria. The tops of her breasts were spilling out of her blouse and her biceps were encircled with the gold border of her blouse.

"You look powerful. And sexy." Neil held out one end of the fabric and walked across the room until the fabric was as taut as the fabric of his pants had been all day. They walked towards each other with the two ends, bringing their corners together.

"I think we're not supposed to let the fabric hit the floor like this," Aria said, taking the sari from Neil.

Neil took the once-folded end of the sari and found the second set of corners, careful now to keep it off the ground. He walked towards Aria, looking straight into her big brown eyes, and then down to her cleavage, enjoying the coming together more than the separating part of the folding dance.

"You know, you don't have to do this much seducing. I'm pretty much a sure thing as your fiancé." Aria took the corners from Neil again, as he straightened out the other end and pulled the material taut.

"We're just folding a sari. I haven't started the seducing."

"Oh yeah. What does seduction look like then?" Neil took the remaining fabric from Aria, folded it and set it down. He moved behind Aria and embraced her from behind, looking at them in the mirror and letting them both feel the line of his cock through the fabric of his trousers and her petticoat. He ran his hands up and down her arms, warming them from the air conditioning that she was unaccustomed to. She looked so good in the blouse and petticoat that he almost didn't want to remove them. Almost. Neil rubbed his own hands together to make sure they were warm and began unhooking the back of her blouse. She tilted her head to expose her neck, without breaking their mirrored eye contact, and Neil kissed her before moving to her front and pulling her blouse forward and off. He loved that she was letting him do this undressing. She had a black bra underneath the blouse. Neil didn't want to remove it yet, though. She was breathing faster, anticipating what would come next. He placed his palm on her chest and caressed the tops of her breasts. Aria exposed the other side of her slender neck and Neil placed his lips on it. From there, he leaned down and kissed the tops of her breasts, moving the cup of her bra down, he took her nipple in his mouth, licking and sucking. Aria arched her back into him and Neil put his leg between hers, sucking to the rhythm she was setting as she began to gently ride his leg. Neil unclasped her bra and let it hang loosely on her arms as he turned his mouth to her left breast, his hand caressing her right. Her elongated nipples felt so good in his mouth. Neil followed Aria's pace, set by her pelvis pulsating against his leg.

They stopped looking at the mirror and started looking at each other. Neil tried to memorize her—her face, her breasts, her body, and pump his body to her beat. Her thighs squeezed his thigh like a vice as she moaned with pleasure and shuddered against him, finally going slack with a sigh.

Neil wanted to get her into bed. He had wanted to be in this exact spot almost for as long as he could remember. He stood and pulled Aria up with him so her legs were wrapped around him. Aria let her bra drop to the floor as Neil carried her across the room. He eased himself on the bed with Aria on top. Aria grabbed his lapels and took off his jacket and then his bow tie. She squeezed him with her legs around him and kissed him on the lips and began to unbutton his shirt. Pulling Neil's shirt off, she grabbed the bottom of the shirt and spoke right into it, grinning.

"Do you want to be inside me, Neil?" Her voice was sultry. Neil nodded. Aria winked at Neil. "Go get a condom." Aria balled the shirt up and threw it across the room. It landed all the way in the living room. Neil knew there were a lot of other microphones in the room and that someone was listening to them, and so did Aria. He didn't care who heard them, as long as Aria didn't mind. He had condoms he had picked up from the Lowland headquarters out of his bag, thanked God he didn't have to use the black market ones from Upland, and took off his pants and boxers. Aria was wearing only black silk underwear that was in the clothes he had ordered for her. He brought the condom back to her and she ripped the package open with her teeth, unrolling the condom down his shaft. Neil palmed her mound and found she was ready. He wondered if she had been that wet since their train ride. He'd been hard the entire train ride and walk in the woods. He'd been waiting for this moment. He pushed her underwear to the side and inserted one finger and then two, feeling Aria's muscles tighten around him and her pelvis rock into him. He took out his fingers.

"Don't stop." The words were magic to Neil's ears.

"Take them off," Neil said. Aria smirked as she complied. Neil touched his tongue to his fingers and tasted Aria's tartness as he watched her slide off her underpants. There was an electricity to her gaze on him, as if she was daring him to keep going.

"Turn over." Aria was on all fours on the bed. Neil used his hand to guide the tip of his penis up and down her slit. Aria was rocking her pelvis towards him. Neil pushed himself inside and leaned forward to grab Aria's breasts again. He followed her lead at first and then sat up on his knees and buried himself inside as he'd wanted to all night. Aria cried out.

"Yes." Neil pounded inside her and felt his balls tighten. He wasn't going to be able to last much longer. "Now." Aria cried. "Now Neil." That was all it took, Neil felt himself empty into Aria. He collapsed on top of Aria and she straightened her legs under him to lie down, turning her head so her cheek rested on the bed. Neil lay on top of her, still inside her.

"So good," Aria said softly, with her eyes closed.

"That was amazing. You are amazing, Aria." Neil reluctantly pulled out of Aria and got up and walked to the trash can to take care of the condom. When he got back in bed, Aria had pulled the covers over her and was asleep on her back. Neil crawled in to join her, and carefully laid his arm around her as he snuggled in. He kissed her cheek. "I love you, Aria Petros. I always have," he whispered before falling asleep himself.

19.
"I HAVE NOT COME HERE ALONE"

—The Peace Poets

Two days before Eamon landfall

The bank of dark clouds outside made the cozy fire less suspicious, as Aria had anticipated. Neil and Aria took breakfast in their room at the small table by the fireplace. Aria had the hotel robe wrapped around her and Neil was, distractingly, wearing nothing but sweatpants. They were slipping each other little notes about who they had spoken to the night before and what they had found, and after each exchange, they were lighting the note on fire. It was all too easy.

"Why didn't she just tell me last night?" Aria wrote.

Neil shrugged and lit the paper on fire with the candle on the table, holding the paper until his fingers were nearly singed, and then standing to drop it in the fireplace. Just like in the Paxa billboards of Neil shirtless, he had the perfect amount of chest hair and muscle tone. In real life, there were also freckles and creases on his back and chest. Aria quickly turned her head when Neil sat back down, hoping it was not obvious that she'd been drinking him up with her eyes. She needed to focus on not getting killed.

"Why haven't they arrested me?" Aria wrote on a slip of paper.

"Because you're with me," Neil spoke aloud. He wrote down "They don't want a scene," before letting the fire claim the paper he wrote it on and watching it go up in smoke. Neil, Poppy, and Gears had all tried to convince Aria repeatedly that the threat of a scene would protect her from Simone Rao, but that logic didn't feel right to her. She tried to put her unease out of her mind and focus on their task. Interspersed with the names of people they had spoken to were sexy notes, the final of which led to a round of morning sex. Neil had written, "I'd like to lick that chocolate off of you." Aria was game. She'd be able to focus better after a few orgasms. She smirked at him, put her finger in the chocolate mousse cup, opened her robe and smeared it around. They had sex in the chair, not even bothering to move to the bed. Luckily it was a sturdy chair.

They were not giving anything away to the surveillance state. Anyone listening only knew they'd had great sex, more than once. Unfortunately, there wasn't much *to* give away. Neither of them had gotten any information the night before, other than that Minister Gupta claimed to be on their side. They were essentially going to have to start from scratch on their quest today.

Since they had nothing on the agenda until the opening session just before lunch, Aria and Neil got cleaned up and retired to the pocket of their suite with their instruments. They began to work on another duet. It had been years since Aria had gotten to play cello whenever she felt like it, and she was enjoying herself more than she should. She felt guilty not working, and anxious about how easy infiltrating this meeting had been so far, but she took the time for herself to recoup. They had a recording of the music and tried to play along with it at half speed, learning the notes as they went. Every little mistake was making them laugh and start over. Aria tried to lean into the joy, as Neil was, with his eyes closed and his brows furrowed in focus. He was so into the music that he didn't hear the sounds approaching. Aria did.

"Did you hear that? Footsteps." Neil opened his eyes and stopped playing, but motioned Aria to keep going. Then they heard her voice.

"Neil, why is your watch off? " Neil's mother yelled through the front door of the suite. They knew she'd be arriving on the second day, but Aria was not expecting the intrusion on their private space. Secretary Rao pounded on the door. "Why are you blasting that music?" Aria was relieved that she didn't have a key or at least wasn't using the key.

Neil sighed. "We can't hide in here forever, sadly." Neil went to open the door, which Simone Rao pushed into and entered with her companion. Simone was one of those people who were shorter than you expected. She stood barely above Aria even in two-inch heels and a tight bun on top of her head. The intensity of eyes and her sharp nose took over the space. Aria put her cello away, retracing the steps she had gone through to take it out, as Neil walked over to Aria standing in their private pocket of the room. The intrusion was jarring.

"Mother! Allow me to formally introduce my fiancée and the mother of your grandbaby."

Aria was not thrilled at the emphasis on the fake pregnancy, but had agreed with Neil that they should keep it simple and stick to the lie they had already told. They had kept that part of the lie from the public.

It wasn't a difficult lie at the moment, because Aria felt like it could have been true. She was nauseous with fear.

Her hands were trembling and sweating so much she could barely handle her cello. She knew she was acting oddly and should turn around to greet Simone, but her body was frozen. She took a deep breath and told herself that her body was reacting irrationally to her first close-up encounter with Secretary Rao. She turned her head up to see Simone glaring at her with a clenched jaw.

"It's nice to meet you," Aria said unconvincingly, finally finding the steadiness to click her cello case closed. She felt cornered. "I'll be right back."

Aria pushed past Neil and Simone to the bathroom. She could feel her heart beat faster with every step, like an out-of-control metronome. The beat was getting faster by the second. She could feel the sweat pouring out of her glands. She could hear her chest wheezing. She got into the massive bathroom and closed the door. She splashed water on her face and looked in the mirror, trying to take deep, steady breaths.

She's just a person. She's just a person. She can't hurt you while you are standing next to her son and she thinks you are carrying her grandchild. She can't hurt you. But an image of her parents the night they were arrested popped unbidden into her head. Tears began to roll down Aria's face and her breathing became shallow again. Her lungs felt constricted. She was hyperventilating and she was getting lightheaded.

Aria felt the cold on her head first. She felt the warmth on her face. She heard Neil's voice. She had passed out.

"Please wake up. Please wake up. Please wake up."

She opened her eyes to see that they were on the bed and Neil was holding an ice bag on her head and was brushing her hair out of her face with his hand. Neil smiled down at Aria and moved the ice pack to the other bump on her head.

"Thank God. You've been out for ten minutes. It felt like hours. I was so scared. I told Mom the first trimester has been like this."

"They're in there, Dr. Reeves," Aria heard Simone Rao's voice and tensed and began to panic again.

"Darling, you do not look good," Secretary Rao said to Aria. "I brought Dr. Reeves. Neil was being such a brute breaking down the door and carrying you to the bed, I knew someone had to be sensible and get the doctor."

This woman had turned Aria into an orphan. This woman had publicly pushed for activists to be gunned down. She would do anything to hold onto power. And she was standing over Aria's prone body.

"I was so worried," Neil said to Aria, not looking up to greet his mother or the doctor.

"Son, you're going to have to take a step back so I can get her vitals," Dr. Reeves said. He was a stout man and half of his square head filled with the black circles of puffy skin under his eyes. He looked like a boxer who put on a lab coat and stethoscope to play the role of doctor. Aria was not buying it.

"Neil, why don't you let the doctor do his tests and join me for the opening ceremony?"

Aria tensed up. She was far too vulnerable in this position and she had no idea who this brute was. She shook her head "no" to Neil, that he thankfully understood. Neil massaged Aria's temples lightly and looked her straight in the eyes even as he spoke to his mother.

"I'm not leaving Aria's side, but I know how important this meeting is for you, Mother, please do go."

Aria relaxed hearing Neil push back on his mother, which was good timing since the doctor began putting a cuff on her to take her blood pressure. Aria felt the constriction not only in her arm, but also in her throat.

"Neil, you were the one who begged to come to this meeting. I wanted you to be my deputy and you insisted that you would only do the audio-visual technology role. You begged to bring your girlfriend and I even went along with that, but I'm not going to find another person to take care of the recording. Either come to the opening ceremony or you two can leave."

"Okay, fine, Mother. I'll go down."

Fine? Shit, was Neil going to leave her with this supposed doctor his mother had brought?

"And I'm fine too! I'll join you," Aria rasped out. Aria's heart started beating faster again. She could not be left alone with this man. She was sure of that. Her eyes landed on the inside of the doctor's bag. There were needles and vials. She tried to read the labels but couldn't make them out. The machine started beeping loudly.

"Whoa," Dr. Reeves said. "Your blood pressure is through the roof, you are not going anywhere."

Aria tried to take deep breaths, willing her blood pressure back down. Another person walked into the room. *Another witness.*

"Anthony, thank God you're here," she heard Neil say. Aria trusted Anthony. He hadn't taken advantage of her vulnerability back in high school or on the roof the previous week. He had gotten them out of the bind on the roof with barely any effort, and he was armed. Aria believed in nonviolent collective action, but *strategic* nonviolence. Getting shot was not strategic, and Aria wasn't an idiot. If someone was about to shoot her, she'd shoot them first. She'd gone through the Lowland firearm safety training, and she'd trained tens of thousands of people in understanding that being committed to nonviolent action does not mean you should not defend yourself. Even Martin Luther King Jr. had armed guards protecting his home. At that moment, Aria needed an ally with a weapon. Anthony approached Aria and Neil and stood by the bed, looking to Neil and Simone for instruction.

"I have to join my mother for the opening ceremony and Aria's ill. Can you please make sure that the good doctor here doesn't give her any medication she doesn't want and keep an eye on her until I'm back?"

"Yes, sir, " Anthony said, taking a few steps, positioning himself between Aria and the doctor. "Aria," he greeted her with a nod. "Doctor, what's the diagnosis here?"

"Her blood pressure is high and she hit her head so needs to be watched for signs of a concussion."

"Got it. I can take this from here, folks," Anthony waved the others off, picking up the doctor's bag as he walked him to the door. Aria wondered what it must be like to be able to just wave off Simone Rao. Neil motioned a "thank you" to Anthony by pressing his hands together and mouthing the words before leaving with his mother and the doctor. Anthony shut the door, and turned the deadbolt, before turning back to Aria.

Aria was relieved to see the doctor and Secretary Rao go, even if she was disappointed that Neil went along with them. She didn't love the way Anthony had locked the door.

"We have a lot to talk about, Fields," Anthony said, using Aria's code name right under all those microphones, and handing Aria a folded piece of paper. Aria's head was throbbing too much to read the paper, so she set it down.

"Why are you helping me again?"

Anthony walked over and helped Aria stand up and walk across the room. He was so much bigger than Aria that he was able to bear the brunt of her weight and cross the room and open the door without breaking a sweat. They were outside together and Anthony's shirt was pinned with a lead clip when he spoke again.

"I'm a gay man who is in a relationship and in love with another gay man, Aria. I joined for my own liberation so that one day I could publicly be with the person I love. But this isn't about me. It's about you." Anthony held the note out to Aria again.

Aria reached for the note and began to read.

Aria, I know you only met me for the first time last night, but I have known you much longer. I had a feeling Poppy would send you here to meet Musa and me. Dr. Reeves is a threat. If he is in the room when you are reading this, get out of there immediately. We need to meet as soon as possible so I can explain the rest. Please dispose of this note and follow Anthony to meet us at the opening ceremony. Yours, Preeti

Aria looked up at Anthony and back down at the note. The words began to swim on the page. It wasn't going to clear up anytime soon, so it seemed she was about to find out what a crowded ballroom would feel like with a concussion.

20.
"I CARRY MY PEOPLE IN MY BONES"

—The Peace Poets

Two days before Eamon

Aria stood across the room from Gupta wearing a black cocktail dress and the *jhumka* dangling earrings that could record a conversation just by tossing her head back. They stopped recording with a vigorous shaking of her head "no." She tossed her head back and heard a tiny beep, then shook her head "no" and heard another faint beep. They seemed to be working still.

She was grateful Anthony had extracted her, but her head throbbed at the jerking motions she had to use for the equipment. She'd taken an aspirin and then a quick shower, but she wasn't in great shape. She was struggling to get to Gupta through the crowd. She moved haltingly to avoid bumping into people. She tried to listen to snippets of conversation but found that she required all her brain power to just put one foot in front of the other.

Anthony had pointed out Preeti to Aria but stayed at the edge of the party with the rest of the security detail. Minister Gupta looked like her silver hair had been cropped even shorter than it had been the night before. She wore a huge bindi on her forehead and was wearing a beige and bronze sari with a spectacularly detailed border. Neil was in a suit on the other side of the room and was busy setting up a camera and checking the microphones. He hadn't seen Aria yet.

Aria scanned the room to make sure that Secretary Rao was not there. She selected a puff pastry from a passing tray. It made her miss Noona and wish her friend had been able to sneak in with the caterers again. Noona was back home holding down an operation getting ready to feed millions of people who'd be destitute after Eamon picked up Lowland, shook it, and put it back down.

"Is it vegetarian?" Aria asked.

"Yes, everything is Star-compliant and vegan tonight." Poppy had told her to watch what she was eating and drinking and that they would try to poison her food. This food was being passed randomly, though, so it seemed safe.

As she bit into the vegan puff pastry filled with spinach and soy, Secretary Rao entered the room and took the stage, stepping up onto a footstool behind the podium. Aria's box breathing technique was working. Secretary Rao's eyes kept coming back to Aria as she gave the welcoming remarks to the BRUINS, but Aria was staying calm.

"Welcome to the first Upland BRUINS meeting in over a decade! My gratitude to you all for regrouping here in West Virginia. Luckily this time the rioters have been contained or kept out," Secretary Rao said and with a laugh. She stared at Aria as she spoke. Aria felt a chill down her spine, took a deep, loud inhale through her nose and placed a serene smile on her face as she exhaled, half expecting the military brass in the room to descend on her. "This week we will rekindle the special relationship between our nations and lay out our vision for the coming decades." Secretary Rao prattled on. No one descended to arrest Aria.

Neil had followed his mother's gaze to Aria a few moments earlier. He was busy with the recording equipment and messing with the soundboard, but his eyes were scanning the room looking for Anthony, and showed some relief when he saw Anthony nearby.

A Nigerian oil executive took the stage next, and Neil's mother was standing to the side of the stage ready to take up her role as emcee again. The man on the stage was talking about how flooding had eliminated most of the villages that were opposed to more oil drilling in his region, and how a massive fire that no one thought possible in the tropics had killed the other activists who were angry about their water supply being tainted by oil extraction. A small group of wealthy Nigerians in Lagos were fully supportive of their plans to extract more oil, and that, he said, was what was most important. Supposedly Upland communities in the US owed it to Nigeria to pay top dollar for the ability to extract Nigerian reserves.

"You Uplanders had your chance to develop in the past century," he said. "In Nigeria, very few of us can have Paxa watches and fine wine. You must buy our oil so that we can develop." He then lamented the success of The Line community in Saudi Arabia and how the project had reduced demand for oil and gas by reducing the living space being cooled. "We are relying on Upland US to buy more petroleum products like plastics and maintain many more internal combustion engines to meet your responsibility towards Nigeria."

Aria felt the scratch in her throat from her earlier bout of nausea and wondered if her disgust would bring another round of vomit. The man's callousness about the Nigerians killed to extract the oil was not surprising, but it was shocking. *Dead people don't need Paxa watches and fine wine.* The world was on fire and the richest of the rich wanted to set more fires and saw the floods as a convenient way of getting rid of their opposition. Aria continued her Ujjayi breathing her father had taught her. It was building heat in her body and calming her nerves. As the remarks wound up, Aria no longer felt the fog of her head injury as acutely.

Aria plucked a glass from one of the servers and turned around to find Minister Gupta handing her a glass of water with a smile.

"I heard you had a concussion, dear, so you might want to stick with water," she said with more of an Indian English lilt to her words than she had had the night before. "I'll take the wine off your hands if you want," she added.

Aria was not interested in drinking water handed to her by this person who she still did not trust, concussion or no concussion; she was better off taking a drink that anyone might have grabbed for.

"I'll stick with the wine, thank you. I'm feeling much better."

"Okay, but please be mindful of your health."

Preeti Gupta took a sip of the water she had been offering Aria. Maybe she wasn't trying to poison her. Aria was annoyed, nonetheless, at the personal nature of her intervention. It was presumptuous even if they had had a conversation the night before.

"Let us go outside for a stroll before the dinner remarks. I'd like to get to know you more."

Aria remembered Preeti's note. *Dr. Reeves is a threat. If he is in the room when you are reading this, get out of there immediately.* "I'd like to see if Neil or Anthony would like to join us. They've had such busy days and could probably use a break."

"Of course, but Neil is setting up the remote participation cameras in the dining hall now, why don't we just have Anthony join us?" With that Preeti looked at Anthony, nodded her head towards the door, and gestured with her hand for him to join them.

It was breezy outside and the sound of the river gushing was a reminder that only a few days remained before Eamon arrived. The stars were obscured by the smoke from the Western fires, and the moon was behind a layer of smog.

Preeti was staring at the sky. "I'd like you to visit India."

"As far as I understand, there is a civil war raging because people are rising up against your Ministry and the Hindu nationalists in your administration. Doesn't seem like an ideal vacation spot."

"You should be more careful what you say to others. You can tell me anything. But always go outside if you don't want to be heard."

"That, and your note, are why I'm speaking freely now. I wish you would as well." Aria gave an impatient look in the hopes that Gupta would get to the point.

Minister Gupta halted her steps for a moment but then seemed to figure out where to start and began walking and talking at a quicker clip. "We can't stay outside and away from surveillance for too long in this weather without people getting suspicious."

"So talk quickly. Where are the seed reserves? Are there also mineral reserves?"

"The seed reserves are at the Beltsville Agricultural Center."

Aria's body tensed with anticipation. She was recording and relaying. She was about to get everything Expectus needed.

"Are there also mineral reserves?"

"Yes, but they are across the continent at Los Alamos."

This was great news if true. The All Pueblo Council of Governors was one of many relationships Aria held across the continent and even if she couldn't get a message to them, she knew they were poised to secure and maintain their sacred lands as soon as Donner was in exile. "How do I know you are telling me the truth?"

"You can confirm my identity with Poppy. She had no way of knowing which of us would be here, but she has met a half dozen of us. I've been a plant inside the administration for decades, since the days when PM Modi took away democratic norms back in the early '20s. We've known since then that we would need someone on the inside. It hasn't been easy, but the land rights movement in India will prevail in this round. They plan a *bandh*—a general strike—to coincide with the US strike when Hurricane Eamon hits Upland DC and the west of Upland US is engulfed by fire. That is likely only a few days away and, from the inside, I can tell you that there is no way that BJP has the steel to stifle this *bandh*. Half of the staff of the military and intelligence agencies have joined up with the movement. Huge changes are coming."

"What else do I need to know?" Poppy could have told Aria more of this information. Aria felt in the dark.

As Preeti spoke, Aria had the feeling again that sneaking into this meeting and talking to diplomats was easier than it should have been. *Why didn't the doctor just take her out? Why hadn't she been arrested? Who was this woman really?* Aria tried to focus on what she was saying but her mind was spinning.

"The movement in India is not so dissimilar to what you have here. There is a large youth movement who are refugees from the areas that have become inundated from glacial melt, and the areas where heat waves have made the region uninhabitable in the outdoors. Speaking of which, it is getting quite windy. Should we start to walk back towards the hotel?"

"Walk back? I need to know exactly where the reserves are and how to get into them. "

Preeti stared intently at Aria. "That's not all you need to know, Aria. There's so much to say. I don't know how to say this in a way that won't be shocking, but I suppose you are right that we should just get straight to the point. They'll be expecting us at dinner in a few moments." The light sound of the xylophone rang from inside, the caterers' indication that it was time to move into the dining room, to the assigned seats.

"Aria, did you hear the man speaking just now during the reception?" Aria nodded, recalling her disgust at his speech. "That man's name is Musa, and he is your father." Aria wasn't sure what she had expected this woman to say to her, but it wasn't this.

"I'm afraid you are mistaken. My mother would never have had an affair with someone with such vile views on humanity. She was a dedicated activist and she loved my father. "

Minister Gupta stopped walking, and Aria turned towards her to let her say her piece. "I am not mistaken, Aria."

"And how would you know? Were you privy to my mother's every sexual encounter?"

Minister Gupta was visibly taken aback by Aria's words.

"Aria!" Minister Gupta inhaled sharply. She looked on the verge of tears again. She'd looked like she was going to cry the night before as well. As a double agent, she would have to always be playing a role. Aria did not believe for a second that the man inside was her father.

A memory of Aria's father flashed, reminding Aria that she had always had questions about her lineage. "Baba," Aria remembered asking him as a child, "Why don't I look like you or mama?"

"You are a princess, my dear," he'd told her, "A princess, who is also a general, like General Leia Organa, and a general who can fly!" Aria's father said before picking up Aria, tossing her onto his back. After she was done giggling, her dad spoke again. "You, General Aria, look exactly like you, like who you are meant to be. Your body is just the vessel for the powerful soul within it. Never worry too much what you look like. It's who you are that matters."

And here was this woman asking Aria to believe that instead that her goofy and cerebral Baba was not her real father. No. Aria was not buying it, even if she had questions in the back of her mind about her parentage.

Aria loved her parents. They had given their lives for her. What drove her every day was her promise to them to take their work forward, and that's what she was here to do. That was what she was going to do right now.

"I think we should head in for dinner." Aria turned around and walked back down the path. She felt bad to hear the rustling of Preeti's sari behind her as she hurried inside.

Anthony opened the door for her when she got to it, giving her a questioning look she ignored as she entered. Musa was standing in a circle of BRUINS diplomats facing her, smiling, likely at something Aria would not find smile-worthy. Aria's stomach sank as she recognized the similarity with her own smile—all teeth with a side of crinkled eyes.

She swallowed back a deep urge to find a way to talk directly to Poppy or Noona, but that would put all of them at risk just to meet Aria's emotional needs. Could she talk to Neil? She felt raw. She'd do what she thought Poppy and Noona would advise. She'd take what Neil had on offer—distraction through pleasure and sexual intimacy. Her other needs could take a back seat until after this mission was done.

21.
"IF YOU LISTEN YOU CAN HEAR THEM IN MY SOUL"

—The Peace Poets

It had been a long day. Neil had finally extricated himself from the boring conversation he was stuck in and gotten back to their suite. He collapsed on the settee, enveloped by the sound of Aria playing Bach's Suite No. 1 again. He could listen to her play just that song for the rest of his life and be content. He'd ask Anthony to get some new sheet music for her.

It was a foreign feeling so it took a while to put his finger on it, but Neil was happy. On the train and the walk to the hotel, they had all the hallmarks of a fun and stable relationship. Their playacting was perfect. Some of their words were for the microphones and others just for each other. That they could manage the complexity was the essence of their compatibility.

Unfortunately, that compatibility had disappeared tonight. Aria froze and then evaded when Neil had asked her about how she felt their relationship was going. She was avoiding going outside with him where they could speak without being heard. Not knowing where they stood gave Neil a sense of angst. And his angst ramped up everytime he saw her flirting with another man or woman.

Aria had spent dinner with her head together with Eniola Musa of all people. She had been laughing at his stories, even leaning into him—flirting with a man hell-bent on destroying the planet. Was he another Expectus spy somehow? They certainly looked cozy. Neil feared that Aria was getting in over her head with Preeti. He suspected Aria might not be telling him everything that she had found out. He wanted to raise these questions with her, but didn't want to ruin their night.

Aria wrapped up the piece and began to put away her instrument. "Thank you for this. It means a lot to have this release and to be able to play with so much going on. It's going to keep me sane for this trip."

"I love listening to you play. Always have."

"Duet?"

Neil wanted to make one last play to get her outside of the room to understand more of what had transpired since the notes she'd passed him that morning. "Another night. I'm worried you're overdoing it with your head injury."

"I'm feeling much better, actually. I think playing jolted my brain back in gear."

"I'll find a cello and violin duet for us, and we'll play it tomorrow, deal? Now let's check out the night sky from the balcony and then get some sleep."

"Sleep? I thought we were going to pick up where we left off, or maybe we can pick up our discussion from the train of how we would handle sexual ebbs and flow in our marriage?"

Aria would not be lured outside for a confidential talk. Neil put on an interviewer's voice. "So, Aria, tell me, how would you handle sexual ebbs and flows in our marriage?"

Aria answered with more of a bedroom voice than a stage voice as she got closer to Neil. "That's an excellent question. My short answer is sex toys."

"Really?" Fulfilled hopes were so much better than the dashed ones."My short answer is pornography AND sex toys. I have to admit the cello isn't the only thing I brought just in case you'd love it and need a distraction. I have a case of brand new sex toys with me." Neil paused, and continued when it was clear he had Aria's interest. "And some carefully selected pornography, if that's your jam."

"How presumptuous of you!" Aria gasped with fake shock, fanning herself with her hand.

Neil got up, walked across the room, and picked up the black briefcase he had packed, just in case, and brought it over to the settee where Aria was sitting. He placed it on the coffee table and clicked it open. Aria gasped when Neil opened the case.

"I thought it was some kind of office work for your mom, not a sexy perv kit." Aria ran her fingers over the silver rabbit vibrator, the handcuffs, and the red satin blindfold.

"We do not have stuff like that available in Lowland. I don't know what half of it is." Aria picked up the handcuffs and swung them around her finger. "I know what these are."

Neil's eyes moved to the bed, scanning the headpost for spots to use those cuffs. Aria smiled again.

"I pick the cuffs and the blindfold and the location—the closet. You pick whatever other toys you want. Just ask me first."

If Aria was trying to distract Neil from having a talk about what the hell was going on with her and Preeti Gupta, she was doing an excellent job. Neil's cock would be doing the thinking for the rest of the night. "A lot happened today. Are you sure you want to jump right in with the cuffs?" Neil would have preferred to make out with Aria, to make love to her without all the toys, but that seemed more intimate than the vibe Aria was giving off. Neil was glad he'd been right to bring the case. She needed to let off some steam with someone she felt safe with after the scare with his mom and her "doctor" and Neil was there to help her do it.

Aria slowed her swinging of the cuffs, and Neil took them out of her hands. He was sitting on the coffee table next to the briefcase of toys. He leaned in to kiss Aria and she met him for the kiss. It started chaste, but then Neil ran his fingers through Aria's hair, massaging her scalp and grabbing a fist of hair to pull her in closer to taste her. She tasted of mint.

Neil forgot entirely about going to the balcony to debrief their day away from the listening devices. He forgot about his discomfort at being in this place with his mother and her colleagues, a few of whom had tried to bed him when he was a college student. He forgot that he wanted to warn Aria that it wasn't safe to flirt with some of these people. He forgot everything except the determination he felt when Aria had told him she wanted to have sex handcuffed and blindfolded in the closet. His body's urge to please her overrode anything his brain wanted to discuss. Neil sat back on the coffee table in front of Aria. He turned the lock of the handcuffs, opening them. Aria held out her wrists. Neil could not believe that she trusted him this much after everything they had been through, but he was grateful for it. He put the handcuff around her left wrist. "You sure?" he asked. "Very," she said. He put the handcuff around her other wrist. He picked up the red satin blindfold, and raised his eyebrows looking for approval. Aria nodded and he placed the blindfold over her eyes. Giving careful instructions and with his arm around Aria's waist, he walked her over to the closet, carrying the briefcase of sex toys in one hand. He left the lights off in the closet, but the door opened so there was enough light for him to see. He could tell when they made out under that tree that Aria was turned on with her arms over her head. One half of the closet was completely empty of clothes. He lifted her cuffed arms up in front of her, and she followed his lead, holding on to the closet rod above her head. It was just the right height. Aria held onto the rod and arched her back in a cat-like stretch that lifted her pajama top above the waist of her underwear, exposing her belly button and back. Neil's cock went rock-hard at the sight of her.

"You are so fucking gorgeous, Aria. Can I take off your underwear?"

"Please."

"You're wet," he observed.

Was she thinking about one of the jerks at the party? He forced his mind to close that thought and return its focus to pleasuring the beautiful woman in front of him. Her trust was a turn-on. This was his high school sweetheart. The only woman he had ever loved. He wanted to make her feel as hot as she was. He got out a collapsible spreader bar from his case. He velcroed one side to her left ankle.

"I velcroed a bar, like the closet bar above you, to one ankle and now I'm doing the other. This okay?" Neil asked.

"Oooh. My first surprise from the briefcase." Aria spread her legs apart to make it easier to attach the bar to both ankles. Neil was on his knees on the floor and carefully velcroed the bar on and asked her to wiggle her toes and fingers to make sure everything was circulating.

"Good girl. Tell me as soon as you need to stop. Okay?"

"Of course. What's my next treat from the case?" Aria asked.

Neil kneeled and kissed Aria's inner thigh, eliciting a moan of pleasure. He massaged her leg as he kissed his way up. He loved the taste of her. Neil licked up and down her opening as he massaged her legs. She was gyrating into him with the limited motion she had; her breath was getting heavy. Neil stood and embraced her from behind so she could feel his hardness through his pants. Aria gyrated back into him trying to get her release. Neil reached for the front of her pajamas and unbuttoned the first few buttons so he could reach in and grab her breasts. Her nipples were hard and she was writhing with need, arching her back and gyrating her hips. Neil was not going to be able to last much longer and he wanted to give her at least one orgasm before he fucked her. He pulled his hands off of her breasts and took a step back.

"No, don't stop."

"I'm right here. I'm just picking another toy out. Can I put this vibrator inside you?"

"Yes." Aria was more than ready.

Neil picked up the rabbit vibrator and turned it on. He put it in his mouth to make sure it wasn't too cold and then ran the vibrator up and down, and around the diamond opening, to make sure she was ready. It slipped right in and Aria gasped with pleasure. Neil turned on the vibration for the extension that was on her clit and began to move it to the rhythm of Aria's hip movement.

"Aaaah. Yes. Yes." Aria was crying out and Neil hoped to God it wasn't just a show for the microphones. She knew that people were listening to them, and she either didn't mind or it turned her on. Everything about her right now turned him on. The spreader bar kept her legs spread, her hands were cuffed, holding on to the closet bar above. She was naked from the waist down, her top was half-unbuttoned, and she was orgasming on a vibrator he was holding. If he never had sex again in his life, he could call up this image and get off at any point. When Aria was coming down from her orgasm, she let out a huge sigh of pleasure. Neil removed the vibrator and set it on top of its cloth case and took a step back to unbuckle his pants. He dropped the belt on the ground and unbuttoned and unzipped his pants, slipping them and his boxers off.

"Are you ready?" Aria asked, hearing the clang of the belt hitting the floor.

"I like impatient Aria," Neil said as he stood up. "I was going to unbutton my shirt, but I'd hate to leave a lady waiting."

Neil used both of his hands to grab Aria's breasts from behind and she let out a pleased sound. He kneeled down, rising until the tip of his cock found her entrance and he inserted just the tip at first to make sure she was ready. She was. He entered her completely, feeling a rush of warmth and tightness, and bringing a cry of pleasure from Aria.

"Come again with me inside you."

"Yes. Yes. Yes." Aria screamed to the rhythm of Neil's thrusts. Neil looked down at his cock entering her and it was a pretty damn sexy sight. He slowed down.

"What happened?"

"Aria I'm going to cum inside you if I don't stop."

"Do not stop."

Neil kept thrusting until he could feel his balls tighten and release right inside of her. He held on to her tightly from behind and could feel her whole body shaking as he came, moaning.

Neil kissed her shoulder. "Are you okay?"

"I'm more than okay."

Neil gave himself the treat of a few more moments inside Aria, holding her from behind, before he pulled out, kneeled down, and released the velcro from her ankles. Aria brought her arms down and Neil got the handcuff key from the case, releasing the handcuffs, and massaging her wrists and palms as soon as they were free. Neil put one arm under Aria's back and picked her up, the other arm under her knees. He used her feet to push the door open and walked over to the bed and laid her down.

"That was really good, huh?" Aria couldn't believe he had to ask.

"Yeah, it was really good."

22.
"WE NEED THE STORM"

—Frederick Douglass

Day before Eamon's landfall

Aria had woken up feeling focused and satiated. She felt a magic in the cells of her body. She was ready to manifest success. It was a gray morning and the Shenandoah and Potomac were raging with power. Eamon would be arriving soon. Aria was running out of time. It was time to get information about how to access these reserves. She realized she hadn't asked Preeti about the water walls yet, and if they could be lowered to even out any flooding impact. Talking to Musa was her best hope of finding the exact location of the reserves Poppy had charged her with saving. She had agreed to meet Musa at 8 am for breakfast and hoped to get more information from him than she'd been able to get at dinner as well as find out what Preeti knew. She heard Neil turning over in bed and went to give him a goodbye kiss on the head. Neil grabbed the end of her *dupatta* she'd quickly wrapped around her neck to go with her *salwar kameez.*

"Nooo. Come back to bed."

Aria whispered to avoid waking him up entirely, and uncurled his fingers from the sheer red fabric. She normally didn't wear so many Indian clothes, but they helped her *jhumka* recording earrings blend in here. "Can't. But you should sleep. Sessions don't start until after ten."

Neil opened his eyes a crack, as Aria went to the door to leave. "Wait. Why are you dressed and out of bed? I was dreaming about spending the morning in bed with you. We need to talk. Or I could tie you up with that scarf and give you multiple orgasms." Aria reluctantly shook her head. "Or you could tie me up?" Neil grinned and held his wrists out together for her.

"That sounds much more fun than a meeting, but I need to be downstairs. I have a breakfast date with Musa."

Neil opened his eyes fully at that. "A breakfast date? You just had dinner with him last night. You had your heads together laughing for more than an hour. What more could you have to say to him? Ditch him. Come back to bed. Let me take that sexy outfit off of you."

Aria looked over at Neil's bare chest as he sat up and her fingers tingled with the desire to run them through his chest hair and down his shoulders. She could almost feel his biceps under her hand. Good Lord, even his forearms were sexy. Neil saw her gaze go down his body and was curving his index finger, motioning for Aria to join him in bed. She felt naked under his gaze, and more than a little tempted by the invitation. But she steeled herself for turning Neil down.

"I'm afraid if I get too close to you right now, I'm going to fall into that bed with you. It's going to have to wait for tonight."

"This is important to me. Please, Aria, choose me right now. Let me keep you safe."

Irritation at the words *important*, *choose*, and *safe*, rose through Aria's gut straight to the tip of her tongue. A fight wasn't a terrible idea for their invisible listeners so she leaned against the suite door and gave into her urge to unleash. "You want me to choose you, Neil? Like you chose to stay with me after I passed out in front of your mother? As I recall, you left me with Anthony and went trotting after her. I trusted that you felt like you had a job to do, but talk about not choosing me."

Neil sat up straight at the accusation. "This is about you and me, not my mother."

"Everything about you and me has always had to do with your mother."

"When are you going to get over what happened in high school, Aria? It was high school. I was a kid. I made a mistake. I can't keep apologizing for it. I'm here now."

"I appreciate that, Neil, I do, but right now I'm late for my appointment. I don't like to leave people hanging."

"So you're just going to leave me hanging? We need to talk. I'm starting to feel like you're just using me for sex."

Using him for sex? Aria stared at him, fuming. That there was a kernel of truth to his accusation only made her more incensed.

"You've gone too far, Neil. If you can't reel it in, I'm leaving and I'm not coming back."

"You can't just run from me, Aria. We're engaged now. We have a baby on the way." Neil evoked their lie and the people listening with his words. "Don't go. Stay in bed with me, Aria. I want this to work, but it's hard for me to believe that we are worth fighting for if you always run away from me."

"So I'm not worth fighting for because I have a prior commitment? Just because we are engaged does not mean you get to tell me what to do." Aria took a breath and put on what she thought was an Uplander tone. "I think we're both finding this conversation to be extraordinarily vexing. Let's take a breather. I'm going to meet Musa, who has been waiting for me for five minutes already. I'll see you later, Neil."

Aria spun around and left Neil in bed. She hoped that her language seemed off enough for Neil to realize that there was something she wanted to tell him about Musa but couldn't tell him right then. A bizarre fight with Neil was not the ideal start to her morning. She needed to focus on her mission.

Downstairs, Musa had indeed been waiting on Aria and had already gotten himself a breakfast plate and sat down.

"Good morning," he bellowed as Aria entered the room. "We must feed you, you are too skinny." Musa stood and placed his cloth napkin on the chair. He was wearing another beautiful dashiki.

"Good morning. Thank you for inviting me as well as for waiting for me. I'll get a plate and be right with you." Aria knew that Nigerian elders needed more appreciation than she was used to giving, from her background reading. She would do her best. Aria knew exactly how to serve coffee in an Ethiopian manner, but wondered if there was a Nigerian way to do it.

The buffet was a feast yet again, and still a shock relative to Aria's normal diet of sweet potato and peanuts that were available in Lowland. Aria picked some shiitake mushroom "bacon" and served herself some baked beans and a tomato. She took a soft-boiled egg from the display of dozens of eggs, each sitting in a unique egg cup that was intricately hand-decorated with gold and silver etchings. She wasn't going to turn down a hot meal on a rainy day no matter what she thought of the wealth and the waste of the BRUINS.

"It was nice to get to know you a little yesterday, Musa," she said as she sat down. "My apologies again for being late, should we pray?" Aria wasn't sure what was culturally appropriate in these circumstances, but her mother had always told her the importance of praying with elders.

"What a good Christian girl you are! I already prayed over our food, but let us thank God again." Musa held Aria's hand while he quietly murmured his prayer. They had both said "Amen" at the end and began eating and talking.

"You have good manners, good character, and a good set of skills. I have heard rumors of your success at the cello at a young age as well. Impressive. You are a testament to your parents, no doubt," he said, not giving away whether he believed he was complimenting his own genes. He continued without pause. "Tell me, how long have you and Neil been courting?" *Again with the personal questions.* Aria tapped the shell of the soft-boiled egg, and tried not to replay the argument she and Neil had just had in her head. She needed to focus on what she was doing and avenging her real parents, the ones who raised her, not this man.

"We were high school sweethearts," Aria shared, divulging only what they'd made public. "Tell me, how are you liking your breakfast?" At least if she could change the topic to food, she could somehow ask about the seed and food strategic reserve and get a few clues to help her in her mission.

"The eggs are delicious, as is everything. You know, I do wish that there was some sausage or other meat available. In Africa, most of us have not been bitten by this Lone Star Tick everyone here speaks of. It is a shame. I used to love the enormous American breakfasts before that little insect ruined it all. Personally, I prefer the *akara* and *pap* our chef makes at home. You need to come to my house in Lagos for Sunday rice one day, and then you will see a real feast!"

Aria whispered, hoping the microphones wouldn't pick up her words. "I actually wanted to ask you about food. What do you know about seeds?"

Musa furrowed one eyebrow and subtly shook his head "no." He moved his head closer to Aria's and whispered back.

"Follow me."

The closet Musa led them to after breakfast was full of mops and cleaning supplies. It was next to the laundry so it was loud, protecting them from being heard. Musa knew nothing about the water walls or how to control them, or so he claimed. He did confirm with Aria where the seed and mineral reserves were located. He and Preeti had been present when they were established. He claimed to know nothing about how to lower the water walls. Aria still wasn't sure what to believe, but recorded his detailed description of the Beltsville seed storage location with her earrings. She pushed back on the water walls.

"I heard you yesterday giving that speech about flooding communities in Nigeria, you know. That scale of damage is why I need to know how to lower the water walls driving flooding towards homes. Water at the scale of this storm will be devastating."

A flash of pain passed Musa's face for the first time that Aria had seen. "I had no power to stop the flooding at home, my child. And I have no information to help you stop it here." Musa reached out and held Aria's hand and looked her in the eye. "After things calm down, I want you to go to my house in Lagos. You must meet my wife and children. You can find them at the *Ikoyi Club.* They know all about you. I have long-ago confessed all my sins to them. You have an older sister and a younger brother—Alika and Obi. It is time for you to visit Lagos and meet them. You will love it. You can teach the children music and Neil can join you if you are married and have a family then."

Aria had no space in her mind for "after" and she was not sure she believed that this man was her father. She wasn't even sure they would survive Eamon at the moment. She needed to scramble if she was going to get this life-or-death intelligence to the people who needed it. She was in the process of jiggling her earring just the right way to get her recording with the location of the reserves to upload to Poppy, Gears, and Noona, when the closet door opened. Aria and Musa spilled out of the closet, right into Neil.

"I see," Neil said, stiffly flashing a glare at Aria before continuing down the hallway without giving Aria a chance to explain. Musa looked embarrassed and mumbled something to a fellow Nigerian diplomat who was passing by about how they'd been looking for the concierge and got mixed up.

"We will meet again later," he said to Aria as he walked away.

Aria went looking for Neil to see if they could get outside even with the rain and she could explain the progress she'd made with Musa. She hadn't felt like talking about it the night before, but Neil could become a liability if he didn't understand what was going on.

The meeting session had begun, and Secretary Rao was on stage speaking when Aria walked into the conference room. Neil was at the soundboard adjusting knobs and levers, and looking at the screens to make sure it was recording and broadcasting. Neil had told Aria that it was a secure broadcast just to the White House for today.

Aria stared at Neil, willing him to look at her. When he finally did, she nodded her head slightly towards a small side room that she entered. Neil followed behind her, leaving his station, even as his mother continued to speak from the stage about the tasks for that day.

The room was scattered with agendas and handouts. There were boxes of meeting materials, and a door to outside if they needed privacy. Outside did not seem like an option, though. The wind was whipping tree branches into a frenzy. They watched together as a huge branch broke off in the wind and crashed down into the swollen Potomac.

There was plenty Aria could say that would be fine for the listening microphones inside. She could at least make it clear that there was nothing sexual, romantic or physical between her and Musa. Before she had a chance to say anything at all, Aria turned to see Preeti standing a few feet from them.

"A/V emergency. The screen is going in and out. Your mother transitioned to a panel discussion so she wouldn't need the visuals, but you'd better come take care of it."

"Let's talk later," Neil called back to Aria as he left to handle the "emergency." He was impossible to read.

Preeti glared at Aria with an expression that admonished her to be more careful, and led her outside to a covered patio area.

"Did you talk to Musa?"

"Yes. He wants me to go to Lagos. I'm trying to save millions of lives and he's talking about vacations."

"He didn't tell you about me, then."

"What about you?" Aria wondered if part of Preeti's undercover schtick was always looking on the verge of tears.

"Aria, I *know* Musa is your father, because I am your mother."

Aria held her breath and stiffened her body. She did not want to have this conversation. She didn't believe her. Aria exhaled a sigh, rolled her eyes, and turned to go, but Secretary Gupta grabbed her hand. "Musa and I asked your parents to raise you because we were deep undercover when you were born on December 5, 2012. At the time the US seemed like it would be safer for longer, but that was before Donner took over and cut off international communications. It's been so hard to be out of touch and cut off. All of that is about to change. Everything is about to change, and it's time that you know the truth. It is critical that you know the truth."

Aria pulled her hand away and took a step back.

"I didn't expect you to believe me immediately, but after the past few days I also knew that your lineage was too visible to deny. Aria, you are an exact mix of Musa and me. You have my nose, and his smile. You have his hairline and my jaw. If a mirror is not enough evidence for you, I can also tell you things about your parents most people would never know, as can Musa."

"Poppy would have told me."

"Poppy didn't know. She only knew what your parents told her, that we were moles on the inside who had been cut off and would be back if there was ever another BRUINS meeting in Upland. Mus and I only met Poppy once, over a decade ago, at a secret meeting in Ireland that the UN hosted for all the non-BRUINS nations to discuss BRUINS defections. Only your parents knew everything. I don't know why they didn't tell you in the end, but I realized the night we met that they hadn't."

The hurt of losing her parents welled up from deep below the surface. Even if Preeti wasn't telling the truth, the pain she was causing was real. Aria felt like she was losing her parents again.

Aria looked out in the brewing storm and thought of her mother, her ema—the woman whose death she was here to avenge—the woman who gave her life for the cause.

It did not matter whose genes she carried. She knew whose spirit she carried. Aria nodded to Preeti, pulled her hand away, and slipped by her in the open doorway back inside and into the main room. Neil was working on the uncooperative A/V equipment. Aria wondered if this panel discussion sounded as offensive to his ear as it did to hers, now that he had been through so much with Aria and the Expectus training.

"It pleases me to note that we are nearing the 200th birthday of the oil and gas industry, coming up in 2059. Many climate activists tried to exterminate us along the way, and the threat from radical climate groups like Expectus means we must come together to ensure that we make it to our 200th birthday. We have taken this glorious industry to annual profits over $5 Trillion Upland Dollars despite being blocked out of all but BRUINS nations, and despite regular attacks on our pipelines by Expectus. These radicals have tried to exterminate our industry and we must in turn exterminate them. We cannot be lenient anymore. It is time to take up arms again. They are vulnerable. They can barely keep the Lowland alive and I predict there will soon be a rebellion of the Lowland people against Expectus."

The room applauded politely as the microphone was passed to Alex Bortnikov, the richest man in Upland, the Russian attaché, and the former CEO of BPShell.

"The people in this room represent all the currently operational fossil fuel reserves in all of the countries that have successfully avoided the United Nations' shame machine. Thanks to us, we have kept oil and gas alive. We have lost our social license to burn coal even within our countries after the air pollution die-offs in Asia, but we are poised to convince our own nations that the 1.8°C of warming above pre-industrial levels is acceptable if they are able to keep their bloodlines pure and their culture—"

Neil looked grateful that Bortnikov stopped just as he was about to turn more hateful, but his relief quickly turned to mortification. A feedback pierced the room. Neil frantically moved plugs around trying to figure out what was going on.

A familiar voice rang through the speakers, and the screech ceased. The screen flickered and Poppy appeared. Aria felt relief and warmth rush through her at the sight of her mentor. The words she spoke were words that those who had been through an Expectus training had heard before. Poppy's voice rang through the room. Her image appeared on each phone. "It's time," Poppy said, looking straight into everyone's eyes.

23.
"WE RISE"

—Batya Levine

Poppy's utterance was all it took for the waitstaff at the Hilltop Hotel. The servers set their trays down and exited the room. A few shrugged off their jackets and filled them with dinner rolls and muffins on their way out. Aria knew that the kitchen staff were all leaving and taking food on the floor below, but the BRUINS were too distracted by the image of Poppy on their phones to even notice.

Secretary Rao was on the stage with the microphone, but it had stopped working. Neil leaned under the table skirt and pulled out a megaphone, offering it to his mother.

"I'm not using that thing. Get it out of my face," Rao said to Neil. "Get the microphones working and turn off that audio."

"I can't, Mother. It's not coming through the system that we brought, it's overriding everything and coming through the internet, the Wi-Fi, and the phones. We'd have to turn all electronics off to cut the sound. Whoever is speaking just said they had control of the airwaves, internet, and all comms channels."

Secretary Rao walked back on the stage. She turned to the nearly two hundred people watching. The crowd's attention moved from the servers' departure and the video to Rao. They quieted to try to hear her.

"I need everyone to turn off your phones. We will need to cut off electricity to the room to cut off this feed."

Musa was in a large armchair on the stage. "Why would we do that, Rao? We are not afraid of these rioters. These workers are clearly brainwashed. They are acting like programmed clones. We always knew workers would be unreliable. We have a plan that is resilient to whatever they do. We have armies and navies. All they have is their words. I think we should listen to these words to understand the enemy better." Musa quoted the *The Art of War*. "If you know the enemy and know yourself, you need not fear the result of a hundred battles. If you know yourself but not the enemy, for every victory gained you will also suffer a defeat. If you know neither the enemy nor yourself, you will succumb in every battle." A mumble of agreement came from the crowd.

Aria reflected on how ironic it was that Musa was using *Star Wars* comparisons and Sun Tzu's *The Art of War* to convince the BRUINS and Uplanders to stick to the fight—the same texts she often referred to in Expectus trainings. She wondered if it was Musa's role as a double agent that led him to using those references or if these Hollywood and Chinese quotes were common among Nigerians. Whatever the reason for using it, it worked on Secretary Rao.

"Fine, Musa. Neil, put it on the screen, but please keep the audio down. His voice is incredibly grating."Aria chafed at the casualness with which Simone misgendered Poppy.

Neil plugged the screen back in and turned some dials. Poppy was on the screen with a group of people behind her.

They were at Malcom X park, a high spot of Lowland that the Uplanders never wanted and left to them. They were standing in the Josephine Butler House. Aria had been there a million times. "I stand here today with faith leaders of many traditions—Christians and Muslims, Jews, and Hindus. We are here with union leaders of airport workers, flight attendants and pilots, train operators, and service workers, as well as all the trades. We are here with business leaders from hotels to technology corporations. We are here with retired Generals who have seen enough. We are here with young people who are fighting for their future. Hurricane Eamon is arriving. We come from different walks of life, but all of us here have agreed that all workers should go home immediately to take care of their families through the floods that are coming and the fires that are already raging in the west. Ground and air travel will end at noon tomorrow. General McMaster has ordered military leaders not to fire on civilians, in accordance with existing law, and we are urging police to stand down as well. Today, Thursday, August 21, 2042 will be remembered for generations to come as the true independence day. From our own Expectus movement in DC to the All Pueblo Council of Governors, our communities have shown that we know how to do the hard work of taking care of each other, identifying needed resources, and teaching our young people, I ask everyone to hold grace and reconciliation in your hearts and welcome those who are ready to live in community with us."

Aria realized she had been holding her breath and exhaled. Poppy had gotten her message about the mineral reserves being at Los Alamos. There was no other explanation for the mention of the All Pueblo Council of governors and the line about resources. Halfway through Poppy's speech, Secretary Rao had had enough. She walked over to Neil, reached under the table, and grabbed the megaphone she had refused earlier. "I think we've heard enough from these traitors," she barked. "Turn off your phones. Neil, cut the internet and all the feeds."

The room hummed as they followed Rao's instructions. Neil flipped switches at a circuit breaker. Though it was still light out, the room dimmed as the power was cut. Rao kept speaking through the megaphone. "We may not have electricity for a few moments, but in the grand scheme of things, they are the ones with no power. Expectus will not stop us. They will engage in some looting and some rioting, perhaps. Remember, the Secret Service is still here, protecting Upland. The military is protecting *us. Us.*" She pointed her finger at herself and then the room. "That was a lovely show, but it was fiction. Let's break into groups by country and go over the plans for extracting enough energy for us to have the power to put down any riots and uprisings in every one of our countries. We'll regroup here in 90 minutes. I expect a detailed breakout report from each group. The breakout rooms are listed in the agenda, and I will be leading the Upland US session."

She was going to go forward with the meeting despite no electricity and no staff in the hotel. *Let them underestimate us.* Aria was not going to let Rao's dismissiveness get to her. Everything was going according to plan. Everything in Upland would come to a grinding halt in a matter of days without Lowlander labor. This is the moment Aria had been working towards for her entire adult life.

Aria wondered how the general strike was playing out in the lowlands of other regions. She had traveled for trainings enough to know that there were some places where Donnerites would become dangerous and deadly to Lowlanders if they felt threatened. She worried about what would happen if they didn't succeed. She worried that some in the military would ignore General McMaster's order not to use military force. She worried that President Donner would find a way back onto the airwaves. Aria thought back to her trainings of insiders for police and military roles. She was confident there would be mass defections. She thought of all the trainings focused on joy and rejecting violence. Their side would keep nonviolent discipline and keep their tenuous hold on the moral high ground.

They had put in the work for this moment. Rao's dismissiveness was not a problem; in fact, it was almost too good to be true. They'd take the country back in a matter of days with barely a fight. They'd be able to hold not just movement elections, but national elections. People's rights were about to be restored. Aria was getting ahead of herself though. She was still supposed to figure out how to lower the water walls before Eamon hit. It wasn't enough to have identified the seed and mineral reserve locations. There was one last thing Aria needed to find out before she left to celebrate with her friends.

24.
"HUMBLY HEARTED"

—Batya Levine

Aria passed the closet she had shared with Musa. Only a half hour had passed but it felt like a lifetime. She looked back to see if Neil was following her, and was surprised at the sadness she felt at his absence. Their room felt empty without him.

Aria had herself trained tens of thousands of people on what to do. She had led them through role-play. She had watched them pretend to walk out, practice getting yelled at, practice being blocked. One of the simplest parts of the action had happened now. Everyone got up and left, and no one stopped them. Why hadn't anyone tried to stop the workers from leaving? The ease of it began making Aria uncomfortable.

Neil hadn't followed her. Was it worth the risk to go back down to the conference to get him? *You need to stop using me for sex.* The words from this morning still stung. If only he'd gotten up and walked with her, hand in hand. If only he hadn't followed his mother's instructions and turned off the electricity. She'd enjoyed their fifteen minutes of being the golden couple. The honeymoon had not lasted long. No, she couldn't go back to get Neil. She'd be risking getting stopped by guards and sending the wrong message to all the Lowlanders who had walked out. They did the right thing even knowing they would lose their jobs over it; Neil had not.

As much as Aria racked her brain, she saw no path to getting information on the water walls. That meant huge swaths of Lowland would flood. It was time to get back to DC to help Poppy and be by her side at this critical moment. She could find the train conductor who'd offered help.

Aria reviewed in her head what she knew. Expectus had the locations of all the reserves. The Russians did not know about the reserves. Musa and Preeti were there for the opening of the reserves. She was missing exactly how to access the reserves and information on the water walls. She needed to make a decision about whether to get out with what she had or try for the last bits. She was thorough. She needed to finish the job. Her mind was ungovernably fixated on Neil.

Aria got up and looked around.

Their suite was empty. She re-checked that she had bolted the front door and latched it so she would have warning if Neil, or anyone else, tried to enter. She walked over to the cello. Playing always helped her think more clearly and it was more enjoyable than obsessing about Neil's behavior. She remembered the story of Nero and fiddling while Rome burned. She was no Nero. She planned to help her people. She just needed to put on some comfortable clothes and play for a bit in order to come up with a plan.

25.
"WON'T BE DIVIDED"

—Batya Levine

Upland DC, day before Eamon

Meet at your appointed emergency meeting location for evacuation. All Donners are eligible for an upgrade from Upland to Upluna.

Joe was confused and conflicted. The emergency family messages kept blaring from his wristwatch. His wife kept calling and texting to tell him to get home and shelter in place with her and the boys. He wanted to be with his kids. If everyone here was going to die, though, he wanted to get his kids evacuated. His wife was never going to leave their kids. His wife was not eligible for a Donner family evacuation because they only had space for "blood relatives" according to the messages he was getting.

The same thoughts swam in a circle in his head. He needed a moment of calm to figure it out. He needed Anthony. Anthony wasn't answering him. He sat in the bathroom of the hotel room they had shared so many times, paralyzed.

Laurie, their producer, had just called a staff meeting to let them know that Expectus had taken over the station, and that no one would lose their jobs. She would be handling broadcasting for the next 48 hours. Everyone would get paid for their time and come back to news scripts written by human beings. There were a few interns with questions about how to close out tasks. Joe took the opportunity to excuse himself. Becca and Laurie probably wanted to talk. He knew the feeling. He wanted to talk to Anthony.

Growing up, Joe had always been browbeaten with images of Russian royalty being dragged out to the woods and shot. He didn't believe that Laurie would ever harm him, but neither did he think that slightly uncomfortable staff meeting was as difficult as the takeover would be. Would that happen to his kids? To him? The broadcast said the police and the media had all peacefully transitioned to working for Expectus and everyone would be safe.

There was also a clear ultimatum. Expectus demanded that the entire cabinet step down or else they would be exiled. Donner allies would be exiled to Russia or elsewhere if they insisted on clinging to power. On the other hand, if the cabinet stepped down, they would be safe, and their families would be too. *But how could that be guaranteed?*

If only he could talk to Anthony and find out what was going on within the Secret Service. There was simply no safe option, so Joe did what felt safest to him. He waited for Anthony to tell him what to do. Going to his kids could endanger them. Taking them to a meeting point could endanger them. Going to the meeting point without them was not an option. He would just have to sit still until he had more information. Joe prayed for the first time in his life. He hoped God wouldn't fault him for all the times he had pretended to do it before.

26.
"WITH SPIRIT TO GUIDE US"

—Batya Levine

Sitting in Neil's sweatpants and socks playing the cello in their beautifully appointed hotel room, Aria cleared her mind of all the drama downstairs and in the world. This was her meditation. She was improvising, giving herself the melody, which the cello so often didn't get in orchestra pieces. Aria was no Yo-Yo Ma, but she sounded good when she gave herself the *cellody*, and she knew it.

Aria's brain synthesized and summarized as she played. She wanted one last chance to get information, but wasn't sure whether Neil, Musa, or Preeti would be her best sources. Alternatively, she could just leave and try to pump information from anyone she saw on the way out. The clock was ticking on her mission. She could hear the metronome in her head. She allowed herself a moment of self-admonishment. With all the drama with Neil and her supposed parents, Aria had failed to make significant progress on the task Poppy had given her.

Done is done. She tried to shift her mind to self-belief, to envision success. With her eyes closed and her ears on her music, Aria emptied her mind of reproach, and focused on the tune she was playing. Behind the music, she thought she heard a sound from the balcony. The storm was getting stronger and a branch might have hit the balcony. Aria opened her eyes, continuing to play, but looking behind her. Her heart was suddenly beating louder than the ticking in her head. The hairs on the back of her neck rose. She was feeling some of the panic she felt when she first met Secretary Rao in person. But no one could be on the balcony; Anthony had a camera on the balcony door he was watching. Maybe Neil was trying to surprise her with another apology. It was just like him to try some silly grand gesture like climbing up to their balcony to make up for not leaving with her. Something told Aria it was not Neil, though, and that she was not alone. She had been chased by police at enough actions to know the feeling of someone being after her. She engaged her earrings' recording and transmitting settings.

"Anthony? Neil?" she called out.

No answer. She got up from her cello and turned towards the balcony. The sound of the storm outside rushed in. The curtains whipped up, nearly horizontal to the floor for a moment before falling back down. The French doors were open behind them. They had definitely been closed. Aria rested her bow on the case and called out to Anthony again. "Anthony?" She moved out of the nook where she'd been playing, moving towards the front door of their room, keeping her cello in front of her. Maybe she could put it between her and anyone out to get her? Cello in one hand, Aria turned and unlocked the latch. She needed to get out of the room. She reached for the door knob, calling Anthony again with more panic this time. "Anthony!" Before she could open the door, a hand covered her face and yanked her back.

Her cello crashed onto the floor as another hand grabbed her wrist and twisted it behind her back. Her mouth was covered with a cloth and her right hand pinned. A pungent smell filled her nostrils. She heard another person moving the cello and twisted to get a look. Her assailant spun her around so her back was to the other person, and suddenly the lights in the room were off, leaving Aria and her assailant in the dark. Aria scratched at her assailant with her left hand, she bit at the cloth in her mouth, catching some of her assailant's finger, she lifted her foot and kicked them as hard as she could in the shins, she elbowed his ribs with her left arm and twisted her body loose. For an instant, she was free of the cloth on her mouth and she screamed again.

"NEIL," and then she felt a searing pain in the exact spot she had hit her head, and then everything went black.

When Aria came to, it was nothing like the last time she had woken up in Neil's arms. She was sitting in mud, blindfolded and bound with the gag toy from the sex kit Neil had brought. It wasn't a toy she was ever interested in, but this sealed the deal on her never experimenting with it. Aria tried to move her arms and realized she was handcuffed behind her back. She heard footsteps nearby. Heels. Simone.

Aria felt her blindfold being lifted. She blinked her eyes, trying to adjust to the dim light of the shed she was in. Secretary Rao was in front of her.

27.
"UP FROM THE WRECKAGE"

—Batya Levine

Simone did not like getting her hands dirty, but she had to see to this hussy herself to be absolutely sure. Everything was going according to plan. Expectus made the nonstrategic decision to call the general strike just before a hurricane. They were too late. It was disconcerting that the hotel management seemed to be abetting their staff, but none of that really mattered. The people who mattered were the business leaders who were ready to take off. She had hand-selected world leaders to go with them. The launch times were staggered so they did not all arrive at the Moon base, *Upluna*, at the same time, but they would all get there, and from there they would regroup for the longer journey to their base on Mars. The unfortunate strike and hurricane confluence would just move up their journey by a few days. All she needed to do was convince Neil to join them, and if this girl was pregnant, she needed to have her knocked out and put on the space shuttle so that the next generation of Raos could be born on Mars. By the time they came back, it was the young ones who were going to repopulate a healed and vacant Earth.

Simone had a few surrogates she'd selected to join them. She had her frozen eggs implanted with top-of-the-line sperm already, and the embryos ready to go, if needed. But if her baby was having a biological child, that child was coming with them. *Where was that doctor?* Simone wanted the pregnancy confirmed or ruled out quickly. She leaned down to Aria, wishing for the thousandth time that Neil had chosen someone less disgusting. The baby would be so dark. She'd told her son a million times about the brown paper bag test, but even at thirty he was still in a rebellious stage. She'd made the same mistake herself, and it was starting to feel like a curse. No matter. They had generations ahead to rectify the matter. Right now, she needed to let this girl know if she was pregnant she belonged with her; and if she was not, she was worthless to them.

"I'm going to take this hideous gag off of you, but I want to be clear that I'll put it right back on if you scream. Do you understand?" Aria nodded "yes." Secretary Rao walked behind her, removed the gag, and immediately moved away, shuddering, repulsed by Aria's coughing and bleeding.

"What do you want from me?" Aria asked.

"Your time with Neil is over. He knows you were using him to distract us from your precious general strike and he's done with you. Now you just need to stay out of the way so that we can complete our meeting without spies among us." It rankled Simone that Aria looked defiant rather than despondent. "Did you think I didn't realize that your precious Poppy sent you to spy? Neil was pretending just like you were. He was using you to get information; and now we have what we want, so we'd like you out of the way."

Aria looked shocked. Maybe the idiot knew even less than Simone thought.

"H-how do you know about Poppy?"

Simone laughed. "You really know nothing. We know all about Poppy's general strike because we listen to everything going on. If we wanted to stop this silliness, we would have stopped it and arrested and killed all of your kind. Your "Expect us" friends are sloppy, and *expected.* As for Poppy, I've known him and his idiocy since his name was 'Paul.'"

Aria had shifted her arms behind her back and, for a moment, Simone worried that she was going to free herself somehow. The guards told her that they used the gag and the handcuffs from a sex kit in Neil's room, which no doubt this little whore had talked her son into using. Simone worried for a moment that they weren't proper military grade cuffs. The last thing she needed was her ex-husband's whore attacking her. She needed to get back to the meeting before Neil noticed she was gone. Her assistant was not going to be able to distract Neil for long. Again, she wondered where the doctor was.

"Him? Poppy's not even here. Why bother with the cruelty of misgendering her and using her deadname?"

Secretary Rao clenched her jaw and growled out her next words, with the purpose of intimidating. "You think I'm cruel, Aria? You haven't seen cruelty. Paul is the one who abandoned me, with a child, no less. I told him that I could pull our families out of the hell that other dark-skinned people were in, but it wasn't enough for him. I managed it even on my own, as a single mother. I did what I had to do to make sure my son had all the best things in life. Paul insisted we could just stay together, and we would live as a lesbian couple even after he had his sex reassignment surgery, as though that was an option. I would have never been appointed Upland DC governor with a sexual deviant in my own home. No. I am not the cruel one between us. Paul made his bed and he has certainly slept in it, and filled it up just fine after I kicked him out. I have done what I can to make sure to stomp out that kind of deviance and prevent gender nonsense before it breaks up families and ruins lives. I'm the only one between us who ever knew right from wrong." Simone's anger at Paul for abandoning her simmered in her blood.

Aria was staring blankly. Simone had no idea what her son saw in her. "You are saying that Poppy is Neil's biological parent and that you left her because she transitioned?"

"You really are slow. Paul is the one who abandoned me, abandoned our family, and abandoned all that we had planned to achieve together. He's spent decades organizing millions of people to withdraw their work and participate in a strike to get back at me, when he was the one who wronged ME. I'm having the last laugh, though. We knew there was no way we could withstand a mass protest and Earth needs a moment of rest anyway before we can continue with our plans. We saw this moment coming. We are getting out of here. All of us. Unless you are really pregnant, you are going to stay right here in the replica shed of your precious John Brown's standoff. We're not even going to have to kill you; you are going to die all on your own when the landslides come. All of you pathetic Lowlanders will."

The hatred in Secretary Rao's voice came through loud and clear, as she intended. Maybe the girl would be properly cowed by the venom she felt towards her.

"What makes you think you are going to survive and we are all going to die?" Aria asked.

"You, my dear, like so many other Lowlanders, are going to be a sad casualty of Hurricane Eamon. The water is already coming up enough to make this floor muddy. The water walls in every community have been raised to drive the flood water into the Lowlands and trigger landslides, as well as to preserve as much of the Uplands as feasible. In a few hours, the water will start to rise steadily, and soon you will drown in here and then you'll be buried in mud. Others will be killed in the fires out west. Many will die in the cholera outbreaks and diseases that always come in the aftermath. Of course a few people could survive if they hoarded resources, but you have conveniently trained everyone to share—to do what you deem to be morally correct rather than what will allow them to survive. As for us, we will survive because we have made sure that our people used the resources God gave us to save ourselves. All the BRUINS leaders at this meeting will be invited to take off for manned flights to the moon landing and later to Mars. We are leaving for various island launch pads as soon as the storm pauses. An hour after we launch, all the seed, food and mineral reserves will be blown up to make sure that the Lowlanders left behind die out before we make our return trip in two generations. If you are pregnant, we will have to take you with us to Mars to extract the baby. The doctor did a test and will be back with it in a moment."

"Poppy will lower the water walls and save the reserves."

"Your faith in him is idiotic. The water walls are locked in place. Not even I could override them now. As for the reserves, HE doesn't even know where they are."

Aria shrugged her shoulders. "SHE told me she had a plan to get the reserves free."

The girl had no idea what she was talking about. "The DC

Upland reserves are so spread out it will never work. The medicines are on the Health campus, the minerals are at Los Alamos, the seeds and food are at the Beltsville facility. They are all protected with biometric security. The only override to the iris scan is a DNA match with half of the BRUINS originators of this plan. And it has to be DNA from a fresh blood sample so it's not like he could get samples and hold them. Anyway, even if Paul saves some of the reserves in DC, there are reserves all over he won't be able to save. His kind will kill themselves in a state of constant war given the huge storms coming. You'll be long extinct before we make our return. Paul knows perfectly well that most revolutions fail and that all revolutions have pain. Were you so naive that you thought we would just step down from power and let you take the reins? You are somehow dumber than you look, which is hard, given your appearance."

Simone was bewildered that this woman had somehow seduced Neil. Paul was a disgusting deviant, so no surprise there, but Neil? She had to admit the girl had pluck, but she was slow to understand they had lost. She needed to be taught that she was completely helpless and that no one was coming to save her or any of them.

"What about all the Uplanders you'll have to leave behind? Did it occur to you that you could stay and we could all share the food and water that's available and heal together? That path you've chosen is to dig, scar, and burn Mother Earth and then take off for Mars. It's not the only path."

Fury colored Simone's vision but she projected calm through it, as she always did. She had discipline. She wouldn't let this girl get to her. "Do you know how hard I worked not to be poor? Do you have any idea how hard it is to be a woman of color in this administration? I've worked hard. I'm not giving all of that up and I'm not letting anyone else have it. I earned all of this."

"You earned the right to blow up food?"

"Paul is trying to exact his revenge, and I'm trying to exact mine. You're just bitter that I play the game better than he does."

Aria sat up again. Simone stepped to the side to ensure that her bound hands were not moving. "This is not a game, and Poppy does not want revenge. She wants to be whole. She wants us all to be whole. She wants justice and liberation."

Convinced that the girl was secure, Simone began to pace with impatience. "*I* want to win. And I have aligned myself with winners. We will be back in a few generations after all of you have died off after failing at this nonsense 'sharing' and 'justice' and 'liberation'. None of that is real. What's real is power and resources, and I have those."

"Why are you telling me all this?"

It was a good question. Simone was still not satisfied with the impact she'd had on this girl. She wanted her reduced to nothing. She wanted Paul and all of his harem dead. "If we leave you here, I want your dying thoughts to be about how you were outsmarted and I wanted you to realize that you are nothing to Neil. We've always had a plan. Even if your whorish behavior gets you a seat on a flight to Mars, make no mistake, you will be there as a prisoner who happens to be carrying my bloodline."

Footsteps were finally approaching. "Neil?" Aria called.

Simone rolled her eyes at the naivete in this girl. "That's not Neil, it's the doctor."

The square-headed doctor entered the shed looking somehow more villainous than he had the day before with his white coat now wet and splashed with mud. He didn't spare a glance towards Aria. Simone was annoyed at how long he took, but pleased that he looked downright sinister with a scowl that he wore more comfortably than his suit and beard. "Secretary Rao, the test was negative. Would you like me to put the patient down before we go? We need to leave to keep on schedule."

So she wasn't pregnant. No matter. Simone let out a sigh of relief that the piece of trash in front of her was not carrying her grandchild.

"No need to waste any medicines on her. Let's go."

Simone turned to Aria one last time. "I suggest you spend your last hours repenting to God for your unnatural behavior, young lady. Maybe if Paul does the same you all will meet in heaven. Otherwise, I'll see you in hell at some point, I suppose."

Things were turning out for the best. It was time to find Neil and see if she could convince him to join them. Once she informed him that Aria was sleeping with his own father—who abandoned him as a baby—he might just agree to come. Every ounce on the flight was scrutinized, but if he agreed to come, she'd bring a violin. He would be an asset and he'd finally see that she supported his music, just not the sin that came with it. Neil could finally take up his birthright as a leader. She shouldn't get ahead of herself though; who knew how much that woman had brainwashed her son? He might not agree to join her. Either way, Simone was leaving Earth for good, and her progeny would be coming back to reclaim it in a generation. The legacy she'd worked so hard to secure was within her grasp.

28.
"ANCESTORS SURROUND US"

—Batya Levine

Aria watched as Rao and the "doctor" left the shed and listened as their footsteps got farther away. The rain was starting to come down harder, and just during their conversation a thin layer of water had covered the ground of the shed. The pounding came in waves against the metal roof, a swelling, clanging percussion. The roaring sound of the storm was disconcerting. It was a reminder that time was running out.

Aria ran through in her head all that she had just heard and learned. Poppy had lied to her about who Neil was to her. Poppy's plans were falling apart. Aria had tried to bluff about Poppy having a plan for the water walls and reserves. Aria had jerked her head right at the start and heard the two beeps indicating that the audio was not only being recorded, but it was being livestreamed to Expectus. Gears would have enough information to make some sort of plan. And everyone listening would know about Poppy and Neil. It bothered Aria that Simone thought that Aria's unrequited crush on Poppy was a full-blown affair. If she died here, Neil and everyone in Expectus might think that too.

More importantly, if she died in this shed, everything would play out just the way that Rao described it. The Uplander leaders would escape to Mars and everyone else would die. She thought of Sadie's daughter, Malin. She thought of all the people back at the bookstore. She thought of the lowland communities she had visited for trainings. It was overwhelmingly tragic to imagine the next two days playing out the way Rao described it.

Aria was too tired to imagine another way at that moment, though. She was ashamed that her mind kept going back to Neil. Where was he? How had she so misread him? Did he really leave Aria again at his mom's request? Was he faking it all? If he wasn't, he'd be here now, so Aria had her answer. Neil had lied to her too. She had no idea who her parents really were and the people here claiming to be her parents were getting on a literal spaceship to Mars with the woman who had her parents killed. What crushed Aria's spirit was that she may have never really known her parents or Poppy or Neil. She loved them. She trusted them too much. But she didn't *know* them. It stung that Poppy had kept her being a parent—and Neil's parent—from her. She'd been a fool. It didn't really matter, she supposed, since they were facing the end of Earth as they knew it. The woman who had as good as killed her parents was leaving the planet and setting it afire as she took off.

As the adrenaline wore off, the fog of grief settled over Aria. She was cold and tired, and her head was spinning. She was tired of fiddling with her handcuffs. The muddy floor began to fade into the distance as she lost consciousness slowly. The sound of her heart began to drown out her other senses, as Aria pictured herself slipping her wrists out of the handcuffs and standing. Aria's parents' image appeared before her like a mirage. They were wearing the traditional Ethiopian and Indian clothes she had seen them in only in photos of their wedding and the time before Aria was born. Looking down, Aria realized that she was in formal wear as well, an Ethiopian white dress with a thick green embroidered border. Aria reached out to embrace her parents and found herself sobbing in their arms. She felt their warmth, their bodies. They were not a mirage, and Aria never wanted to wake up.

"Is it true?" Aria finally spoke between sobs. "Am I really not yours?"

Aria's mother rubbed her back with her warm hands, squeezed her tight until Aria was warm and dry, and held her face. It was her father who finally spoke.

"Not having our genes doesn't mean you aren't ours Aria. We are a family and we made each other who we are." Aria's father spoke as a teacher as he had done so many times in Aria's life. It annoyed her as a teenager, and she'd said rude things about how all he'd ever done was run a restaurant. When they'd died, she'd realized how much she missed out on by not listening. She relaxed into listening to her dad. "Remember I told you the story of how Krishna loved his adopted mother fiercely? You may not be our biological child, but you are ours. You have done so much for us, for our memories. You are not done dear. It's not time to give up."

"Baba, Ema," Aria said, immediately feeling the warmth from the words she had not said in so long. "I don't know what more I can do. I think my role here *is* done. I don't know if we can win. I don't know if I believe it." Aria's mother continued to rub her back as her father nodded.

"You don't have to believe it all. Just take what serves

you. There is another story of Krishna in battle. Do you remember? He told Arjun to keep fighting, and chided him, reminding him that we are not promised the fruits of our labor. You must be even-tempered. Continue the work without anxiety about the result." Aria vaguely remembered the story. "My friend Rabbi Levitt shared with me many times the words from the Talmud that said the same." That quote Aria remembered her father saying over and over. "Do not be daunted by the enormity of the world's grief. Do justly now, love mercy now, walk humbly now. You are not obligated to complete the work, but neither are you free to abandon it."

"Rabbi Levitt was there with Poppy to call the general strike, and so was Imam Abdellatif. So many of your friends were there. Did you know that? What do you know?"

Finally, Aria's mother spoke. Her voice melted Aria's heart. "You are my heartbeat. You know what I know." Aria leaned into the endearment as her mother first spoke and then kissed her forehead. "You know what you need to do, my love. Just fold your hand, slip the bangle off, and go to your friends. You are strong. You are competent. You are needed." Aria's father joined in as they repeated the last lines, *You are strong. You are competent. You are needed.*

Aria felt the cold and wet before she realized she was no longer half asleep. She closed her eyes and willed her parents back. She hadn't yet told them that she appreciated all the sacrifices they made. That she understood why they stood up to Donner. That she forgave them for lying to her about her biological parents. That she would finish what they started. She had so much more to say, but it wasn't going to work. They were gone. The searing pain in her arm demanded her attention. She opened her eyes and saw she was lying in a pool of blood. One hand was free of the handcuffs. Aria used her free hand to wrench her other arm free, then wrapped her bloody arm in the bottom of her shirt, stood up, and stumbled out into the rain.

29.
RISE—IN HOPE, IN PRAYER, WE FIND OURSELVES HERE

Neil had seen the way that Aria looked at the video of Poppy calling for a strike and immediately suspected that Aria had feelings for Poppy. Knowing that this woman existed was one thing. Seeing her, and seeing Aria gaze at her with adoration was a whole other thing. How had he been so blind? He was in love with Aria, and Aria was in love with Poppy. He was in a love triangle where no one loved him. Aria had disappeared and hadn't even told him where she had gone, or invited him.

After the interminable breakout sessions ended, Neil decided to go for a run to clear his head. He ducked into their suite and pulled on his workout clothes from the bathroom floor and got out of there. He guessed that room service had gone on strike before they got to their suite. He'd clean up later. He needed to get out.

Outside, Neil realized it was beyond "not running" weather, but he welcomed the discomfort. Spontaneous rivulets had formed on every hillside. Neil followed one towards the train station and beyond. Every one of Eamon's raindrops seemed to drop with urgency. Neil pounded out each step, running up the stairs to Jefferson Rock and finally back and around to the Hotel. He was soaked through, but calmer now. He'd just do what he always did and find Anthony and come up with a plan. First he needed to get out of his wet clothes.

Walking back into his suite, Neil saw that the place was not just a normal mess. He was so distraught when he had come in before he hadn't noticed the room had been ransacked. *What the hell?* The sex toy case was open. Neil walked over to it and saw that the cuffs and the gag were gone. *Super weird things for Aria to take.* The thought of Aria made Neil walk over to her cello. The case was closed and lying on the settee. Aria would never leave her cello on a couch, where it could fall off. Neil unzipped the case and found that the neck and bridge were broken inside.

How had he missed all these clues that something was amiss? Neil was too panicked to chastise himself for long. He scanned the room for clues, and checked the closet. *Fuck.* Anthony was sprawled on the floor. Neil checked for his breathing. Anthony was alive. He got out his Paxa knife and cut off all the restraints. He couldn't move Anthony, so he got a wet washcloth and washed off the cuts and scrapes, checking for other injuries delicately. He was determined not to lose Anthony. Suddenly, Anthony opened his eyes and tensed, grabbing for the washcloth, before realizing he was with Neil. His body relaxed.

"You're okay," Neil told him.

"I'm fine."

"I don't know where Aria is. Someone took her. I was outside the door guarding it and watching the camera for the balcony, when the video feed went out and I was attacked by five guards I've never seen." Anthony pulled himself up.

He tried to stand and crumpled back to the ground. "I'm too weak to go look for her. You need to go, Neil."

"Where?"

"Ask people where they've seen your mother going. I'll be okay. Just go now before any more time passes."

Neil followed Anthony's instructions and ran out of the room in his wet running clothes, trying to nonchalantly ask people if they'd seen his mom. Guests were wandering the halls seemingly lost without electricity or hotel staff.

"I need to talk to her about whether we are reconvening the meeting tomorrow," Neil told her secretary.

"There you are. Your mom told me to make sure you didn't leave the building."

Then she left the building. "I'll just hang out in my room then," Neil told the secretary, before changing directions and leaving through the back door of the hotel. There was only one road into town and he had just run along it. He retraced his steps. He tried every closed door, and tried to think like his mother. Where would she take Aria?

That was when Neil heard the train arriving. He ran towards the station, hoping that the limping figure he could barely make out was Aria. Neil picked up his pace to a sprint down the stairs and arrived at the platform just in time to see a bloody and bruised Aria board the other end of the train. He sprinted again towards the open door of the train and saw the conductor they had met when they arrived.

"I need to get on!" Neil had never pushed his body this hard. His heart was pounding.

"Go on then. You barely made it. I'll sell you a ticket once we get going." Neil jumped on the train and looked in both directions.

"Thank you! Where did Aria go?"

The conductor pulled up the yellow step stool from the

platform and closed the door before turning around to look Neil up and down, taking in his soaked running clothes and panicked expression. The train had begun to move. Apparently done with his assessment, the conductor finally spoke.

"Room 13. That way. I'll bring dry clothes and any other provisions I can find. She's lost a lot of blood."

30.
"UP FROM THE WRECKAGE"

—Batya Levine

November 2011

As soon as she got off the bus, the crisp fall air hit Simone's cheeks, and she called Paul. She didn't want to call near the Paxa building since she knew that calls were monitored inside, and she didn't want to call from the bus because she hated all those people listening.

It was safer to be on the phone with Paul while walking, though, since the neighbors liked him. Ever since she had turned in two of their neighbors to the cops for dealing drugs, she didn't feel safe in her own neighborhood. Everyone knew and respected Paul, though, so she spoke loudly to him on the phone if she was out on her own. They never talked about much on the phone because Paul said it wasn't secure, but their banter was a balm.

"Hey, hey gorgeous." Simone loved how Paul answered her calls.

"Hey, hey stud—I'm almost home! What you got in the pot for dinner?" Simone listened to Paul describe dinner over the phone as she walked and only hung up after she opened the door and Paul's real voice began to clash with his phone voice.

Their basement apartment smelled like a home-cooked meal. Simone's fatigue and nausea lifted in Paul's presence. Paul's vegan gumbo was one of her favorites.

"I have news!" Simone could barely contain herself as Paul hugged her.

"I have news too." Paul released her from the hug. Simone wished he would wear more masculine clothing, but had to admit he looked good in the floral pastel pink button-down shirt. It was a looser fit than he normally wore. At least she had put an end to his cross-dressing nonsense. This was a compromise she could live with.

Paul put the pot of food on a cardboard coaster in the center of their small table and put out two bowls and spoons and served them.

"No money for sour cream or cheese today, but we had flour and vegetable ends and peppers so I had what I needed to do my magic." Simone wondered if Paul was still mad at her about "being a snitch" as he'd called it. " I did talk to Ms. Esther." Simone did not particularly want to hear about Ms. Esther's sad story. She wanted to get to all her good news, but she let Paul continue.

"She was going to give me the eggs from those chickens she's raising surreptitiously, but now she doesn't want to be associated with us. We need to figure out how to make it right."

People were so petty. And gross. The chicken shit all over a dense neighborhood was just gross. That sort of thing did not happen in Georgetown. Simone couldn't keep in her good news any more.

"We don't have to do that, Paul. I got the job at Paxa. They were so grateful that I gave them the list of DSA members who were on their staff, that they made me the head of the DC office. It's not even the government relations job I was applying for; it's head of the entire office. And the job comes with a huge house in Georgetown! A moving truck is coming Friday, but they already gave me the keys to the house! No food worries. No rude neighbors. Just a beautifully furnished house for our family. We need to pack after we eat and say any goodbyes that you want to share."

Simone waited for Paul to rise up and wrap his arms around her. *That's amazing news, gorgeous.* She could almost feel the embrace and that was before she even shared about being pregnant. But Paul was only getting up to get some pepper. He sat back down. He did not look happy.

"Simone, did you accept that job without even talking to me about it?"

"I was in the room with Donner's staff, like directly with his staff and they said they needed a decision on the spot so they knew I was all in. What was I supposed to do?"

"How about telling them that you'd talk to your partner and get back to them?" Simone did not like how unappreciative Paul was being.

"Well I didn't and it's done and it's a great deal so let's just finish dinner and pack and then we can talk about it in our huge KING-size bed in our Georgetown house. I want to go check it out tonight."

"Nope. I'm giving this a hard pass." Paul was shaking his head. He was stubborn and this was a disappointment but not a shock to Simone. He'd come around. He'd come around on this too.

"Fine you can join me later, Paul, but I'm going tonight."

"I'm not joining you later, Simone. Georgetown used to be full of Black people but I'd be one of the only Black people now. I'm not going." Paul shifted in his seat. He looked uncomfortable. "Also, they won't even let me attend events at Paxa. You can't take this job and be married to me, I'm afraid. I have news too. I started hormone therapy six weeks ago. I talked to Doc and she has an opening for me to have surgery soon. I'm finally going to be able to transition, Simone. I'm finally going to be able to live the life I've always dreamed of."

Simone was stunned. When had they started keeping secrets from each other at this scale? Paul had brought this up before but it was impossible. Immoral. She had to change his mind. Simone was planning to wait until they were settled in their furnished house in Georgetown, but it was time to share the other part of her big news.

"I'm pregnant." *That should do the trick.* Of course they needed a house in Georgetown and a stable job.

Paul looked stunned. Shock and annoyance flashed on his face before he finally did what he was supposed to do and got up and came over and embraced Simone.

"We're having a baby? You must be pretty far along ... it's been a few months."

Simone began to cry, knowing Paul would comfort her, and he did. Paul's embrace only reminded Simone of how infrequently his embraces turned sexual. Why did she have to cajole so much for her husband to want her? She pulled herself away. "I'm eleven weeks. And to be clear *I'm* having a baby. I'm moving to Georgetown, I'm getting a huge promotion to be head of the DC Paxa office. You can come or not, but I'm calling an Uber."

Paul had tears running down his face as he released the embrace. He sat down on the floor, not even looking for a chair, and leaned back against the wall. He didn't bother wiping his tears until they got to his chin. They sat in silence for what felt like an eternity. "Simone, please stay. Don't do this. They will never accept me in that world. It's not safe for me. Don't leave me. I'll get a job as soon as I graduate and we can stay in our home and raise our baby here. We don't need the Inheritance Institute and we don't need Paxa." Paul hugged his knees and dropped his head onto them. He knew that was not an option for her.

There was no choice here. How could she stay in Edgewood with Paul and the chickens as he transformed into a woman? She wasn't gay. She didn't sign up for this. He was the one betraying her. She'd get fired from her job at the Inheritance Institute for being associated with him and live in poverty. On the other hand she could go live in a huge beautiful furnished house in Georgetown and raise a family there. Paul would come to his senses and join her and stop the hormone therapy. She didn't clear her dish, Paul could do that. It wouldn't take long to pack up her things from their 500 square feet. She packed her garment bag that held her prized suits, a small suitcase with her pumps each carefully rolled in sheets of her *Wall Street Journal*, and grabbed the framed wedding photo off of the wall. Paul was still on the floor crying, but there was nothing she could do. The car had arrived.

"I'll send a car for you at 8 pm tomorrow, Paul."

"Why is this all so rushed? I love you, Mona. I can't go where you are going. That world is not for me. It's not right the way they talk about us."

"I can't go where you are going either. You will come, or you'll suffer more than I will, Paul." Simone didn't know why it was all so rushed, but she had already accepted their timeline and she wasn't going to back out.

She tried not to look back. She did not like seeing Paul suffer. She just had sense that he seemed to lack. She could see the writing on the wall, and where the power was. Paxa was going to rule the world soon. She wanted to be on the winning team. Surely Paul would come to his senses eventually. And if Paul never joined her, she'd pour her love into their baby.

Neil Rao was born at 4:17 am at Sibley Hospital in Northwest DC on June 17, 2012. Poppy was by Simone's side as he was born, but dressed as a woman, and going by "Paula," so Simone had introduced her as a friend. She refused to put Poppy's name on the birth certificate, which she now referred to as her deadname. Simone refused to use new pronouns or new names for Poppy. She didn't care when Poppy said she was hurting her. She could see Poppy loved their baby, but she was furious that Poppy had abandoned her for a harem of trans friends who were living together in what had been their home.

When Simone returned to work she allowed Poppy to take care of Neil during the day, and even had her driver take the baby out to Edgewood and bring him back after her evening meetings. By the time Neil was 18 months old, Simone demanded that Poppy detransition and told her she could never accept her. Poppy went ahead and had her last surgery. After the surgery, Poppy barely talked to Simone other than to let her know about Neil's bowel movements and eating. Paxa had found her a nanny so even that communication would be unnecessary soon. Simone was a rising star at Paxa. She did great on TV, and she ran a tight ship in the office. She was an asset to them because she was willing to do things others weren't *and* she was a woman of color who was a single mother. She showed their tolerance. But their tolerance only went so far. Neil was all she had and she wasn't going to let Poppy ruin Neil's life or put all she had built in jeopardy.

Poppy confessed one day to Simone that she desperately needed a loan and had become a sex worker to make ends meet. That was the last straw for Simone. She gathered some evidence, created other evidence, and pulled strings with the police to have Poppy arrested for sex trafficking. Poppy didn't stay in jail. Simone told her she wouldn't stop there if she didn't leave Simone and Neil alone. At 18 months old, Neil wouldn't even remember Poppy, but if she waited any longer she might endanger Neil's future prospects.

31.
"WITH TEARS AND WITH COURAGE"

—Batya Levine

Just as Neil stepped into Room 13, the train jerked its way out of a tunnel, sending Aria into Neil's arms with enough force to push them both back into the seat behind them. Aria winced from the pain. Her body was sore from being attacked and from the process of extracting herself. The skin of her wrist had road rash, and she was still bleeding. Water squished around her frozen pruney toes. She had no idea how Neil had gotten there, but she barely knew how she had gotten there.

"You're okay now, Aria. I'm here if you want to tell me what happened," Neil said, rubbing her back lightly. "I'm so sorry."

"Your mother needs to be stopped, Neil." Aria didn't know where to begin to tell Neil all that his mother had done and said to her and all that Aria now knew. She was exhausted, and couldn't resist resting her head on Neil's chest. Simone had been lying. Neil was not heading to the moon with his mother. Tears of relief slid down her cheeks.

"I have a lot to tell you."

Neil continued rubbing her back. "We need to get you out of these wet clothes and check your wounds first." Neil gently moved Aria directly onto the seat as he stood up halfway, bending his knees to avoid hitting the bunk bed above. The lines of his thigh muscles smoothed as he stepped towards the door so he could stand erect. The dark skin of his legs around his taut muscles reminded Aria suddenly so much of Poppy. Neil reached up to the bunk bed and grabbed two blankets, which he threw on the chair facing Aria, as he began to undress under the dim reading lights in their roomette.

Neil took off his shirt and shorts, and was standing in his naked perfection a foot away from Aria, trying to dry himself off with his soaking wet shirt. He gave up and grabbed one of the blankets wrapping it around his waist like a towel. She could still see his cute little happy trail leading down. There were definitely some big differences between him and Poppy even if they shared the same strong thighs and smile.

Now that she knew the truth, Aria wondered how she hadn't seen it before. It was just like when she first saw Musa's smile and realized her own parentage. The genie was out of the bottle. She couldn't unknow the truth, and she couldn't decide what it meant about her relationships with Poppy, with Neil, or with her parents. Poppy had likely known that Neil would be at the party she sent Aria to scope out. She had explicitly told Aria to have sex with Neil and explore the relationship. Now that she was with Neil, she couldn't imagine ever being with Poppy. Maybe that was what Poppy intended.

Neil knelt down in his blanket in front of Aria.

"I don't want to push you too hard, Aria, but we need

to stop the bleeding and you need to get dry. May I?" Neil's fingers were grasping each side of her shirt. Aria nodded her approval and Neil pulled her shirt over her head. Aria lifted her arms over her head to let him take off the shirt. She winced as the soft material hit her left wrist. Neil threw her shirt in the same bag he had thrown his clothes and reached for the antiseptic and bandages the conductor had given him.

"I could kill her for doing this to you," Neil said quietly.

"Technically I did that to myself, getting out of the cuffs that you bought," Aria said as Neil carefully bandaged her wrist, taped the bandage, and positioned her wrist over her head.

"That should stop the bleeding," Neil said before continuing his previous thought about his mother. "She may not have been the one who tied you up or cut you, but she did this. If she ever tries to hurt you again, I will kill her. And we will stop whatever she is trying to do, Aria. We'll do it together."

Neil leaned Aria forward and dried her back. He leaned her back on the chair and ran his fingers through her hair along her scalp, looking at his hand afterwards. "There's a pretty big bump, but no blood so far other than your wrist."

Neil reached for the second blanket and threw it over his shoulder. "May I?" He asked again, reaching for her bra straps. Aria nodded and he leaned down and deftly unhooked her bra and removed it. "I swear I'm not just saying this because I like getting you naked, Aria, but you need to take off your clothes." Aria was tapped out and tired enough to sleep in wet clothes.

"I like making you wet, but this is all Eamon's doing!" Neil winked.

Aria chuckled despite herself and stood up, moving next to Neil in the doorway so they could both stand straight. She lifted her arms and held onto the bottom of the bunk bed above her.

"My wrist hurts, can you get it?" Pain was radiating from her wrist and she was light-headed from the blood loss. Neil pulled down her pants and underpants and knelt on the floor in front of her to pop her heels out of each pant leg.

"I just thought of how adorably embarrassed you were last week when I found you were wearing adult diapers. Hard to believe that was a week ago." So much had happened in a week, Aria realized she should apologize for how suspicious she'd been of Neil back under that tree. Neil did not seem to be looking for an apology, though. He looked up at Aria, dried off the water droplets. He handed her a blanket.

"Let's warm you up."

Neil stood and supported Aria's waist, helping her climb up into the top bunk. The ceiling was only a few feet above her head, but she could sit up, and crawled over and sat at the foot of the bed, making room for Neil. Neil climbed up and could only lie down in the small space.

"Under the sheets and blanket to warm up you go. It's a short trip, so we need to get you dry, warm and ready for whatever's ahead." Neil laid down under the sheets on the window side and Aria crawled in beside him, pulling her blanket over both of them as Neil pulled her towards him. How did she feel so safe in the arms of a man whose mother had just tried to kill her? Neil's body was warm and Aria melted into his shape, spooning him as he rubbed her arm. Aria could feel her body getting dry and warm. Neil kissed her neck and her hairline, and her cheek. Aria moved her arms to grab the straps that were holding the small bunk in the air. She wasn't sure how she had ever doubted Neil. In just a few days, Neil had become her home. Neil's heart was going to break when he found out everything that Aria knew about his mother's plans and that his father had been so close all along and never reached out.

"We need to talk."

"Shh. Aria, you've lost a lot of blood. Just rest and we can talk later."

Aria was going to have to tell Neil that Poppy was his parent before the two of them met. Maybe she could delay that until after the crisis. "Neil, I think it would be easier if you and I split ways right now. You should hunker down for the storm. We'll talk after Eamon passes, after I find the reserves."

Neil tried to sit up, but hit his head on the ceiling of the roomette. "Ow. I'm not going anywhere. I'm going to be there the next time and my mother will not be able to hurt you," Neil said. "I'm no Humphrey Bogart, or whatever his character's name was. I'm not letting you run away into someone else's arms because of your commitment to the struggle. I'm staying with you. We're going to win together."

Part of Aria wanted to clarify for Neil that there was no one else she wanted—there was no Victor Laszlo. Part of her wanted to take his help. She couldn't do that to him, though. Expectus would have heard Rao giving the location if her earrings sent the recording. They'd also all know that Poppy was Neil's parent. They'd all think she was sleeping with Poppy, as Simone did.

Poppy was probably gathering a team to go bust out those reserves and was not expecting her long lost son to show up there. *That* was what Aria needed to focus on. There was too much at stake to have some kind of old-timey trashy talk show reunion. She needed to part ways with Neil and get her work done, as much as she hated it. Lying next to each other spooning was not the right way to do this. Aria was in pain and tired, but she knew what she needed to do. She needed to focus on the fight ahead.

"Neil, please, if you care about me at all, let's part ways for now. We were just pretending so I could spy, but we don't need to do that anymore. Right now, I need to focus, and to do that I need you to get out of this bed."

Neil looked as wounded as Aria felt.

"I'm going to tuck you in and go look for dry clothes for us, but don't think for a second that I'm going to just leave you because you ask me to. This is my fight too, Aria. My mother has hurt all of us, including me. We can focus together."

Aria tried to think of what would help Neil move on without her. "Neil, I'm not who you think I am. Remember, I was the one behind the action who kept you out of Lowland when you tried to defect a decade ago. Your whole band was blackmailed because of me. You're better off without me."

"That was a decade ago. Why are you trying to get rid of me, Aria? Is it because I was being an idiot this morning? Is it because I couldn't protect you from my mother? You can't begin to imagine how sorry I am about both of those things. This morning I was being insecure. I should have followed you to keep you safe. I thought you didn't want me and that thought took over my brain. I'm sorry. I don't want us to waste any more time being apart."

Neil kissed Aria's cheek and climbed down from the bed, removing his warmth that had been so comforting. Aria knew she should tell Neil about Poppy being his parent, and for that matter, about her parents, but she didn't have the energy. She needed to focus on getting to the reserves and freeing them, or else, there wasn't going to be enough food or basic materials to be able to establish a government. All their resistance work would be for nothing if she did what she wanted and ran off with Neil after confessing everything she knew. She was not going to take that route, as tempting as it was. She was going to keep Neil in the dark about Poppy for the time being. Once Neil realized how much information she was withholding, he would leave her forever. Aria was going to break his heart and save the future. She had always wondered what it felt like to be a martyr. Now she would know.

32.
"FIGHTING FOR LIFE"

—Batya Levine

Aria had been asleep when Neil returned with her dry clothes. The train conductor was a miracle worker. Neil needed some more miracles. Now that they were back in DC, Aria was still trying to break it off with Neil, and he did not understand why. He also did not want to push her farther away, so Neil quietly let Aria know he was not leaving her side and did not push her to explain herself.

When they'd gotten off the train at Union Station, it was nearly morning and the wind and rain had picked up. The train ride was normally only an hour, but had taken almost four hours because of the weather conditions. Neil was grateful for the time since Aria had gotten a solid three hours of sleep, a full REM cycle.

When they alighted the train, a large group of what Neil presumed to be Expectus leaders were there. As they got closer, Neil realized that he knew everyone. Laurie, who had been the producer for the state media interview they had done, was there. His ex-girlfriend from high school, Sadie was there, as was Noona, and the young man he'd met briefly at the bookstore, Cole. Noona hugged Neil, surprising him.

"Thank you for taking care of her."

"I didn't do the best job." Neil pointed at Aria's bandaged wrist.

"Neil did great and is going to go rest up and meet us later," Aria said, ostensibly to Noona, but staring straight at Neil. Neil did not move. He was not leaving. He'd already decided that if he had to, he'd follow her at a distance, but that he was going wherever Aria was going.

The rest of the group had clearly already made a decision to move. Aria and Noona were talking as they followed, and Neil followed behind them. Aria turned around and nodded her head to him to leave, and he shook his head. Neil wasn't sure where they were going or why, but he was determined to stay with Aria as the group moved to the metro station and underground to board, not bothering with the checkpoint. They were ignoring the guards and talking loudly about storm provisions and getting sandbags, which seemed to Neil to be a ruse.

When they got on the metro, Neil could see that there were a half dozen guards on each train, carrying automatic weapons. DC was on severe lockdown compared to when they had left. There were checkpoints on every road and guards on every train. The guards were not harassing the riders, Neil noticed. They were quiet. Neil approached Aria and sat next to her. Maybe she'd given up on telling him to leave. Neil was pleasantly surprised that she let him hold her hand, after her insistence on the train that they could not be together. Noona was in a seat perpendicular to them, right next to Aria. Noona leaned over and whispered.

"People were in the streets all day and night in the rain and wind. Gears is on their channel and heard Donner and

Rao give the police and military orders to shoot into the crowd. So far they haven't, but they also haven't given over their uniforms or weapons."

"Where is Donner?" Aria whispered. They were making Neil uncomfortable with their lack of discretion. There were guards everywhere and they needed to be more careful.

Gears heard her question and leaned forward from the seats behind Aria to answer.

"No one knows. There are crowds barricading the bridges and perimeter streets of Upland in DC and in every city chanting '*Hey ho, hey ho, President Donner's got to go*,' and singing songs, but none of our channels can locate him. We know he's left the White House, because our people took the building and the whole complex over once they realized guards weren't shooting. We have the building secured and we have Pinky on the inside with all the White House staff who were Expectus spies. They're looking for information and securing assets. Based on the intel you gathered, our best guess is that Donner was in a single passenger drone that landed a few hours ago at Andrews. We think he'll try to join Rao and other BRUINS at the offshore launchpad," Gears said, nodding his head towards Neil as he spoke of his mother. "Good riddance," Gears added.

Neil wondered if they were headed to the Air Force Base. That was the direction they were riding. He needed to find out without being kicked out. "What intel did you gather, Aria?"

Noona raised her eyebrows. "Didn't you debrief him on the train, Aria? Poppy told us Neil was onside with us, and trained, and that you'd have him up to speed. What were you doing that whole time if not telling him what the fuck is going on?"

Neil couldn't help himself at the word fuck. "I wish I could report there was fucking going on," Neil murmured. "She needed sleep and rest on the train. She still does." He wanted to defend Aria, but realized he did not need to defend her from Noona, after fielding a withering glare from Noona.

"We're almost there. Tell him now," Noona demanded. Aria shook her head "no," and Noona's momentum barrelled forward with the truth. "I shouldn't be the one to tell you this. Your mother is planning to go to Mars for a few generations and is trying to blow up all the reserves of seed and minerals, so that we all kill each other and die back here." Neil blinked. It would take a minute to absorb the information that his mother was fleeing the planet. "There's more. It's about Poppy," Noona continued.

Neil had at least guessed this part. "The Expectus leader. I've already guessed that she and Aria are lovers," he said flatly.

"Nope. They're not. And it turns out Poppy is your parent."

It was Noona who broke the news. Aria was looking at the ceiling and had not opened her mouth to confirm or deny.

Aria must have lost more blood than Neil had realized. She was sitting mute while Noona claimed that her lesbian lover was Neil's parent. There was no time to clarify what Noona was talking about. The train had stopped. The chime signaled and the doors opened. An announcement crackled over the speakers on repeat. "This is the last station stop. Metro service will be suspended until further notice due to Hurricane Eamon." Noona pulled at Neil and Aria's arms, ushering them all off the train onto the platform where they could now see the scale of the wind and rain.

"We may have to find cover and wait to get to the reserves." Noona yelled over the sound of the wind as she walked ahead, leaning her head forward, pulling Neil along, with Aria and the rest of the group following.

They were heading to the reserves. So much of the group's conversation had been coded that Neil did not pick up on where they were going until now. Aria needed rest, not to be out on a mission right now. They were in the middle of Hurricane Eamon, in the middle of a coup attempt, and if Neil knew his mother, things were about to get ugly. They were in a group of six people, all with their backs to the side of a concrete tunnel, as wind and rain gusted through the underpass. Neil could only hear Noona on his left, who was between him and Aria. Aria and Laurie were talking with Sadie and Cole behind them, but he couldn't hear them.

"Once we get over to Beltsville, we'll need both of your blood samples," Noona said.

Was Noona talking to him? Neil had no idea what was going on.

"Let's just focus on getting to shelter right now."

Before Noona could answer, Neil saw a military uniform and a gun aimed at them and pointed.

"GO!" Noona yelled. Neil had no idea how he had wound up in the front of the group. Escaping a gunman was going to be nearly impossible under these conditions. Things had gotten much worse since they'd gotten off the train. Huge metal signs that had been bolted down were now flying through the air. Running into the wind was more like a slow motion walk as the wind was pushing them back towards the gunman. Then the wind shifted and was almost carrying them forward, forcing their jog to safety into a sprint. Neil's legs were spinning like a wind-up-doll that had been wound too tight. His arms were linked with Noona's and he looked back every few seconds to make sure Aria's arms were still locked with Noona's and that the rest of the group was there. He didn't hear any bullets or screaming, so the gunman may have decided it was not worth following them into these weather conditions.

Neil heard a gust of wind that was somehow stronger than the prevailing wind, and turned to see a highway sign being lifted in the air in the distance. The signs that looked so tiny on the overpass turned out to be enormous. If an object that massive came at them, they'd be dead. Neil realized they had to stop. The wind was going to pick them up if they stayed upright. Neil gestured to Noona and Aria to get down with his free hand, sat, arms linked and laid flat a moment later to avoid the wind picking him up. An explosion, rather than the wind, lifted them off the ground and slammed them back. A car had crashed into the last two in their group, breaking Laurie's arm linkage with the person behind her. It took Neil a moment to realize it was Cole who had been struck, and that Sadie had been behind him. He couldn't see them.

"Fuck. Go!" he could barely make out Noona and Aria both yelling, but he got up, relinked arms and ran. A huge metal highway sign that was taller than Neil crashed in front of him, and he went around it.

Neil had never seen anyone die before. All he could think of was keeping Aria safe. He linked arms with Noona even tighter and motioned for her to link arms with Aria tighter, and for Aria to link arms with Sadie, who Aria had grabbed, and needed to be pulled with them. Once their arms were firmer, Neil kept pushing through the wind and rain towards the only shelter he could see, the corner house at the end of a trail. It was just a few feet away, but it took them almost a half hour to reach it, and it was dumb luck that the rest of them weren't impaled by a flying object in transit.

The porch provided little shelter. They were soaked and injured. They needed to get inside. When no one answered his knock, Neil kicked the door open, and was stunned when it cracked and gave way. Neil pulled everyone in and used his entire body weight to shut the door behind them. He saw that he, Noona, Aria, Laurie, and Sadie, who he'd thought was dead, had made it to the porch and inside the house. They weren't alone though. A woman, who was presumably the owner of the house, was standing at the top of the stairs pointing a gun at them.

"Put your hands up," the woman said as she walked down the top step, pointing her rifle. "Who are you and what do you want?"

33.
IN HOPE, IN PRAYER, WE'RE RIGHT HERE

"I'm Neil Rao, ma'am. These are my friends. We just needed shelter for a few minutes." Neil was hoping, for once, that the person he was meeting had seen all the state media around him being the most eligible bachelor.

"Neil Rao?" The woman scanned the group, her eyes stopping on Aria. "Aria is that really you? It's me, Julia."

"Oh my God! Julia? It's been so long." Aria made what Neil now recognized as the Expectus sign and Julia returned it in kind. Julia had also lowered her gun, come down the stairs, and embraced Aria.

"You're injured. I'm so sorry for the violent welcome."

"It's okay, Julia, but we actually need to keep going. We just lost a friend back in the lot and we owe it to them and everyone who's fallen to keep going." Aria's mind was, as ever, on the mission at hand. She was soaking wet again for the second time in as many days, and she was injured, but she wanted to keep going. Neil was replaying the last few minutes in his head. Was there something they could have done to save Cole? Should they go back to see what happened to him?

"I'm going back to get Cole," Sadie said. Her arm was bleeding.

"You need to stop that bleeding. It's too dangerous to go by yourself and we need to keep going to the reserves." Aria's answer made Sadie clench her jaw. They were both bleeding.

"Where are you trying to go in this storm and in that state?" Julia asked as she ran to get supplies.

"Beltsville Agricultural Center," Noona yelled.

"Turns out the Donner Administration had the Upland DC strategic reserves of seeds and food right under our noses. We have a team already there, just waiting for us to be able to save the reserves before the blow up. They are set to explode as soon as Eamon passes," Aria said. She finally turned to Neil. "Your mom thought I was as good as dead so she gave me a lot of information that's been relayed to Expectus."

Aria's apparent friend, Julia, looked at Aria's injured wrist and seemed to be taking in the cuts they all had on their exposed skin from flying debris.

"Aria, you can do almost anything you set your mind to, but I don't see how you can make it to Beltsville with Eamon pushing against you. You still have two miles to go. My windows are all boarded up, but even in here, we should be in the internal rooms." She looked at Sadie, and her wounded arm, now being compressed with a towel. "I'll go with you to check on your friend when the storm dies down, but you need to stop the bleeding from that arm."

Saide didn't seem convinced. "If he's alive, he won't survive that long."

Aria walked over and held Sadie's hand. "I saw it. He's gone. It was a direct hit from the car. He died doing what he thought was necessary to save us all. May he rest in power."

"Rest in power, Cole," Noona said, followed by Laurie. Neil repeated it as well, and finally Sadie said the words through tears. "Rest in power, Cole. I'm sorry I couldn't pull you out of the way. I tried."

Aria was still holding Sadie's hand. "Blame Eamon and the fossil fuel companies that superpowered him, blame Donner and Simone Rao for making us have to scramble through Eamon, blame the rest of us if you need to, but don't blame yourself."

Julia had a pile of towels and first aid materials laid out for them. Neil hoped that someone would convince Aria to take a break, and luckily Laurie did. Noona was the least injured and took charge of cleaning wounds.

Laurie took Julia aside. "Thank you for all of this. It's nice to meet you. I go by Gears and produce media and handle tech for Expectus. I don't mean to be rude or ungrateful, but can I ask what it would take for you to be willing to give up your weapon and welcome neighbors in?"

"Look I'm really sorry about that."

"Don't be. I'm just curious if you'd be willing to share the story of your reaction and why you wish you'd had a different one."

"That's a great idea, Gears," Aria said. "This scene is playing out all over Upland right now, even with Expectus-trained folks. Let's get out a video asking everyone to lay down their arms and explain that if we can get the food reserves, everyone who lays down arms will have food delivered as soon as Eamon heads back out to sea."

Laurie had found something to slow Aria down, whether or not that was her intention.

"I have experience with a camera. I can record while you two do the interview," Neil offered.

"Given who you are, Neil, it would be pretty powerful to

show that you are on our side and want people to lay down their arms. Can you do the interview with Julia?"

If Neil did this video, his mother would see him as the enemy. No one in the administration would speak to him ever again. If the coup failed, he'd be on the losing side. Neil looked over at Aria and realized there was no question that he was going to do this. He would protect Aria. He would do anything for her.

"Happy to do it as long as Aria dries off, puts on warm clothes and cleans her wound while we shoot."

Aria nodded in agreement. "Deal," she said. Laurie started briefing him and Julia on how they would shoot and what she wanted them to say.

34.
"ALL OF THE CHILDREN"

—Batya Levine

The water and wind were threatening to knock over the shed Aria was standing in behind Julia's house. Their situation was going from bad to worse. Even Julia, who Aria had personally trained, was so scared she was taking up arms against people in need rather than helping them. Julia wasn't just in a single training. Aria had spent a week with her at a camp where they were on a team blockading a pipeline. Julia even ran some of the trainings.

That Julia had taken up arms against people who might have been neighbors indicated that a lot of people were too scared to act in accordance with their training. On top of that failure, Aria had not gotten the water walls down before Eamon hit, and their chances of saving the reserves were slim. Then there was the trauma that Aria was trying to push out of her mind for now. She couldn't shake the image of Cole's body exploding upon impact with the car. It was running on repeat in her head. Who knew how many other lives Eamon had already taken, and this was just the beginning.

Events were unfolding just as Simone Rao thought they would. A part of Aria wanted to concede, to admit that the Donners had caused enough chaos on Earth to make it unlivable. If they would lose no matter what, she could just pull Neil into a closet and hold him while things fell apart. She remembered her paternal grandparents' story about the Partition of India and the death and destruction left when colonizers finally retreated. Millions of people died during partition, but not everyone died. Her grandparents were little kids, and they managed to stay alive. Her maternal great-grandparents survived the brief Italian invasion of Ethiopia. Even if they turned out not to be her biological grandparents, the ancestors gave her strength. She would stay alive too. She remembered Poppy's words. "It's never over unless every tree is burned to the ground and every last person is dead. There is always hope."

Aria checked the bikes that Julia was lending them again. There was a tandem bike and two single bikes. If the shed held up, they could use these to get to Beltsville. It was only a ten-minute ride under normal conditions, but now trees and electrical wires were down everywhere. One of the bikes was huge and likely Julia's son's bike. Neil would have to take that one. That meant that Aria and Noona would do best on the tandem bike and Laurie and Neil would be on the individual bikes.

Was Neil coming with them? Neil had shot the video urging people to lay down their arms. He was still with them after she'd pushed him away and failed to tell him about Poppy. What was keeping Neil there? He must understand that there would be no going back once that video was out showing Neil above an Expectus logo. Aria remembered that his only condition was that Aria take care of her wound.

He was being protective and caring even after Aria had tried to dismiss him on the train.

A moment of silence came suddenly. The wind had died down to almost nothing and the rain was slowing. Just as Gears anticipated, the eye of Hurricane Eamon had arrived. This was their only chance. Aria signaled to Noona that she should come and started rolling the bikes out.

The streets were abandoned as everyone stayed inside in anticipation of Eamon's eyewall striking down. They had to pick up the bikes and pass them over downed trees a couple times, but they still arrived quickly, leaving their bicycles at the fence, and climbing over into the Agricultural Center. The vaults holding the seed reserves were on the near side of the creek that was now a raging river. Aria had never been there, but Noona had and was leading them. There were Expectus activists everywhere, yelling instructions. They were trying to saw a hole in the side of the reserves. The building was made of some kind of metal. It did not seem to be working.

"The backup battery power has kicked in. We need to try the security panel," Gears said. "We probably have less than an hour before the next eyewall hits."

Noona nodded and led them to a ladder at the side of a silo. There was a buzz of work around them. Everyone seemed to be focused on their role.

"The panel at the top should open everything if we have the right biometrics," Noona said.

"I'll go first," Neil said.

The steps of the ladder were slick from the rain that had disappeared. Neil was first, which Aria suspected he insisted on to protect her, not because he thought he could open the reserves on his own. Aria was close behind Neil. They had made it up around three stories already and were close to a platform that looked like it held a touchpad for security. Gears and Noona hadn't started climbing yet, and were waiting on a signal from Aria. They were following Gears' advice and not looking down when they both saw it at the same time. On the platform they were climbing onto, a Donner Secret Service guard had Poppy at gunpoint.

Time stood still for Aria. How could this be happening? Poppy should have been better guarded than anyone. Why was she up here by herself?

The guard pushed the barrel of his gun into Poppy's head. "If either of you make a move I'll blow his brains out."

"Let's all calm down," Poppy said, and began a long monologue about the importance of staying calm in stressful situations. The guard was holding her tighter with every word and looking warily at Neil and Aria.

Poppy looked from Aria to Neil, nodding her head slightly in support as Neil pulled himself to the top of the platform and moved his body in front of the ladder to protect Aria, preventing her from climbing up onto the platform.

Aria had gone from angry to terrified as she took in the scene. Poppy had a gun to her head and a huge arm around her pinning her still. This was worse than having a gun to her own head. Neil had moved in front of her as a protective shield, but she needed to see this guy and calm him down. Aria tapped the back of Neil's leg to let him know she was climbing up. Neil made space for her, but pulled her behind his body. As soon as Poppy finished her filibustering speech about the importance of calm, Aria made her own effort, using the name on the guard's badge.

"Amos, listen, Upland has fallen. President Donner is in hiding. Secretary Rao sent her son here to let the Secret Service out here know that the SS is standing down. Your supervisors want you to stand down. You'll be safe if you put the gun down. I promise. You have nothing to fear from us," Aria said, using the insider term SS that she knew die-hards called themselves.

Aria needed this guy to step away from Poppy, but couldn't think of what else to say. The buzzing of the helicopters had been masked by the rain and wind at first, but as they got closer they were unmistakable. They, too, were using the pause during the eye of the storm to make a move. Aria, Neil, Poppy, and Amos all looked up to see three Marine One olive green helicopters flying past them. It was President Donner. No other figure was important enough to have two decoys flying alongside them. Aria looked from Amos to the helicopters as they buzzed by, hoping the guard would realize he didn't have anything to defend or fight for anymore. Amos's face showed only disgust and anger. Aria knew that face and it scared her.

"I don't care if Donner's flying away, I'm not," Amos said. "And no way I'm letting a bunch of darkies and cross-dressers take over on my watch. God is with us and will make sure we prevail. He's our only boss. That's what Donner always says."

This guy was a wingnut. He was probably a conspiracy theorist and Aria felt in her gut she wasn't going to be able to talk him down. She saw in Poppy's eyes that she realized it too. Poppy's hair looked like it had recently been done in box braids that were pulled back into a bun atop her head. Her high cheekbones stood out, regally. Rain drops covered her face but did not mask the tears Aria saw slip out of her eyes, before her eyes were fixed with steely resolve.

"I love you both more than you'll ever know," she said. Then she jerked her body to the side, twisting around and reaching for Amos's gun. Amos pulled the trigger. The shot rang out across the sky, above the noise from the helicopters. The bullet hit the side of the silo across from them. Aria lunged towards them but Neil held her back, securing her in his arms.

"No, Aria. There's nothing you can do."

Poppy and Amos were wrestling over the gun one second, and the next second they went over the edge. Time slowed down for Aria when Poppy went over. She was mouthing something as her body flew back. Aria could not make out what what Poppy saying. She pulled against Neil's arms to try to get closer, but as he held her back, Poppy pushed Amos off of the top of the massive metal storage tank. Amos did not go down without a fight. He grabbed Poppy's arm and pulled her with him. One moment Poppy was there and the next they were both gone. There was no way anyone could survive that fall. Aria screamed. She pulled away again and found Neil's arms had gone slack and she could approach the edge. She still couldn't see. She couldn't think. Maybe Poppy was still alive.

"No, Aria. You'll fall. She just gave her life so we could get the seed reserves. Please, Aria. You have to live. She'd want you to live."

Neil was right. Poppy had given her life. She was gone. Forever. Aria was not entirely sure she wanted to live in a world like this. The cruelty of Amos' words rang in her head. *No way I'm letting a bunch of darkies and cross-dressers take over on my watch.* The man didn't even realize that the people he idolized were trying to blow up all the food and leave him for dead. His hate had stolen Poppy—her vivaciousness, her beauty, her unparalleled ability to strategize, to reach people—none of that mattered to Amos. He just wanted her dead. He just killed her. Out of a hate and rage that Donner had sparked and now stained the entire country. A hate and rage that had just killed Poppy before her eyes. Aria fell to her knees and laid down on the roof. She let the despair in her heart spread through her body, behind her eyes, and finally come out as tears. The world around her melted away. There was no point to any of this without Poppy.

35.
"WE WHO BELIEVE IN FREEDOM CANNOT REST"

—Bernice Johnson Reagon

Gears climbed onto the platform and approached from behind them looking stunned. "I-I-I filmed the whole thing from the ladder and broadcast it. I'm such an idiot. I should have come up to help instead of filming. All of Upland and Lowland just saw that."

Aria finally looked up. She registered what Gears had said, and turned it over in her head a few times. She had never heard Gears sound so flustered. "I wish the people full of hate blamed themselves with the same passion we all seem to do it with. It's not your fault, Gears," she said through tears that were starting to subside.

"Maybe. Two people we love are dead, but a lot more are going to die if we don't move. Let's go put your blood sample in the sensor and hope we can open this. Then we'll go down and see if there's anything we can do. Most of the team is down there."

Aria let out a sob against Neil's body, , whch was suddenly behind her. "Fuck. She's gone. I'm so sorry, Neil." Gears was looking from Neil to Aria with an expression that moved from shock to frustration.

"We don't have time to process this, Aria, we have to open the reserves. Fucking Eamon is on the move. NOW FIELDS!" Gears yelled, shaking the bag of supplies she had extracted from her pocket in Aria's face to get her attention. Aria hadn't heard her code name in what felt like forever and it woke up the disciplined activist in her. She wiped her tears with the back of her forearm, trying to avoid her injured wrist. She took the knife and the vial in the bag Gears handed her and sliced a small cut in her left pinky finger. She filled the vial, put ointment on her finger and wrapped a bandage around it that matched the bandage on her wrist. Her arm was more bandage than skin at this point. She turned to Neil.

"Let's try yours too."

Neil grabbed the bag with the vials and repeated the actions Aria had just done.

Gears took the bag with both vials and climbed to the raised platform that Poppy and Amos had just fallen from, carefully crossing to the biosensor. The eye of the hurricane had given them a moment to complete the mission, but no more than a moment. The wind and rain were threatening to return. Gears added a drop of Aria's blood to the sensor, and nothing happened. She wiped it off with her sleeve and placed a drop of Neil's blood, which took an extra few seconds to be rejected by the computer. Gears added a drop of Aria's blood to Neil's as a last-ditch effort. As soon as both bloods hit the sensor, it was obvious it had worked. A huge metallic screeching sound started, with a larger-than-life clunk. They heard Noona's team below cheering.

"They must not know about Poppy, yet, on that side of the building," Aria said.

They sounded ecstatic. Aria could hear Noona giving instructions for how to use the machinery and transfer the seeds as quickly as possible to the trucks that were lined up below.

"I need to go down and get the trucks moving to the train car. I have enough of your samples for any other biosensors we come upon. You two should head back to Julia's house and get some rest. I'd guess we have a half hour left of Eamon's eye. Go before it's too late or we'll end up sheltering here for days," Gears said, looking hurried but sympathetic.

"We'll just go into one of the buildings here so we can be nearby to help with the transfer," Aria said.

"No. We'll need you well rested to get through the next few days. Please go process this and rest. We got this from here. We'll be right behind you and we'll go get you if we need you." Gears was insisting and Aria was too numb to argue.

36.
"NOT NEEDING TO CLUTCH FOR POWER"

—Bernice Johnson Reagon

Aria and Neil only spoke the words necessary to navigate to Julia's house. Aria wanted Neil to take control. She craved a dark room and a weighted blanket, and letting Neil take the lead seat on the tandem bike was the closest she could get to that sensation at the moment. After they had gotten settled and moving on the bike, they saw a flash in the sky. It was an explosion, but it was so high in the atmosphere that they did not hear it. Aria might have missed it if she wasn't looking up. The trail of light was thicker than a firework. Aria let the shock and numbness sink through her body.

First Cole, then Poppy, and now this. She suspected the explosion was a rocket launch gone wrong, and she suspected that Neil's mother was on that rocket. If she was right, Neil had lost both of his parents in the span of fifteen minutes. Aria knew that feeling. She did not want that feeling for Neil.

As they rode in silence, Aria's mind replayed the moment of Poppy going over the roof a dozen times. She willed her brain to stop tormenting her with images of death, but she also didn't mind having Poppy with her so vividly. As they arrived at the house, the eyewall of Hurricane Eamon arrived as well, and the sky went from daylight to dark in an instant. Aria hoped that her friends were being careful out at the reserves and taking precautions. She trusted them to do their jobs and do them well, just as they trusted her to do the same, so she tried to put her worry for them aside.

Julia gave Aria her bedroom and, seeing that Neil didn't walk in immediately, offered him the guest room. He thanked her quietly and shut the door behind him. Aria was numb and lost in thought. She laid on Julia's bed, listening to the rain drumming on the house.

Was it done? Had she avenged her parents' deaths? Had she done what Poppy had asked her to do? Could she have done anything to save Poppy or Cole? Why was she alive while they were dead? Was Neil angry with her? What was Neil thinking?

As far as Aria could tell, it took fresh blood from both her and Neil to open the reserves. That must be because it was set to open if Preeti, Musa, and Simone were all there together. They didn't trust each other enough to allow any one person to open the reserves. Together, Aria and Neil could now open all of the reserves, not just the food reserves. That gave them, together, the power to start afresh on this land. They could return to the indigenous name, Turtle Island, and they could form communities that took care of each other again. If Aria's theory about the explosion was right, they were both also now orphans, and she was an orphan twice over.

Aria woke up to Neil sitting on the bed gently shaking her shoulder. Where was she? She looked around and remembered, Julia's house. *How much time had passed?*

"They have a path cleared to get us back. Expectus sent a car for us. Do you think you can get up and make it?" Neil asked.

Aria nodded that she could. An entire day had passed. She groggily got up and changed into more of Julia's clothes, thanked Julia again, and walked with Neil to the car, hoping they would not pass the spot where Cole had been killed.

Neil played with his seatbelt, pulling it out and letting it retract.

"So that was my parent back there?" Aria nodded yes. "Were you lovers?" Aria shook her head "no." "How long have you known that Poppy was my parent?"

"Your mom said it when she had me locked up. She was saying all kinds of things because she thought I was as good as dead."

"What else did she say?"

"She said that it took three BRUINS leaders to be present to open the reserves. My theory is that you have her blood and I have Musa and Preeti's and that's why we could open the reserves together."

"You have Musa and Preeti's blood?"

Aria realized she was laying too much on Neil all at once. "They told me they were my biological parents at the conference."

"And you found out from my mother that Poppy is my biological parent? Did Poppy never mention me to you?"

Aria wasn't sure what to say. Did she owe Neil honesty? Or did she owe Neil the love and protection she wanted to give him? Aria thought back to her last real conversation with Poppy before going down to see Neil. She replayed it in her head. *Neil cannot know who I am.* Poppy had insisted. How could Aria tell Neil that? She wanted to be authentic, she wanted to be honest, but she didn't want to hurt Neil even more. She decided to share the part that was positive.

"I think Poppy and Anthony wanted us together. That's why they had me scope out that party."

"Anthony?"

"He's with Expectus I think. He told me he was gay in Harpers Ferry."

"Not even Anthony was ever on my side then. He never trusted me. Poppy never wanted me. They both chose you."

Aria held Neil's hand. "I'm here for you Neil. I've been through losing parents. It's disorienting. Tell me what you need."

Neil removed his hand from Aria's and stood up. "I need a break."

37.
"I'M A WOMAN WHO SPEAKS IN A VOICE, AND I MUST BE HEARD"

—Bernice Johnson Reagon

Two days later Aria found herself giving her third live interview to Joe and Becca Donnner. She was about to use the platform to plead for information about Neil's whereabouts, when she saw Pinky march him into the side door of the Oval Office, and watched Anthony sigh with relief and make his way over. Even from a distance, Neil looked like he hadn't slept or showered in two days. He was a mess.

Aria on the other hand, had been plucked, tweezed, and molded by stylists hand picked by Gears to appeal to the Upland public. She looked ridiculous. In the course of forty eight hours, Aria had been convinced to step into the power vacuum left by Poppy's death. The formerly dormant Upland Congress had actually convened and nearly unanimously elected Aria President in Donner's absence. It was absurd, and it was all orchestrated by Gears behind the scenes, who told Aria it was the only option and it was only temporary. Taking over the capitol was the sign to other Lowland areas that people should coordinate and govern themselves rather than central coordination, so the position was a formality to attempt a peaceful transfer of power, Gears had assured Aria. Neil would have heard all this through the news by now no matter what rock he'd been hiding under. Aria wondered if he'd also heard that Gears wanted them to continue with their fake dating and get married. Aria was willing, but also worried. She and Neil hadn't had time to set anything between them—they were like two clay pieces that hadn't yet been kiln-fired. She'd do it for the movement, but they weren't solid enough for a marriage. And Aria didn't even believe the kind of marriage her parents had could exist in the mess of a world they lived in. Neil did not look like he had come back ready to get married either.

Aria's eyes locked with Neil's scowl as he approached. She heard Joe make an excuse to end the interview. Something was wrong.

"Let's take twenty minutes and give Aria and Neil a chance to talk, everyone," Gears yelled out.

Aria rushed off the set, through the room, ignoring the praise she was getting for her interview from the staff in the room. She was focused on where Neil had walked off to. In the hallway, people gave them space and even Anthony stepped back. Aria grabbed Neil's arm and opened the first door she saw. It was a small conference room filled with photos and busts of confederate soldiers, photos of Hitler and a huge portrait of Donner. Aria tried to ignore what was on the wall and focus on what was important.

"Where were you? I was worried."

"You're the one who told me to leave you, Aria, and then sent your people out to hunt me down and pull me into the White House of all places. I fucking hate this place. Why did you want me back in this world? Because you need me for something?" Neil looked crazed, and Aria wondered if he had slept at all since they had last seen each other.

"Gears says if we get married publicly using Upland and Lowland traditions it might calm the violence and give us a chance to get more governance in place."

"So you need me for a fake wedding?"

"Yes, and I wanted to see you." Aria was confused about how this conversation had gone so wrong. She missed Neil. She wanted him by her side.

"Aria, would you marry me if Expectus didn't want you to? If the public didn't need a wedding?"

"Neil, I think this conversation got off on the wrong foot. I want to be with you. I care about you. We're good together and we've been through a lot together. I'm sorry I tried to push you away before. Why are you making it sound like I'm using you?"

"Look at you Aria. You are in the fucking White House. You may not be just like my mother now, but you will become like her if you stay here. I've seen what power does to people. Listen to you. I heard you on TV preaching to people about property and currency. This isn't you."

"This *is* me, Neil. I do what I have to do for the movement. They only asked me for six months."

Aria thought about her interview and the moments she was proud of.

What I want to save is humanity: our ability to make beautiful music together, our ability to tell fantastical stories, our ability to cook food for each other.

Neil had ignored all that and focused on the bits she had maybe flubbed.

"Six months of this will change you. And what happens then? Do we get divorced in six months? Real talk—Would you marry me even if it hurt the movement?"

"That's not the scenario we are in!"

"Answer the question, would you marry me if none of this pressure from 'the movement' was here?" Neil used his fingers to show air quotes around "the movement." It grated on Aria more than it should have. *What was so wrong about caring about the movement? About having a philosophy?* She needed to know if Neil was in or out.

"Neil, you want me to be honest? I don't even believe in monogamy, much less marriage. It's an unequal, oppressive institution, but this is what the people need, so I'm willing to do it. You were willing to do it before to protect me from your mother. Are you still willing, Neil? Are you willing to marry me?"

"No."

"No?"

"NO. I CAN'T DO THIS. I HATE IT HERE." Neil's voice struck her in the chest, and Aria's heart broke.

"So is that what you came here to tell me? That you don't want to marry me?"

"No, Aria, I don't want to FAKE marry you. I don't want to do this unless it is real. I'm trying to understand if this is real for you. I love you. It's real for me."

Aria stared at Neil for a second then looked away, needing a break from the intensity in his eyes. *He loved her and wanted her to commit to a monogamous marriage for the rest of her life?* It was one thing to do what the movement needed and put on a wedding for the people. That was just going through the motions in an emergency to buy them some time. It was an entirely different thing to commit to Neil that she'd live a life of monogamy with him. Aria was queer, she didn't believe that one person could ever meet another person's needs entirely, she believed in open relationships, she hated patriarchy. She thought about saying all of this, but decades of surveillance culture had created a habit of only truly speaking her mind when outdoors. Aria couldn't break the habit in the moment.

She and Neil seemed to not be on the same page about any of the things that Aria held most dear—the things that kept her alive after her parents were killed—the things that made her a good leader. She needed to understand Neil's expectations and let him know that she had different expectations in a relationship. She broke the silence that engulfed them, speaking softly. "Can you define what you mean by 'real' Neil?"

Neil did not match her soft tone, coming back with more force than Aria could handle. "I mean I want us to exchange real vows that we mean with all our hearts, in front of God and everyone. It means I want us to design the ceremony to represent our commitment to each other, not design it to calm the world. It means I want us to agree we're going to build a life together and raise babies together. It means we are real."

Babies? Babies were what Simone Rao had wanted from her too. Aria tried to put herself in Neil's shoes and felt sympathy for all that had happened. She thought Neil didn't even believe in God. She placed her hand on Neil's shoulder. "Neil, is this a grief reaction? You just lost your parents."

"Forget my mother. Now that she's dead there's no one desperate to keep us apart, but honestly, she has nothing to do with this, Aria. This is just me being real with you and finding that you don't really want me. It has nothing to do with my other dead parent. It has nothing to do with my dead parent, Poppy, who you clearly loved more than me, and who never gave a shit about me. This has to do with us, you and me, and the fact that we want different things from each other. I've told you I love you twice and you've said nothing in response."

"I didn't know you were keeping count," Aria muttered, pulling her hand back. Aria wasn't sure she could turn Neil's anger around, or for that matter, her own. She thought of her de-escalation training, and took a deep breath. She used his name again and reached out to him.

"Neil, I'm asking you to marry me. I'm prepared to do this. I just also want fewer people to die so I want to do it in a way that calms the country down. Is that so wrong? We can figure out the details of the ceremony and our partnership, but if you're willing to do it then we aren't in such different places. The reality is that the people on general strike will not accept just any outcome, they want some concessions from Uplanders, and the Uplanders won't trust that they won't be imprisoned or worse unless there is a show of unity and reconciliation."

"The *reality* is that you're not understanding me, Aria. I don't want you to be *prepared* to marry me. I want you to want to marry me, be desperate even to marry me. I'm not marrying you unless it's real."

Aria was not going to be bullied into giving up her agency. She snapped. She was no longer in control of her words. Her anger was in the driver's seat, anger at a world of oppression that always seemed to trap Black women no matter how much power they held. "You may want to marry me, but you want it for all the wrong reasons. I want it to save people and you want it to ... to ... I don't know, to break me, to force me to abandon who I am, to strip me of my queerness and my loathing for patriarchal institutions, and to watch me give in to your world."

Neil glared at Aria. "You will always think the worst of me, won't you? I don't want to break you, Aria. I want you to marry me with the same passion that I want to marry you. I'm sorry that we don't feel the same way about this."

Neil opened the door to leave but found a guard blocking the door.

"I was told no one was to leave this room."

"Let him go," Aria said from behind Neil. "I'm not going to use armed guards to make him stay."

38.
"I NEED TO BE ONE IN THE NUMBER AS WE STAND AGAINST TYRANNY"

—Bernice Johnson Reagon

Two weeks later

Neil slowly made his way through standing water towards an unmarked row house with his team. His gas mask and gaiters gave him the sensation of being in an astronaut suit, protected but separated from his surroundings. After one day of disaster response, he had been made a team leader, leading volunteers through diseased standing water, looking for survivors and finding mostly dead bodies. He'd been at it for a week.

The wind and water damage and the rest of the infrastructure destruction were palpable reminders of Eamon. Neil did not envy his team's uncertainty about the fates of their families, neighbors, and friends. At least Neil knew his family was dead and he had no friends. The coup and the storm coming together meant that everything had changed for everyone overnight. It was a lot to absorb. Every able-bodied person was asked to help out with search and rescue or in other volunteer roles.

The work was simple in a way. At least the local council had revived a nearly forty-year-old protocol from Hurricane Katrina, which was probably all that they could think of as precedent. When Hurricane Ilsa had hit Miami a decade earlier, there was such chaos that there was no search and rescue at all—they just cordoned off and abandoned Miami.

There were thousands of volunteers making sure that wasn't what happened in Anacostia, as they now called the combined Upland and Lowland DC. They were determined to find every last survivor. The teams marked each house with a large X when they finished going through it. Inside the v-shaped space at the top of the x, they listed the date and time they left the house. On the right they wrote what hazards were inside—usually rats and mold, on the bottom they had two numbers, the top showing the number of survivors they found and the bottom showing the number of bodies they had found. The only modification from Katrina was that now they were looking for shelf-stable food and noting if there were salvageable materials for shelter, and they were noting that in the left along with their team ID. There were few top numbers in the X shapes, and Neil wondered again that he and Aria had survived that train ride and trek to the food reserves in the middle of the storm.

Thinking of Aria made Neil wince as if he was in physical pain. He could not remember the last time he had slept, and he didn't care. He had a lot to make amends for, and if he stopped, he would have to think about his conversation with Aria last week and remind himself that Aria didn't love him.

As his team worked through the largely dry second floor of the house they were in, they built a pile of cans and sealed bags of food. Neil passed out the sheets to inventory the pile, as the crew chatted and brought items in, checking expiration dates and seals.

"Did you hear they found Donner's remains?"

"That coward literally tried to run away to the moon, how could they have found remains? That's BS. Did Aria say that?"

"No, but someone on my last shift told me."

"Unless Aria said it, don't believe a word of it."

It irked Neil that they used Aria's first name so informally. He wanted to correct them to say 'President Petros,' but he didn't care for the title and didn't want to engage.

"I like the way she talks. She's right. There is still stuff to save, and we are worth saving."

Neil couldn't help but feel pride in overhearing praise for Aria. Even if he hated that she was taking up this mantle.

"Did you hear they've already uncovered two plots to assassinate her plus that full blown plot to kidnap her? I give it a week before she's taken out and we're on to the next one. She's driving around in that tiny van with no security."

"Yeah. The first Black woman in the White House should probably be more careful. Some people are popping mad she's there."

Neil had been avoiding news about Aria as best he could, but the last snippet he heard had gotten his attention. She was in danger. He was moving out of earshot to the next room and nodded to his partner behind him to signal that he was going to enter.

Neil knocked on the door as a precaution and opened the door a crack. A putrid smell emerged, and Neil could already see one body lying face down on the bed. That was why they had masks. He entered slowly and saw a smaller body curled up next to the larger one. It was a child. Neil rushed over, turned over the body, and checked for a pulse. The girl was alive. Her pulse was weak, she was barely breathing, and she seemed to be asleep, but she was alive. Neil lifted her small body and checked her back and head for visible injuries. Seeing none, he lifted her and walked towards his partner.

"She's alive."

"Thank God."

"MEDIC!" Neil cried out and passed the little body to the medic on their team, who placed her on a table in the main room where they had been taking inventory of the food supplies.

"She's breathing. Pulse is weak. I can't wake her up. We need to get her to the medic tent."

"I'll take her." Neil volunteered because he needed to get out of there. He needed to save this girl, and he wanted to be alone.

The medic tent was quieter than it had been for most of the past week, as the number of survivors had been dwindling. Once they dropped off the little girl, medics and healers rushed around her to check her vitals and insert an IV drip.

"Is she going to be okay?" Neil asked.

"We don't know yet," a medic answered.

"This is the address where we found her." Neil took his tiny Moleskine notebook and a Sharpie out of the top pocket of his gaiters and wrote the address down along with his own name. "The rest of the family is dead."

The medic looked at the paper "Wait, are you actually Neil Rao?"

"Depends who's asking."

"A friend was here looking for you. It was just before you walked in. He went that way."

Neil's family was dead. He had no friends to speak of, and the love of his life had rejected him. He was utterly alone with nothing to show for his life. Maybe it was Anthony looking for him.

"A tall bruiser with brown hair?" Neil asked, but the medic had moved on to listen to the little girl's heart and shushed him. Neil decided to let the medics work.

"Call out for me if she wakes up and needs anything."

Neil turned in his gaiters and his gas mask for the day after leaving the tent, and washed up at the hygiene stand. He was spent. He wandered outside and walked over to the shade of a tree. He leaned his back against the trunk of the tree and sat down. He watched the long line of people requesting help slowly creep forward. Most were reporting missing family members or that they were in dire need of shelter. Community members were gathering for a spokescouncil meeting in an abandoned parking lot that was turning into a meadow, across from the medic tents. Neil rose to join the observers on the sidelines. He felt like a foreigner in a foreign land. His only exposure to spokescouncils was in a role-play he had done as part of his Expectus training. The elected commissioners stood in a semicircle with their constituents behind them. They were hearing complaints that seemed to come from the table of volunteers taking in concerns and triaging issues. A young man came before them first. He wanted to be signed up for food and water drone delivery again after being caught stealing a package of food and leaving six families on his block without breakfast this morning. As the young man closed his opening remarks, the commissioners' questions began. Many of them were reading notes their constituents were handing them.

"Do you have the support of any of the families who went without breakfast?"

"One of them is here to speak on my behalf."

"We'll hear that later," the apparent chair of the meeting noted.

Another speaker chimed in. "How do we know we won't be back here tomorrow or next week after you stole again? Do the family members you stole the food for now have a plan for signing up for their own drone delivery of food?"

"As I said in my opening comments, my family isn't causing any trouble. They had Upland jobs and got food in Upland before and never signed up for food delivery since they wanted to keep their guns and didn't need the food before. They don't have beef with anyone. They don't get in fights. My family stays to themselves. They just don't want to give up their guns for central storage on the block with the block captain. They think they will be in danger with the guns in a safe. So, that's why they can't sign up for drone delivery. They've already agreed to all the principles, but they want to keep their guns."

"How many and of what type?"

"Handguns. Each of them has one. They thought about lying about it and signing up, but they figured it would just come out later."

Finally, the commission decided to reinstate food delivery for the young man. To Neil's surprise, they also decided that if the family came to the commission that day that the rest of the family have access to food even without turning in their arms for a one-month period. During that time the family with guns would need to talk to everyone on the block to understand why the consensus was to keep firearms in the neighborhood safe. Their neighbors were the ones who had made the rule and the family needed to listen to them and understand why. The speakers wanted to hear a compromise where everyone felt secure on the block by the end of the month and the speaker who represented the block in question indicated she would knock on every door and try to find a solution as well.

Neil's mind couldn't absorb the scale of all that needed to be done. This one tiny issue that involved maybe five people was taking dozens of people and weeks of time to resolve. He could only focus on the people right in front of him that he had the power to help, and this young man was not that person. Neil thought of the little girl he had saved. She had to make it. He pushed himself up to head back in to sit at the girl's bedside when he heard Anthony.

"Neil!" Neil looked up but kept in motion towards the tent.

"Hey, Anthony." Neil spoke without emotion. He had been expecting someone to come find him when it came time to access other reserves since accessing secure sites seemed to take his blood and Aria's together.

"Don't 'Hey Anthony' me. People are dead all around us, both of your parents are dead and somehow, we are still alive. Get your sorry ass over here and give me a fucking hug."

Neil had missed his best friend, and decided to allow himself the bear hug he knew he was in for. The feeling of Anthony's arms around him released something in Neil that he didn't know he'd been holding. He coughed, hoping that would be enough of a release, but then he felt his torso convulsing and couldn't hold it. He let out a sob in Anthony's arms.

"I know, buddy." Anthony was patting his back and

tightening his bear hug. "I've been looking for you for more than a week."

"I ditched the shoes and the watch so you couldn't find me," Neil said, backing out of the hug and wiping the tears from his face.

"We need to talk, Neil."

Anthony and Neil walked into the dive bar and sat in a booth with Neil's back to the 3-D VR images of the weather report. Neil had just been outside. He knew it was hot as hell and sunny and didn't need more information. The dark crisp air of the bar felt good. Anthony began to talk.

"I'll get to the point. I'm sorry I lied to you about your dad."

"You knew." Neil had wanted to believe that Anthony was not in on the lies. He felt abandoned and alone being reminded that wasn't the case.

"Yes, Poppy and I had been friends for a long time. She's not going to win any awards for best parent, but she loved you in the way that she felt she could. I owed her, so I spent my life protecting you on her behalf, and you became my best friend in the process."

Neil tried to absorb the information, but it didn't match his life. His voice cracked as he spoke, but he'd already cried all the tears he had in him, so none came out. "I don't feel like she loved me. She abandoned me with a control freak who was a murderer and ruined my life. I appreciate all you've done for me, but honestly it hurts that you did it at her behest. You're just another person who didn't really love me for me. You realize that my entire childhood, my entire life, I've never had a single person who loved me?" Neil felt pathetic saying it out loud, but he might never see Anthony again, and he was determined to be honest and find out the truth.

Anthony was searching Neil's eyes as he spoke. "That is not true, man. I love you. Aria loves you. Poppy loved you and your mother loved you in her own way. Now, your mom loved you in a super creepy way so I've never let you spend a single night alone in a house with her because I was afraid she would chip you or freeze you or something. I never would have let her hurt you, Neil. I would have been right there by your side with your mom every day of your life, even if I didn't owe Poppy."

Neil reassessed the man in front of him. Anthony had given up having his own life to watch over Neil. He suddenly felt like an ungrateful asshole and a spoiled brat. How had he missed that Anthony was the only person who cared about him? That Anthony had been acting as his parent all along? Neil suddenly needed to know this man who raised him. His voice cracked again, and he squeezed his eyes shut as he spoke. "I wish I'd known all of this. What happened? Why did you owe Poppy?"

Anthony sighed and took two swallows of his drink. "It's a long story. Poppy came out to your mother when she was pregnant with you, but she didn't know your mom was pregnant. Your mother was disgusted and kicked Poppy to the curb immediately. She had nowhere to go and began the stroll."

"The stroll?"

"She was a sex worker."

"A sex worker?"

"That's how we met. One day I was out there on K Street hiring another sex worker. The young man I was with and I were both shot by some hateful puritanical neighbor. The young man died that night, but I survived because Poppy took off her dress and held it over my shoulder until the bleeding stopped and somehow got me to a medic. Like I said, I owed her."

"That's horrible. I'm so sorry your friend died." Neil knew he should stay in the sympathetic head space, but he couldn't. "So, what happened? When I was born, Poppy told you to be a surrogate dad for me? Did that take care of her guilt?"

"She loved you. She went by Poppy her whole life because it was what you called her when you were a baby and she never wanted to forget her responsibility as your dad. She thought about trying to get you back when you were a toddler, but she was living on the streets at first and couldn't give you a safe life. She thought she wouldn't be good for you when you were a kid. She didn't think she knew how to parent. And later, we had a few plans to get you kicked out of Upland, but Poppy was always afraid of hurting you, and so was I. Poppy never had enough food or medicine the way your mom did. At some point, we got so deep in our lies we didn't know how to get out. We just knew we had to protect you."

"We? What do you mean we? YOU protected me. Poppy ditched me and turned the only girl I ever loved into her protégé. She didn't protect me. She fucked me up in every way she knew how, probably to get back at my mother, who I get was vile, but still."

"Neil, it wasn't just Poppy who decided to push you and Aria together, it was me too. We both thought you'd be good for each other. I'm sorry we manipulated you, but all we did was make sure you were at the same party together once. You two did the rest."

"So, what, Poppy realized Aria had a crush on her and figured she'd let her down easy by letting her have the son instead and it would be the same? What the fuck were you two thinking?"

"It wasn't like that Neil. We were just talking about how to get you out of that job you'd taken with your mom. Poppy was ready to extract you by force, if necessary, but we weren't sure how you'd react. Poppy shared that she was also trying to get Aria back in town because she needed her here for the escalation. Then I remembered how you forced me to sneak her into her parent's prison cell, and wondered if you were still soft on her. You're both so talented, too, and had given up too much of your music and joy to the political mess around us. We just wanted to see if there was something there. And there was."

"Did Aria suspect that I was Poppy's son before my mom told her?"

"How would I know? You need to talk to Aria about that."

"She doesn't want to talk to me, Anthony. She doesn't want me. Not like I want her. She doesn't love me."

"Who says she doesn't love you? Does anyone other than you believe that? Neil, she got on national television with Joe and said that she was going to marry you. She gushes about you to the public all the time—how talented you are, how caring you are. How much more evidence do you need that she wants you? Seriously man. You can be mad at me all you want, and I am sorry I lied to you. I did what I thought was best for you and Poppy, and the movement. Maybe I was wrong, but I did what I did out of love. Aria loves you too. You need to get your shit together and go talk to her. Frankly, she puts herself at unnecessary risk without you and every day she insists on no security and traipsing out to dozens of public events could be her last. She's going to get herself killed if you don't do something Neil."

Neil didn't believe he had the power to stop her, but he heard Anthony out.

"I don't know what I can do."

"Can you at least take this phone, so I don't have to stake you out for a week to find you next time?"

Neil took the phone, wondering if he would ever decide to dig up his shoes and watch that he'd buried. He preferred to leave them in the past, but also knew how valuable they were.

"I'll take the phone. But first, tell me, is there anything else about my life that is a lie?"

"There's a lot you need to know on the phone. I loaded the annual video messages that Poppy recorded for you on your birthdays. Every year there was always some reason not to upend your life and deliver them. I realize it was a mistake now not to tell you all along. The last one is from three months ago."

Neil was floored. "Have you listened to them?"

"No. It wasn't my place. And I have a lot going on myself. Listen to them and then I'll answer any question you have."

They chatted for a while longer in the dark bar, until Neil finally excused himself. His curiosity was piqued. He'd listen to what Poppy had to say.

39. "STRUGGLING MYSELF DON'T MEAN A WHOLE LOT"

—Bernice Johnson Reagon

Neil began to walk to his room in Georgetown. It had been less than two weeks since he'd packed up his things to head to Lowland to live out his life. So much had changed since then. He had no idea if his home was still intact, but it was a destination. It would take him the rest of the day and into the night to walk from Deanwood to Georgetown. The walking was helping him process. Neil popped in the earbuds that Anthony had given him and pushed play on the recordings.

As he listened to Poppy's voice, he felt that he knew her better with each minute. Poppy knew everything that was happening in Neil's life at every stage of his life. She had recorded a congratulations message each time he was concertmaster. She knew his repertoire. Not even his mother had ever paid that close attention to him growing up. What would it have been like if she'd actually reached out to Neil instead of hiding behind these recordings? The voice of a dead parent who cared wasn't enough to make up for a lifetime of missing out on parental love. Neil wished he could have been Poppy's son and heir. Instead, Aria was the heir. He didn't want it to rankle, but it did. Neil didn't want to covet what the woman he loved had. He wanted to covet her. He did covet her. He wanted to spend his life bedding Aria and dancing with Aria and making music with Aria. His lack of rational thinking about her and Poppy was a serious obstacle.

He wanted to earn Aria's forgiveness. Poppy was gone now which meant that one layer of Aria's support system was gone. The guys on the search and rescue team had said there was a plot to kill Aria, and Anthony had intimated the same, that she was in danger. Neil thought of the little girl he had saved that morning. He imagined it had been Aria passed out in his arms and clenched his gut as he let himself picture an assassination attempt. He could see it clearly because he had lived it a few times—Aria nearly dead in his arms—while he could do nothing about it.

His need to keep her safe flashed out from his core. Aria was becoming beloved to most people, but not everyone by a longshot. A famous, beautiful, and widely respected Black woman was going to be in danger. Everyone either wanted Aria in bed or wanted Aria dead. Neither was going to happen on Neil's watch, if he could help it.

Aria might still want to marry him for the sake of Turtle Island as she was now calling the country. Neil might be able to make a deal with her—he'd go through with the fake marriage if she agreed to stop traveling without guards. Neil walked with more purpose now straight for the White House.

By the time Neil got to the White House he was desperate to talk to Aria. "I need to talk to Aria Petros." Neil announced to the guard at the 17th St NW gate. The area was still covered in debris and Neil realized that Aria had not prioritized clean up around these monuments.

"ID?" Neil handed over what he had—an old Upland ID. The guard scowled.

"Sorry, we don't have you on the list."

"Could you just call her and let her know I'm here?"

"Sir, even if you were Oprah Winfrey come back from the dead, I would not interrupt my boss and tell her to interrupt the President to tell her that you were here because, you see, I'd like to keep my job."

Neil did not need this obstacle. He'd never had trouble entering the White House before. "Don't call your boss then, call someone else in there. Just tell them Neil Rao is here."

"Sir, my records show that the last time you were here you were volatile, and the time before that was for a photo opportunity with President Donner. Don't push your luck. You need to get out of line and let the other people past."

Neil had a feeling he was about to get tackled and backed off. Aria would know exactly how to sneak into this place. Neil's approach was not working. He looked down the street and saw the water wall was still up, so he couldn't go around to the south. He walked around to the north to try a different tactic at the Pennsylvania Avenue gate. He was deep in trying to come up with a plan when he literally walked into someone.

"Excuse me."

"Neil?"

"Laurie! Can you help me get in? I need to talk to Aria."

"Why?"

Neil recalled the conversation he'd just had with Anthony.

"I heard that you and Anthony and your partners all cleared the air and things are working out and I just want a chance to do the same with Aria."

Laurie looked at Neil with sympathy. "She's not here."

"When is she back?"

"Tomorrow. And it'll take that long to get the smell of death off of you. You look like you crawled out of a trash bin. Let me help you get cleaned up."

"Why would you help me?"

"Oh, I don't know, because you saved the reserves and therefore all of us, and because Aria is a mess without you, or maybe because I can tell you love each other? I want to help you because I don't want you to fuck this up. Come on. Let's get you credentialed and inside the White House, get you showered and cleaned up and then you and I can do some role playing."

An hour later, Neil felt more human and was sitting on a loveseat talking to Laurie, who was pretending to be Aria in the chair next to him, but had come out of character.

"No. No. No. Do not ask that. Why do you need to know that?"

Neil had asked if Aria had been in love with Poppy and had ever wanted to sleep with her. "I feel like I need to understand if she loves me or just because I'm a poor substitute for Poppy."

"Why? Why do you need to know that? Who cares? You're being a child. Aria didn't know Poppy was your parent at the time you two got together. You're being as puritanical as your mother, and you need to drop it."

"Harsh."

"You need some hard truths right now. I made up an excuse to get Aria back here early and you are going to fuck this up, and then Aria is going to do something stupid and risky and then we're all going to be sad and fucked."

Laurie was not pulling any punches. "Okay let me try again. 'Aria, I want to make a deal. I'll marry you in front of the country like you want, and in exchange, you stop risking your life by traveling with no protection."

"HOW are you so bad at this, Neil? A deal? You want to make her a deal? I thought you were supposed to be some great charming flirt? Where is that person? Let's take a step back. What do you like about Aria?"

"The same things everyone in the whole damn country likes about her. She's hot, she's smart, she's brave. Why are you asking this? You know her."

"Okay, and what do you think she loves about you?"

"I don't think she loves anything about me. I think she wants to marry me out of a sense of duty to the movement and the country. She loved Poppy, not me."

"You are blind as a bat. Aria loves you."

Laurie was the second person that day to insist Aria loved him. "Then why hasn't she said so? Why won't she marry me?"

"Why do you think? What has she told you?"

Neil tried to remember what exactly Aria had said.

"She said something about marriage being a patriarchal institution."

"Does that sound like she thinks you are an obligation or that she loves Poppy more than you?"

"I suppose it could be seen as just a critique of the institution, but then why was she pretending to be engaged to me if she had that critique?"

"You two need to talk about this, it just can't be the first words out of your mouth okay? She needs you to support her right now."

"I need her too."

"Then tell her that. And DO NOT ask her if she ever fantasized about sex with Poppy—not as your opening line, and ideally, not ever. Stop punishing her for having loved Poppy. A lot of us loved Poppy. She was lovable. I hope you'll come to love her too, even after the fact of her."

"You got to experience a relationship with Poppy and so did Aria. I didn't, and I guess that hurts."

"Then tell her that, Neil. Tell her the truth. Be vulnerable. And don't fuck it up."

"Got it. I've got this."

"You do not have it. Do not be overconfident."

Laurie took Neil's phone and entered her number. "Go get some sleep. I'll text you when Aria's back and rested so you can have a conversation. I put my number in so you can call if you need me." Neil now had two numbers in his phone—Anthony's and Laurie's.

Neil was walking back to the room he'd been given in the White House when he heard the guards saying the honey badger was in the fields. It had to be that Aria was back. Laurie had told Neil to wait, but he couldn't. Laurie was still watching him from the doorway when he took a turn down a hallway that was definitely not where his room was.

"What? Where are you going Neil? You're not ready yet! You're going to fuck it up!"

Neil had a head start, but he could hear Laurie running behind him. Neil had been in the White House plenty of times in his life, but he had never had free reign, so he didn't know his way around. Miraculously, he found his way through the labyrinth at a fast walk that was still faster than Laurie and managed to look confident enough to not get stopped. Neil was relieved when he found the double doors that led to the helicopter pad, but when he got to the door there was no helicopter there and the doors were locked. Right. That wasn't how Aria would travel. He had lost Laurie at some point in his speed walk. He needed to get to the other side of the building and tried one dead end before finding a corridor that looked promising. Finally, he turned a corner and saw the double doors and a small van unloading. Aria was in the back unloading her cello by herself as guards tried to help. She was smiling and flirting with the guards.

"Don't touch it! I know you want to use those big muscles for something, but I've got it."

She laughed and blocked the guards from touching her instrument. He loved her laugh. Neil had no idea why he had left this woman who he loved. His eyes filled with tears at the sight of her in one piece grousing about her cello. They'd been through so much, had so many people taken from them, and survived it all.

"Aria," he said quietly as he approached her. She was holding the cello in front of her, in its case.

He had her attention. "Can I give you a proper kiss when you aren't holding that cello as a line of defense?"

Tears were streaming down Aria's face, as she nodded yes. They stared at each other for what felt like an eternity. Neil was taking in the reality of her in front of him.

"I'm sorry." They both said at the same time.

"I love you." They said again, their voices overlapping.

"I love you, Neil Rao."

"I've been waiting to hear that. I'm super fucked up Aria, and I need to process a lot of what went down with my parents. But I know I want to do it with you. On whatever terms you lay out. Now can you ditch that cello please?"

Aria suddenly noticed that Gears was there.

"Did you get him to come home?"

Laurie shook her head "no." "It was all him." She stepped forward to take Aria's cello, and then she whispered in Neil's ear. "That was much better."

40.
EPILOGUE: "WE WHO BELIEVE IN FREEDOM CANNOT REST UNTIL IT COMES"

—Bernice Johnson Reagon

Ten years later . . .

"That was good," Aria said, wrapping her arms around Neil. They were both slick with sweat. After a moment of nestling into Neil, Aria started to push herself up to untie her ankles. Neil pulled her back down to the bed.

"Not so fast," he said, plunking Aria back down onto the bed. Neil had gotten on all fours above Aria and was licking his lips as he scanned Aria's body, making her laugh.

"I would love to go again, Neil, but remember, the kids are going to be home any minute and Anthony and Joe are expecting us for brunch."

"Then we better get showered," he said, leaning back and untying Aria's feet.

"Our shower is small for steamy sex."

"I'm up for the challenge if you are."

"And what if Phoenix walks in?"

"They are thirteen years old. They know to knock."

"And what if they can't stop Poppy from barging in?"

"She can't even reach the doorknob," Neil said, kissing Aria's neck, which he knew would put a pause to her protests.

Neil had missed Aria so much on this trip, not just the pleasure they could extract from each other, but also cuddling and talking with her. He had missed their kids as well. They had adopted Phoenix, who was the child Neil had found unconscious in the flooded house after Hurricane Eamon. Since the child didn't know their name, Aria and Neil sat with them and picked a name. Phoenix suited them. Poppy was their biological child, a human representation of their ability to forgive and love. At three years old, they were like an adorable little toy to Phoenix.

When Neil heard the front door open and the voices of his kids, he realized he did want to give everyone their gifts. "Okay, here's the plan: we'll get dressed, greet the kids, and give them their gifts, have a glorious day with Joe, Anthony, Laurie, Becca and their brood, but after dinner we get back in bed."

"Deal. And tonight, you want me to tie you up?" Aria asked, eyeing Neil's lean, muscular body.

"Yes ma'am I do." Neil answered with a sloppy salute.

Aria and Neil sat up and grabbed their robes. Aria started putting on her layers—a t-shirt, a long-sleeved sweater on top, long johns, and jeans on bottom, with a down robe on top that had been a hopeful gift from Neil years earlier.

"I love how cozy this robe is, and I love that it's chilly enough to enjoy it."

"Don't get too excited. It's just a few La Niña years. We haven't properly gotten winter back. Or at least that's what

Joe said on his show." Neil had pulled on his own layers and dug Aria's most recent present out of his bag, handing it to her. It was a pillowcase that had been hand embroidered to say "You had me at Cello."

"It's to match your 'Don't get in Treble' pillow on the love seat in your office."

"Aww. I love it babe. Now let's go say hi to the kids and get them some hot cacao to warm up."

"Noona sent this for you too." Neil handed Aria a small bag. Aria peeked in and squealed with delight at the package of dried mango and ginger. "We should go tour the farm as a family this summer. She's done wonders with it. The kids will love all the animals."

"Let's do that. I want to give Noona a big squeeze and then eat all the mango she'll give us."

They were planning for their future. There were flurries outside in the air, but warm inside their house thanks to the new passivhaus-indigenous inspired design of the building that held their flat. Their home was stabilizing, and their family was full of love. Neil pulled his robe on and reflected on his trip out west and his pleasurable homecoming. Turtle Island was recovering too. Winter would come back, and they were already living a full and beautiful life.

NOTE FROM THE AUTHOR

As *The Revolution Will Not Be Rated G* goes to publication, courageous individuals all over the US are joining together in movements for justice. People are rising up in the image of the movements that took out Pinochet in Chile, apartheid in South Africa, and Milosovic in Serbia, British colonizers in India and around the world, and Jim Crow laws right here in the US. I wrote this book to provide a story of how movements can succeed against long odds; not only in the past, but in the future.

The table of contents and chapter titles are songs and chants that I like to use in the streets to bring grounding, joy, and camaraderie in moments that might otherwise feel chaotic and fearful. I also tried to weave a few best practices into the backdrop of this story, from the work to build alternative systems and take care of community needs, to the emphasis on training. It was important to me to incorporate the use of noncooperation and strikes, and the groundwork the movement has to lay for mass defections, and for each individual defection, like Neil or Joe's defections to the movement in the story.

While I wrote Neil and Aria's story a few years ago, I wasn't sure if I would publish it, both because I wasn't sure if I wanted to, and because I wasn't sure if I would find a publisher for a cli-fi, speculative, romance that ends with a general strike that succeeds. Just a few days before the Presidential Election I got a call from Dede Cummings at Green Writers Press saying they were interested. I loved Dede and the whole teams' positive energy. By the time I got the offer in writing, I knew that we were moving towards fascism, and in that context, I wanted this story to be out in the world, and I wanted to work with the Green Writers Press team to make that happen.

I love "second chance" romances and "fake engagements" as tropes for telling this story. Romance is the perfect genre for exploring heavy topics like authoritarianism and climate change, because in a romance novel, readers are assured that no matter how bad things get, the end will be a Happily Ever After (HEA) or at least a Happy For Now (HFN).

And it's not only in romance that we can get an HEA or HFN. I wouldn't do this work—the writing or the activism—unless I truly believed one of my favorite street chants, which I like most when it is repeated with clapping, jumping, and dancing:

"I believe that we will win."

ACKNOWLEDGEMENTS

Thank you for reading *The Revolution Will Not Be Rated G*, and for being a person who believes in freedom and cannot rest until it comes! There's a sex double entendre to be had there, but I don't want to force it. I hope that this book brought some joy and fun into your life in this difficult time.

My deepest gratitude to Dede Cummings and the amazing team at Green Writers Press for bringing this book into the world. Birthing a book is a lot of work! Thank you to Allee Pineault for the cover art that screams "hurricanes and sex inside," to Dede and Allee for letting me have so much input, and to the dozens of dear friends who helped me decide which elements I liked in all the options! Thank you to Ferne Johansson for pushing me for needed backstory and for forcing me to leave so many of my darlings on the cutting room floor where they belong. What a bonus to have your expertise in agriculture and seeds. Thank you Becky Tsadik for the cultural accuracy read, and for copy editing out almost every superfluous "a little," and to Charlotte Williams for proofreading. Thank you to my friend Jacob Johns for picking up the phone any time I had questions about appropriately honering Indigenous terms, and to my friend, Stevie O'Hanlon, for an additional sensitivity read.

Any lingering errors or insensitivities, should there be any, are my own responsibility. Thank you Britt for the tireless promotion to bookstores, romance genre influencers, and more. I'm constantly floored by the kindness with which the whole Green Writers Press team has treated me as a debut fiction writer whose activist life has had to take priority over my writing life.

Thank you to my alpha readers, Stosh Cotler, Mikhiela Sherrod, and Mona Hatoum, who were so into this project from the jump that you somehow got through my extremely rough first draft, when I thought it would be more fun if the characters had sex in every single scene. Thank you to Afabwaje Kurian for teaching my only formal course on writing and revision, and for my first exposure to writing groups. Thank you to my writing group, the Beyond Bud crew, who welcomed me and nurtured my writing so I could get to a second draft—Denise Robbins, Ericka Taylor, Chuckry Vengadam, Jeremie Amoroso, Marissa Fretes, Raisa Johnson, Christina Tudor, and Mike Lauer, and also to the Le Salon de Things crew for practical advice through early humps. Thank you Fran Liebowitz, who I connected with on Reedsy and loved connecting with in real life as well. You got me to a vastly improved third draft! Thank you Bill McKibben for reading an early draft of this book and then writing a blurb that kept me going through moments of overwhelm and writers block. Thank you to everyone who wrote a blurb for this book: Ericka, Jeff, Connie, and Julia! Thank you to the Sunrise Movement and Arm in Arm leaders, past and present, who inspired the Expectus slogans, and so much more. I am so filled with gratitude for you and for all the people with Free DC, Freedom Trainers, so many allied organizations, and our champions in philanthropy, for doing the work that will prevent a dystopian future. Bless you. We won't end up in this future because of you, and I'm so thankful for you every day.

Thank you to my family for enabling me to become the person I am today, a topic I could write another entire book on! I'm grateful to my late father and my sister for, among so many other things, keeping shelves of formative books around the house when I was growing up. I could not have written this book without my mom holding down a serious amount of grandparenting at a difficult time.

Thank you to my teenage son, Siddharth, for teaching me so much about life, including about classical music. I may not always show it in the moment, but I appreciate the constant vigilance with which you ensure that I keep in check my own tendency towards being an authoritarian over your personal agency. I'm so proud of you.

Thank you to my husband, Andrew, for showing so much grace while in the crosshairs of fascism at work, for making me tea, pumping up my bike tires, and surviving the embarrassment of my publishing a sex-filled novel that everyone in our lives will forever ask you questions about. You don't have to answer, my love :)

Thank you to Aya de Leon and all the authors of romance novels, who represent women of color and delve into politics. You have brought me so much joy and inspiration. I first imagined this book while reading *Rebel,* a Beverly Jenkins novel about reconstruction. Finally, another note of gratitude to you, the reader. Thank you for giving this romance novel about climate change and authoritarianism a chance. And a special shoutout to my newsletter subscribers! Thank you for following me on this journey!

ABOUT THE AUTHOR

Keya Chatterjee is executive director of Free DC. She is an avid reader, an author, and an activist for climate justice and democracy. Keya is committed to imagining and creating a thriving and inclusive future full of joy and caring. She started her career at NASA and was Executive Director of the US Climate Action Network for almost a decade, where she was a key voice in civil society for strengthening the Paris Climate Agreement and the Inflation Reduction Act. Keya also served two terms as a hyper local elected official in Washington, DC, where she lives with her husband and son. She previously published a nonfiction book, *The Zero Footprint Baby: How to Save the Planet While Raising a Healthy Baby*, and op-eds in many outlets including *Newsweek*, *Reuters*, and *Huffington Post*.